Darren Coleman
AUTHOR OF THE SMASH HIT 'BEFORE I LET GO'
PRESENTS:

Do

Or

Die

a novel by

Washington, DC • New York • Detroit

Nvision Publishing

PRINTED IN THE UNITED STATES OF AMERICA

Do

Or

Die

a novel by D

Nvision Publishing
Washington, DC • New York • Detroit

AN NVISION BOOK
PUBLISHED BY NVISION PUBLISHING
A division of NVISION INCORPORATED
P. O. BOX 274, LANHAM SEVERN ROAD, LANHAM, MD 20703

NVISION PUBLISHING and the above portrayal of a boy looking to the moon and the stars are trademarks of NVISION INCORPORATED.

This novel is a work of fiction. Any references to real people, events, establishments, or locales are intended only to give the fiction a sense of reality and authenticity. Other names, characters, and incidents occurring in the work are either the product of the author's imagination or are used fictitiously, as are those fictionalized events and incidents that involve real persons. Any character that happens to share the name of a person who is an acquaintance of the author, past or present, is purely coincidental and is in no way intended to be an actual account involving that person.

Book and Cover design by Darren Coleman & Les Green for Nvision Publishing. Cover Art by Anthony Carr. Photography by Curtis Catrell.

Library of Congress Cataloging-in-Publication Data;

D, A novel by
Do Or Die: a novel by ⅅ
  For complete Library of Congress Copyright info visit the nvision publishing web site.

www.nvisionpublishing.com

ISBN 0-9724003-7-0
Copyright © 2004

Do

Or

Die

A novel by

In Memory Of

Wilbert N. Lee, Jerome Segars, & Lawrence Marshall

Dedication

This book is dedicated to all of the fallen soldiers who were misled into thinking that they *had* to do wrong to get ahead or survive. 'Fallen' doesn't always mean dead, as some of us are blessed with the opportunity to right our wrongs, repent, and endure.

It is also dedicated to every person who has ever lost a loved one at the hands of violence. Lastly, it is dedicated to those who have found strength in God's hands in Do Or Die circumstances.

Acknowledgements

I want to thank you, the readers, first. I love ya'll for real. The first sistah I see on the subway reading this book is getting a hug and a kiss. Without out you there would be no stage for me to perform my passion as an artist. I would have to work a job rather than live a dream and I've realized that I'm no good at that. From the bottom of my heart I wish you all the greatest of blessings and I humbly ask for your continued support. I hope that I can return the love that you show in some measure with this offering. It may sound strange but I would like to surrender the credit of this story to My Creator, Jehovah. Through divine inspiration I was commissioned to do something remarkable. It's not me… it's through me, no doubt.

Second, I would like to thank my three test readers Chad, Lowe, and Monica. You became my dream team and the support that you gave was truly needed and appreciated. Never underestimate the value of the feedback you provided. True, I knew I could do it, but you all made sure I did it right!

Since this story is created from the energy of the hip-hop world, I feel that I should thank the hip-hop community. Each day I as I banged on the keyboard I used your music and your artistic expressions to inspire me. Shawn Carter, Nasir Jones, AZ, G Unit, Scarface, the Notorious B.I.G., DMX, Cam'ron and the Diplomat's, the list could go on but these names had to be mentioned. For those sex scenes, big shout to R. Kelly, the baddest mufukka ever to make music. Get at me if you want your biography done right.

To Sistah Souljah, it needs to be said; Donald Goines and Iceberg Slim started it (they are the kings), but you re-birthed it with *The Coldest Winter Ever*. I tip my hat to you and thank you for setting a high standard with this urban fiction. If it weren't for you people would probably think that some of this garbage out here was good.

I want to send a shout out to ALL the vendors on the streets getting their grind on from coast to coast. People don't even understand that it is you all who keep this industry afloat. To my man Massamba pushing books out on Jamaica Ave… keep holding me down brother… stay strong in faith. Thanks to my friends at Culture Plus, Larry and Gail, it's always a pleasure. Kevon, keep your eyes on the prize and finish your book. Thanks to A&B and Afrikan World Books. To all the black owned bookstores who keep the doors open for the love as well as the dollars, Diana Books, and Junior out in Brooklyn, Mrs. Villarosa at Hue-Man up in Harlem, Mr. Evans at Expressions in B-more and to every store owner who works hard to make it happen. Thanks to Yao, Simba, Lee and the entire staff at Karibu Books in the Nation's Capital, thanks for the support, especially Trina, Jay, Rico, Le Roy, Tiffany, & TeMac.

Thanks in advance to all the radio and TV stations across the land for having me on your show. Justine Love in the Nations Capital, I love ya'. Free, D loves you baby, I'll be the first author to turn 106 and Park out. Big Tigga can I get a shout? Wendy Williams, big up to you because you do your thing and don't give a damn what anybody says.

Shout out to Tiffany, Phyllis, and the entire Don Diva staff. BIG UP to Essence magazine, the Source, F.E.D.s, Felon, Sister 2 Sister, Vibe, King, XXL and all the magazines that give the book industry a push talking about books… you need to talk about this one.

To my partner in crime… Zach Tate, author of *No Way Out* and *Lost and Turned Out*. You don't even realize how much the advice you give to me means. If I had never read your work I would have never been compelled to bless folks with my story. Thanks for keeping *me* plugged into Nvision's vison. I'm trying to see what you and the Queen see. To Darren Coleman author of *Before I Let Go,* and CEO of Nvision Publishing, thanks for letting your other side shine through.

I have had a chance to meet some truly positive people in this industry and you all have been an inspiration to me, the beautiful and talented Vickie Stringer. Much love to the entire Triple Crown Family. Shannon Holmes, thanks for all the support you've shown. I know you aren't loose with your endorsements or your friendship… I am proud to have both. Shout out to K'wan… you have a bright future my brother. Dewayne Joseph, stay focused. Azarel, author of *A Life to Remember,* I loved your book… keep it up!

I have too many friends to thank so I just want to thank **each** and **every** one of you for the support and love. **You know who you are.** Really you do. Tressa Smallwood, you have been a blessing in my life. I wish you and Tony a multitude of blessings. Shout out to Tam, and to Danielle… you are mission impossible… even with a watch you still don't know what time it is! Yo Yo, congrats on the crib! Lori Carter good looking out all the time, special thanks to you for all you do. You showed me that you will scrap for a nigga … that's scary. Get a computer in 2004 and get started on that book. U can doooo it. Lynn Thomas, Walter Jernigan, D. Brown, John Graham, Big Al, Butter and Shaka, thanks in advance for pushing *Do or Die.* Richard at Sepia, Sand & Sable in B-More, you been waiting so here is some fire for ya'. Shout out to Shawn & Lawn Chase, to Tracey Phillips in Chi-town, Tenia Tucker in the ATL, Alura Jeffries in Bama', Tasha Helair in L.A., Lea Williams in Houston, Shanequa Jordan in Brooklyn, ya'll stay sweet and thanks for that coast-to-coast support. Much love to Turning Heads and all the sistahs in the hair salons across the nation.

Ma, I know you were my biggest fan even when I was begging for gas money as a grown assed man. We don't always see eye to eye, but always know

I love you more than anything.   Big Sis, I love you and if don't nobody else understand me I know you do. Lil' D, by the time you're old enough to read this you'll have that Hummer you're always talking bout. To all my extended family, cousins, aunts and uncles… thanks for your support, it means a lot to me that you're proud and I love you all. Shout to all my peeps at the shop; Pop, E, Louie, Tone, Mr. H, Pete, Ed, & Gina. Books_spring, sunshine 4ever!

June, you bless me even while you fight the madness up north. You have taught me more than you will ever know. We've all done bad things at times, some of us have paid a steep price for our actions in this life, and some will pay the ultimate price later, but at the end of the day there's always a lesson to be learned. It takes a real man to share for free the lessons that cost him the most to learn. Thanks for that. I'll pick you up in that whip and get you out those mountains in a short. Shout out to Borne and to J.O. stay up.

Thanks to the Nvision Publishing staff for making this happen. No man is an island! My editors, Lisa Richardson and Angela Oates, your love for this book shows in the way you fought (smile) with me over each item… Gangsta! Les Green thanks for the incredibly hard work on the web site and cover design. Nigga you better than me staying up all night, but I love you for that. Anthony Carr I am so pleased with your artistry on the cover art. You are the man!!! I am so grateful that you made sure each detail was precisely how it should be. You're something like a phenomenon. Tahisha, the newest member of the staff, welcome aboard. To Danette Majette, author of *I Should Have Seen It Coming…* you got next!

I was about to let a few chumps have it in this paragraph… a couple of writers who are green with envy and a few niggas around the city yapping like chicks. After talking to my man D with the original beard… he said to me, "D, why even give those weak brothers any energy? They aren't doing what you're doing and are mad cause they can't." Then I thought about it and realized that the hating only gets worse from here on out… If I respond now then I will be wasting energy from here on out. I realized then that I had a choice to make. I decided not go off and to keep my cipher sucka-free. So ya'll brothers keep on running your mouths and going to bed worrying about what I'm doing. I'm wishing you the strength to sustain the storm I'm bringing, cause you are going to need it.

Lastly, to my brother Jim. You may not ever read a page of this book and I respect that fully. I just want to acknowledge how your presence in my life has been one of God's greatest gifts to me. Thanks 4 everything.

Love to one and all,

D

ONE

Determination describes what it takes to survive in a cold and unforgiving world. Determination plus a gift is what it takes to flourish. The world is full of those who are determined to survive or merely exist, but those who flourish make a fortune on the backs of the so-called survivors. It can be the hood or the White House. No matter what circles they live or travel in, those who flourish hold the gold and make the rules. The bible says, "The meek shall inherit the earth." The question is though ... what will be left of it when the rulers are done?

As a kid, I hardly ever went to church, and when I did, I seldom listened to a word the preachers said. One Saturday night when I was around eight, I spent the night at my best friend Abraham's house. The next morning when his grandmother woke him up for church, she literally dragged me along with them. At the time, there wasn't much that I cared to recall about church or religion, but that day I somehow did remember hearing this old preacher say, "We aren't living in these projects for no reason at all. It is part of God's Master Plan." He also said that the ghetto would present each of us a gift and a way out to a better life. Those words had an effect on me. The amazing thing was that there wasn't much that could have been said in a church to affect my life at that time.

Rap music, video games, and whatever my mother said was the only religion I knew. I was about eight years old when I heard what that preacher said. Living the way I did and seeing some of the shit that went down where I was raised, it was no small wonder why I spent most of my childhood looking for that gift. When I finally found it, I ran with it.

I grew up in the Greenberg Towers Housing Projects in Bedford Stuyvesant. Bed-Stuy, the home of the Notorious B.I.G., was at one time referred to as the largest ghetto in the world. Drugs, violence, corrupt police and politicians thrived. Of course, there are some beautiful people there to go along with some of New York's most beautiful brownstones, but that's not the part I knew.

Greenberg Towers wasn't the largest of the housing projects, but like the Marcy Projects, Red Hook, Queensbridge, and St. Nick Housing, niggas from Greenberg Towers were well known and respected throughout the city. Greenberg Towers was divided into two sections. The towers, which were built in the fifties, were seven, 23-story, brown, brick buildings. The high-rise buildings encased a courtyard that had a playground, several makeshift junkyards and a parking lot. On the other side of the parking lot was a gated basketball court and several rows of mid-rise apartment buildings. The courtyard, which was like the express lane for drugs, was controlled day and night by the crack dealers. The playground and the junkyards, which had everything from pissy mattresses to burnt-out cars, were controlled by the niggas pushing dope and the fiends. Any parent worth a damn kept their children out of those areas. Used needles could be found on the sliding boards. Empty red-top containers littered the area by the merry-go-round.

In the neighborhood that I called home, the schools had books that were older than the principal and there wasn't a park or live tree to be had. The kids who came up there were bred and raised to be one thing or the other: victims or survivors. No gray area. No in between. Aside from Don Greenberg, who owned the Towers, the young hustlers selling drugs 24/7, the crooked cops, and the Koreans were the only ones getting paid. The poor got poorer and the thieves got richer. To say that there was an addict of some kind in almost every house was no exaggeration. In the Towers, there was a generation of us kids growing up watching violence on television, that wasn't shit compared to what we saw on the streets, and there was epidemic drug use that was destroying some families while feeding others. Most of the month, the little ones were being raised on a diet of hard reality. Around the first of the month though, when checks came and everything was sweet, they might get blessed with some fried chicken wings with mumbo sauce from the Korean carry out.

It was a serious situation growing up there. The way shit started out for me and my best friend Abraham, there was no way anyone could have guessed that either of us would do any better for ourselves than the average kid coming out of the Towers. My little sister, Toni, was well on her way to becoming a statistic and a victim. She was pregnant at sixteen. A twenty-five year old Jamaican cat, named Quentin, who lived upstairs and used just as much crack as he sold, had lured her into his apartment and his world. She told my mom she was raped, but Moms didn't buy it. Toni had brought too much designer clothing into the house and my moms, a.k.a. Lindsey Vaughn was much too smart for that. My moms had been in the projects all of her life and she knew the game. When she saw my sister come in the house with the first Macy's bag, she had told her to remember that you don't get something for nothing. My sister obviously had to find out for herself.

As far as Moms was concerned, once she had hipped us to the game, we were on our own, sink or swim. My mother had warned Toni, "Keep your motherfuckin' legs crossed, 'cause if you bring a baby up in here, you got to go." And to me she said, "If your ass gets locked up for anything other than self-defense, don't waste your phone call on me because I won't be comin' to get your ass." That was as deep as the parenting got for us in the Vaughn household.

That was just Lindsey's style. Love it or leave it. Most people left it. I had never seen Toni's father or my own. My youngest sister, Jade, was the only one of us who was valued at all by her pops. I had only seen him in photos since he was doing twelve years upstate for armed robbery. He did however send Jade books every couple of weeks. He even had a friend who would come by and drop clothes and food off for Jade. I wondered if Jade's father knew that his friend would come late and sometimes stay all night. My mom was the type that did what made her feel good and didn't give a damn about whose feelings she hurt.

We were in the projects like everyone else, but we had decent furniture. My uncle had gotten a job at a furniture rental place long enough to confuse the deliveries of apartments full of furniture for every one he knew. He got fired when they discovered he had misplaced the invoices for fifteen apartments full of furniture and television sets. My mother was as proud as you can be in the projects. We even had cable. She kept our place clean because when she wasn't at work, she was at play most of the time in her bedroom with somebody she met at work. She said she had suffered without as a child and that *she* deserved to have some level of comfort. Now that her babies were grown and could take care of themselves, she said it was time for her to be happy.

Lindsey got paid in cash and collected welfare, so unlike a lot of other families, we almost always had plenty of food to eat. My moms would run around always bragging about the fact that she was getting money. As far as I was concerned, if she was seeing money, she was a selfish bitch because every time me or either of my sisters asked for anything, the answer was "Hell motherfuckin' no!" That's how she talked to us. Lindsey wasn't afraid of the welfare department because they made appointments, but never showed up in our neighborhood. They were too afraid of the stick-up boys, dope fiends, and all around crazy mofos walking through the courtyards. If they actually made it to one of the buildings, then the smell of piss and prostitution would make their asses turn right back around.

When my sister got pregnant, Moms held up to all of her tough talk and promises. She put Toni's ass out. It was December, five days before Christmas when my mother found out, and on the 26th, my moms packed her stuff and took it upstairs to Quentin's apartment. She told him to take care of the situation and his unborn kid if he didn't want to catch a rape charge. Knowing my mother, it was likely that she threatened him with the police in order to bleed him for some cash.

Even though my sister was a few flights upstairs, I hadn't seen her for three months. My mother forbade me to go up there. She promised to throw me out too if I was caught up there or talking to her. I figured that the Jamaican should take care of his responsibilities anyway. I loved and missed my sister, but if she hadn't been doing her own thing, then she wouldn't have gotten pregnant. After all, she had been warned. I also knew that it was likely that one day, innocent or guilty, I would take a ride in a squad car, just as Toni had to know that one day she would uncross her legs and make a baby. I also knew that I would remember Lindsey's promise

5

to me when it happened. With that same reasoning, Toni had to know that Lindsey would put her ass out, as promised, and there would be nothing that anyone could do. That being said, what good would it do for me to be put out behind dealing with Toni?

One afternoon, I was over Abraham's house, lounging after school, playing Playstation 2 and enjoying life as we knew it. We didn't hang outside with the drug boys because neither of us owned a bulletproof vest and there was always the chance of catching a stray. Every now and again, we would get up early and go shoot some ball before all the hardcore thugs came out and took over the basketball court. It wasn't that Abraham and I were afraid to go out, we just knew that life was much easier if we remained outsiders to the game. Most, if not all of the teenagers hanging out in the courtyard, were already getting their grind on or were training for the *life*. Most were strapped and ready to take a life or lose their own in the game; or so they thought.

Abraham and I had never been warned to stay out of the mix, it was just something we had learned by watching some of the kids we went to school with die and get sent up north from messing around in the courtyard. Our parents stopped guiding and babying us around the age of eight, with the exception of Abraham's grandmother who did all she could to keep her influence over him. But just like most of the other teenagers in America, TV and video games were bigger influences. I'd seen a lot in the projects, but hadn't got sucked into a life that would either destroy me or free me. The Towers would make or break a young man coming through them on his way to manhood. The verdict was still out because they hadn't made me yet. It hadn't been determined yet whether or not I would be a survivor or be a victim.

I was leaving Abraham's apartment, taking the steps down because the elevators took forever if they were working, and he only lived on the third floor. It was almost 6:00 and I had to go and pick up Jade from the sitter's house. I ran down the three flights and when I reached the door to leave the stairway to enter the lobby, I heard a girl's voice and stopped in my tracks. Her voice was coming from the steps below me near the laundry room and it sounded familiar. She was crying and begging, "No, stop, pleaaasseee." I heard the voice yell out, "No, don't do that. I don't want to do that."

I moved down the steps slowly, because you didn't run up on folks where I lived unless you wanted to get hurt. When I walked into the laundry room, my heart began to pump wildly when I realized that the voice was my sister's. I saw Phil Boogie holding her by the hair.

Phil Boogie was the worst kind of nigga in the game. He was an enforcer, a dealer, and a stick-up boy. Every man, woman, and child tried to steer clear of him. He didn't live in the Towers, but spent almost all day, every day, around there doing his dirt and wreaking havoc. As my sister squirmed, he yelled, "Listen up, you little bitch. I told Quentin yesterday that if he didn't have my money that I was going to kill him and you. Now I am doing you a favor. Would you rather die or let me fuck you in the ass everyday until I get paid?" My sister was whimpering as if she was thinking things over. "Yesterday you said you didn't know how to suck a dick but you learned quick. Now what's up, you little trick? Do you want me to use that?" He turned to point to the gun that he had left on the folding table.

His eyes ballooned when he looked and saw me standing there with his gun in my hand. His pants were down around his ankles and he pulled them up slowly. My sister, who had just turned sixteen, had on nothing but her bra. Her stomach was starting to show and she looked bad. Quentin had dragged her down quickly. "Bitch nigga, what the fuck you doing? I'm gonna whoop your ass." He started toward me and Toni grabbed him and begged, "No, that's my brother."

"Shut the fuck up!" He swung and punched her in the throat. She began to gasp for air and he said, "I don't give a fuck, I'm gonna kill his punk ass and you too, bitch, after I finish with him. He swung at her once more, striking her again across her face, knocking her to the floor. Phil's face showed all the rage that lived inside him. He held no more regard for our lives than that of a dog on the street. As he approached me, I saw the grimace on his face and the evil in his eyes.

Instead of the fear that should have been present, I had the irresistible urge to smile at Phil Boogie as he approached me and I did. In that very instant, I felt powerful as the projects revealed my gift. I saw my sister on the floor. I saw hatred and reckless violence waiting to be unleashed on my sister and me. In the seconds it took for him to charge toward me, my whole life flashed in front of my eyes. It was as if all the anger and disappointment that I had ever faced, ignited inside of me and burst into one flame. With that flame, came a roar. In a fraction of a second, I saw that old preacher's face and heard his words about the projects giving me a gift echoing inside my head and then I heard GOD coming. He came in a clap of thunder. The sound was deafening, but still he clapped again. He clapped fourteen times in all, each time into a different spot on that thug's body, but mostly into his head and chest.

He had moved toward me, but the force of the first few bullets had frozen him in his steps and the next few knocked him backwards into the washing machine, which was where he laid still as his blood leaked out. I walked up to him and noticed that his eyes were still open. Suddenly as I stood over him and realized that he was indeed dead, I felt good. I felt released. I wasn't scared or shaking, but instead I looked at my sister, who was trembling and somewhat in shock, and saw all of the pain and hurt that she had ever been through right along with me.

Then and there, I made up my mind to straighten out our lives and to protect her and the baby she was carrying. "Put your clothes on and come on." When she stood there frozen, I yelled, "Hurry the fuck up!" I didn't realize that I was still holding the gun and scared her, but she moved quickly. I don't even know where the instincts that kicked in came from, but I immediately stooped over the body and went through the nigga's pockets. He had $1,800 in a rubber band and three bags of crack. In his jacket pocket, I found another clip full of hollow tips.

"Come on," I said to her a lot calmer than the first time and nodded my head toward the door. Toni was nervous but functional and put her clothes on quickly and stepped over the Phil's body.

"Where are we going?"

"I need to go up to Abraham's to borrow a change of clothes and then we gotta go pick up Jade from Mrs. Easton's house." As we headed out of the laundry room, I walked back over to the lifeless body to take one last look. I peered into his eyes and felt no pity or remorse. I did notice that blood was running out of the corners of his mouth. Strangely, the brother looked like he was at peace and I wondered who would be coming to mourn him later in the week. I wondered if his family or friends loved him and would miss him. As I reached down to double check his pockets, I realized that I couldn't care less. He was a rapist, a drug dealer and a notorious murderer his damned self. My mind was clear as I crossed over the first of a series of imaginary lines that marked the path

I was headed on. The hood had made me. I was going to thrive here if nowhere else and I embraced my gift ... Ruthlessness.

Abraham opened the door. "Man, why the hell you banging on my door like that?" He took a look at me and his eyes showed his shock. He glanced over my shoulder and saw Toni standing behind me looking tattered.

I pushed past him through the door. "I just killed that nigga."

He was staring at the blood on my hands and the drops that were on my face and shirt. "Who? You ain't lying. Who?"

"That crazy nigga that be robbing everybody who come through the Towers."

Toni joined in and said, "Phil Boogie."

Abraham's mouth dropped open. His expression showed a mixture of disbelief, fear and respect. If I hadn't raised my voice, he might have been still standing there. I told him that I needed a change of clothes to cross the courtyard. I explained everything to him as if I was a vet at this while Toni sat rocking back and forth on the couch like Rain Man. We talked for a minute about how to keep everything on the hush. At first I was going to take Toni home with me, but after thinking it over, I felt it would be better if Toni stayed over in his apartment for the next couple of days. I didn't want anyone claiming to have seen Phil with her last. If she was out of sight then she was out of mind. In a week, there would be another murder or police raid to talk about in the Towers and then things could go back to normal. We talked some more and I think Abraham began to feel less nervous about what had happened. Things happened in the hood all the time, but it was just hitting a little close to home for him. All in all, Abraham wanted to have my back. He assured me that he could hide Toni out because his grandmother didn't come in his room and his mother never came home. I knew he was happy to have her, even with her budding crack habit. Toni was beautiful and even though he was older than she was, Abraham had a crush on her from the time we stopped saying "uugghh" about girls in kindergarten.

I headed out of his building as the sun was setting. People were coming home from work and hustlers were working on the benches and on the playground. It was only a matter of time before someone went to the laundry room in the basement and found Phil's body. My walk had a little more bounce in it as I walked past the young slingers on benches. I normally walked on the sidewalk to avoid them, but I was feeling a bit amped up from the work I had put in. They didn't notice me as I watched them out the corner of my eye.

I realized that I had always avoided them because I was afraid they might notice me and get up and kick my ass simply for recreation like they did the dope fiends occasionally. But today, I had one arm inside my jacket and my hand on the chrome nine. I felt real safe. Then my mind went a step further. I thought about the fact that I was so close to them, that I could have whipped the pistol out. The mere fact that I wasn't out there slinging meant that I wasn't on their radar.

As I moved past them, I wondered if I was fast enough on the draw to pull the pistol out and spray the four of them before they could respond. I was betting that I could and imagined myself doing so. Then BOOM, BOOM, BOOM, BOOM! Four shots rang out in an instant. Two of them, I hit in the head, one center mass, and the last one I hit in the stomach. He was still alive and kicking his feet in pain. I walked over to him because he was squirming, trying to get away. I stood over him and put my foot on his neck and looked him in the eye. Mad at myself for having to waste another bullet, I pulled the trigger once more. BOOM! I smiled at the last one as I cleared the bench and said to him with a glare, "Today's your lucky day, nigga."

"What?" Only one of them heard me. He stood up, but I just glared at him as I entered my building. Then I mumbled under my breath, "Today, I'll let y'all chumps live."

TWO

Faith goes a long way. In the worst of times, sometimes it's all you have. It has to be built up and put to the test in order for it to be the kind of faith that the Creator appreciates. Experiences, good and bad, are often the results of the works of men themselves, happenstance, or of the transgressions against him by another. The way a man handles himself through those experiences shows what kind of heart he has. Of little faith, of little heart. True faith walks hand in hand with heart, and often by the time you notice that you've lost one... you've already lost the other. And who can survive without either?

I was on my knees in front of my bed praying. Malik Vaughn was the only real friend that I'd ever known. Since we were little kids, everything we'd done, we'd done together. I always hoped that it would be that way forever. But now he'd killed a man and I knew he was headed to jail. My Uncle Tye spent his whole life in the joint and he used to send me letters warning me what they did to youngsters when they went to jail. I didn't want any of that to happen to Malik. He was a good person and like a lot of brothers who made one bad decision, he didn't deserve jail.

After all, it wasn't like the world was going to miss Phil Boogie. He brought nothing but pain to the projects. He sold weed, crack, and dope to anyone who would buy it—pregnant women, kids, whoever had cash—was his customer. He was a heartless cat. He would beat niggas down for next to nothing and the rumors were that he had robbed and killed at least ten people in the last four years. The kingpins had given him free reign in exchange for his policing the Towers. He was their hired gun and psycho robot all in one. Once they turned him loose, most everyone in the Towers feared him. I guess everyone except Malik.

Malik called me a couple hours after he left my crib. He spoke as calmly as any other day when he told me that he was feeding Jade and waiting for his mother to get home so he could go down the hall to get his hair done. I told him that the police had just arrived and people were gathering around my building.

"Good," he told me, "the sooner, the better. This whole thing will die down pretty quick. You know there is just another clown waiting to take his place." I was hoping that he was right about Phil's murder blowing over. Even though I tried to have heart like Malik, I was nervous about the whole thing. I even felt guilty for helping Malik cover it up. I knew God didn't like murder and there probably could have been another way. Don't get me wrong, I wasn't going to snitch, but I felt like the police might understand if we just told them how it had happened.

It was difficult for me to assess what state of mind he was in. Malik seemed different, which was understandable due to the circumstances. The strange thing was that all of a sudden, he was all business. He told me to go outside and see what was going on but not to seem too curious. He made me feel worse when he said *our* lives depended on it. He said that too many people knew we were best friends and if Phil's crew came after him, they would soon get me too. He was right.

"Put Toni on the phone before you go outside. I'll see you in the morning."

"You goin' to school?" I asked.

"Yeah, nothing changes. We gonna act normal and do what we always do. Now put my sister on the phone," he barked playfully. I gave her the phone as I started getting dressed to go investigate.

"What's up?" Toni asked.

"This is what's up. I know you been messing around with that shit and all, but I need you to keep it together and stay in Abraham's room for the next couple of days. Don't leave unless you are going to the bathroom. I gotta make sure all this shit blows over and I don't need you out there acting nervous. I don't want you talking to the Jamaican either." Malik's tone was harsh as he yelled loud enough for me to hear him through the line. "Keep in mind, this whole thing happened because of you. So I won't tolerate any slip-ups by you. This is my life on the line now."

Toni nodded her head while she held the phone. "Okay," she answered as if she was talking to her father instead of her brother. We all had our orders courtesy of Malik.

Word spread quickly about Phil's murder and the next morning the courtyard was nearly deserted. Usually the courtyard was full of hustlers slinging, catching the morning rush, but because no one knew who had killed Phil, they were leery. The word was that the stick-up boys had taken him into the building, robbed him and left him for dead. There were no witnesses to speak of and the rest of the hustlers were afraid that whoever had been ruthless enough to walk into Greenberg Projects, rob Phil Boogie, and empty fifteen bullets into his body, might be coming back.

The next morning, I walked out of my building at 7:45, just like usual. Like clockwork, Malik walked up to me. "Ready?" His hair was freshly braided and he had a black bandana tied around his head like a headband.

"Ready as I'm gonna be," Malik said slapping me five. We walked in silence the first couple of blocks before Malik turned to me. "So how was my sister last night? Was she buggin'?"

"What you mean? About you killing Phil...."

He cut me off. "Look, man, stop saying that shit. I didn't kill anybody. You understand? Don't even let those words come out your mouth again." He shook his head in disgust. "Plus I ain't talking about that anyway. I'm talking about her little problem. Did she try to go out in the courtyard?"

"Nah, she chilled and talked about you all night until she fell asleep."

"Yeah? What about me?" Malik asked sounding curious.

"Mostly she kept saying she didn't know you had heart like that. She said that she was proud of you for taking care of Jade while Lindsey be working and running the streets." I reached in my jacket pocket and pulled out a Three Musketeers bar. I offered Malik half. He declined, so I bit into it. "She said that she is going to get herself together and start going to school. Said she wants to be a beautician."

"Word?" he asked.

"Yeah. I told her that would be real cool." We talked some more about Toni spending the next couple of nights with me. Of course it was cool with me. I let him know that I wasn't sure if she'd be able to stay on the weekend though because my grandmother would be home. My grandmother worked two jobs, Monday through Friday, and only left the house on weekends to go to the grocery store and church.

We were almost to school when I stopped Malik. I turned to him and asked, "So how do you feel... I mean, what was it like killing him?"

Malik paused and stood silent for a few seconds. He stared right into my eyes and then he grew a half smile on his face and said, "Abraham, I never did anything more perfect than killing Phil Boogie. It was by far my finest day." He then turned and headed up the steps to Marcus Garvey High School.

THREE

Misery is a terrible thing. It sneaks up on folks cloaked in darkness poised to strangle everything we need as human beings to survive. There are no such things as joy, hope, and peace where misery dwells. It's contagious in nature because like they say, it loves company. If you don't make sure your resistance is strong, you will catch it like an airborne disease.

Lindsey Vaughn was miserable. You couldn't tell by looking at her. She was thirty-six but still held her shape from her twenties. She had the kind of hair that didn't need a perm and had passed it on to all three of her children, myself included. When she wanted, she could always get money from the men who wanted a piece of her. She was a fiend for attention and had a set of even more miserable girlfriends who kissed her ass like she was the ghetto Claire Huxtable.

The only way to tell she was miserable would be to listen to her beyond all of the bullshit that she talked. The way she begged niggas on the phone at night for their attention, and the way she talked to my sisters and me when she got rejected. She had no idea that things were about to change in our house. She would need to get with the program or shit was going to get funky around here.

She woke me up at 7:00, same as every morning, but this time I rolled back over. "Malik, get your ass out of bed. I am not trying to deal with the school calling here because you are late like it's my damn fault." I heard her through my open door and started to stare at the ceiling. "Maaaaalik!" she yelled this time.

I made my way out of the bed to the toilet to pee. When I came out, I walked into my mother's room. "I ain't going to school today. I got something important to do." I turned and went back into my room and began to lie across the bed. Lindsey came walking into the room behind me.

"Excuse me, but you had better get your ass dressed before I go off up in this camp." I watched her face as she spit her usual verbal abuse. The funny thing was that before what happened with Phil Boogie on Monday afternoon, her assaults used to rattle me. Now I just stared at her. "Boy, did you hear what I just said? Don't make me go upside your head."

I stood up and moved toward her. "Do what you gotta do, but like I said, I ain't going to school today. I was only telling you because I knew you would be off work today and if the school calls, I didn't want you to be surprised." Garvey had an automated truancy device. Too many late arrivals and absences and a phone call would come, sort of a computerized snitch.

Lindsey looked at me like I had lost my mind. Maybe I had. It felt good though, to disrespect her the way she routinely disrespected her children. "Boy, I will beat you into next week. You have lost your motherfucking mind talking to me like that. Don't you ever disrespect me like that again. I saw her swing at me and I ducked. The second time she swung, I grabbed her by both wrists.

"Look, Ma. I am too old for this shit. Don't put your hands on me anymore. If you can't speak to me like you got some sense, then take your ass in the room and cool off," I rattled off in my harshest tone. There was shock on her face when she looked up into mine and saw a man in front of her. It was obvious that somewhere along the way, she had lost track of the fact that I had grown up a lot. "If I say I got something to do, then I got something to do." After a pause, I added, "I ain't gonna be able to pick up Jade today either so make some other arrangements." I let her hands go. She was trembling and ran out of my room and towards the kitchen. I figured she was going to get the cordless phone to run her mouth to my grandma until I heard the drawers open and shut.

Lindsey's ass had grabbed a butcher knife and was at my door looking like she was about to hyperventilate. "The day you put your hands on me is the day you die. I brought you into this world..."

"But you ain't gonna take me out." I had Phil Boogie's gun in my hand. I didn't point it at her, but I kept it by my hip. "Look, Ma. I love you, but if and when I die in these projects, I'm going out shooting. I don't think you're ready for that type of drama. Always know that we're family and I got your back, but you are going have to relax around here. Live and let live. All of that cussing and fussing... I'm not even trying to hear too much more of that shit."

Lindsey was holding her chest trying to catch her breath. I just shook my head. "Go put that knife away before someone gets hurt." I walked right past her and headed into the bathroom to take a shower. When I got out, she was on the phone in her room with the door closed. I took my time getting dressed and reached into my tennis shoes that were on the shelf and pulled them down. I grabbed half the money that I had taken off of Phil Boogie and put it into my pants pocket. I put on my backpack and was about to head out when my mother's door opened.

"So what's up? I don't have a son any more? Is this all I have left, a thug?" She had tears in her eyes.

"Listen, Ma. Everything is cool. We are going to talk later on tonight. I'll watch Jade if you want to go out." I remembered it was Friday and Toni wouldn't be able to stay at Abraham's. "There is one thing though. Toni has to come home for a couple of months until she can get a place of her own."

"What? Are you out of your mind? You got a gun and you think you are going to hold me hostage in my own house. I will call the police and have you put away before I allow you to call the shots around here." Lindsey was snapping but in a different way. I noticed four sentences without being cursed at.

"Hold it, Ma. Sending me away wouldn't be a good thing. I got to tell you that snitching on me is not an option. I will do anything for this family. Anybody that goes against this family from now on is asking for trouble. We are a family of four, plus Abraham makes five. But if we lose a member for the good of the whole, then that is how it has to be."

"Malik, is that a threat?" I headed towards the door. "I said, is that a threat!?" she shrieked at the top of her voice.

"I'll see you tonight and Toni will be with me." I slammed the front door so hard that pictures fell off of the wall. I didn't bother turning my key to lock it before I headed to the elevator.

I was standing in line at Phil Boogie's wake looking around to see if anyone was crying. There was a short line to the front of the funeral home. I was behind a wide woman and her husband and when they stepped to the side, I made my way to the casket. It was closed, of course. I stood there for a moment and placed the flowers that I had picked up from Marty's Grocery on the corner. I wondered what Phil Boogie looked like inside of that casket. I could imagine the mortician trying to put the back of his head back together in order to have an open casket. I had lit him up pretty bad.

Again, I wasn't religious and wasn't all together sure if I even believed in God, but I took to my knees in front of everyone there and began to pray silently, *Dear God, I am not praying for Phil because on the real, he was a heartless nigga and deserved to die. Instead, I pray for the innocent people I hurt: his mother, his sister, his daughter and even his girl. They didn't deserve to hurt so I ask that you ease their pain. I also ask that you forgive me for killing him. Last and most important God, I thank you for letting it be him in that box instead of me.* I stood up and walked away wondering if Phil was even going to see God or if I'd sent him straight to Hell.

I turned and headed up the aisle toward the exit. When I reached the lobby, I saw a girl sitting in the corner by the guest book. She had on a baby blue dress and set of earrings with her name in them. She smiled at me and I walked over to her. "Hey, Angel. How you doing?" I pointed to her earrings, tipping her off as to how I knew her name.

"As good as can be under these circumstances. Phil was my brother." I swallowed hard.

"I'm sorry to hear that... I mean what happened to him."

She nodded in appreciation. "How did you know Phil? I never saw you with him before." She stood up and pulled a piece of gum out her purse.

"Everyone in the Towers knew Phil. We kind of looked up to him. I'm surprised more people didn't come." I was staring into her face. She was trying to smile in response to my comments. I could see that she had one deep dimple on the right cheek but not the left and a small mole on her cheek. She was beautiful. I figured she had to be at least sixteen as phat as she was, even though in the hood the young girls fill out young. *All the steroid-injected chicken and McDonalds does a body good like milk,* I thought to myself. "Listen. You must see his daughter a lot?"

Angel nodded her head. "She lives with us now. My mom takes care of her and I help out." She paused and said, "Why do you ask?"

"I wanted to give you a little something to help out with her." I handed Angel $200. Her eyes lit up. I could tell immediately that very little of that money would go to Phil Boogie's daughter. I really didn't care, my motive was to get a chance to see Angel again. "You got a number?"

Angel wrote her number down and gave me a hug. She told me she had seen me praying by the casket and thought it was the most powerful thing that she had ever seen. She told me that she had a boyfriend in Rahway that she was waiting for but she definitely wanted to be friends with me. She put a smile on my face as I walked out of the funeral home and headed around the corner to White Castle where Abraham was waiting for me while reading the Post.

"How was it?" he asked when I slid into the booth.

"It was alright."

"I still don't know why you wanted to go. That's kind of sick." He sucked on his soft drink. "Did you pray like I suggested?"

"Yeah, I sure did and I was rewarded." Abraham looked puzzled.

"How so?" I slid Angel's number onto the table and started laughing.

"Who is Angel?" he asked still unimpressed.

"She's Phil Boogie's younger sister. And let me tell you she is cute as shit."

I saw Abraham frown up. "That ain't right man."

"Come on, man, don't start. We got a big day. Let's roll." We headed out onto Atlantic Avenue and hopped the bus to downtown Brooklyn. Abraham's saintly ass had no idea what he had waiting for him. I had to get us on the same page and I knew just how to do it.

FOUR

Destiny rules us all. There is no sense being afraid of what lies in wait around the corner. Whether it is good or evil, it will be there waiting patiently. It may be the blessings of life's treasures or a beast in the shadows waiting to pounce and slaughter you. No sense trying to run, hide, or go in a different direction. If you have prepared yourself spiritually or physically, you have already done all you can. Neither prayers nor the weapons of man will guarantee survival. God, for his own reasons unknown to man, allows the good and the young to die or sometimes suffer. Other times, the wretched and evil are allowed to thrive and dominate.

I looked over at Malik. He was caressing the gun like it was the source of life and not the agent of death. I couldn't figure out why he was still carrying it around. It was evidence in a recently committed crime. I had to admit that it was a nice looking tool. It was a chrome Smith and Wesson with a pearl handle. He was sitting in the seats across the aisle from me and was in his own world. I held my head down and started to pray, "Dear God, please release Malik from these demons of violence. Please let him be safe and keep me safe while I am with him. Also, please forgive him for what he did to Phil Boogie, and me for being a part of it. Dear God I also wanted…"

"Man, what the hell are you doing over there? Wake your ass up." Malik slid his body to the edge of the seat and kicked me in the leg. He startled me and I totally lost my train of thought.

"Man, I ain't sleep." I shook my head. I wanted to finish my prayer but I didn't want to hear Malik clowning me all afternoon.

"We here. C'mon." We jumped off the bus on Flatbush Avenue and crossed over to Fulton Street. I followed Malik into the Athlete's Foot shoe store.

I looked around the store and noticed the salesgirl was checking us out. "Man what are we doing up in here? I ain't down for no window shopping."

"Can I help you?" the sales girl asked as she walked up on us. I figured that we might have looked too young to be shopping in the middle of the day. I started to answer her and tell her we were just looking when Malik jumped in.

"Yeah, get him a pair of those Jordans in an eight and can you get two of those sweatshirts down off that rack?"

She cracked a smile sensing her commission might look good after all. "Which one, the black or the gray?" Malik pointed to the black hooded sweatshirts and told her to make them XL's. Just then, a heavyset guy with cornrows in his hair walked in and motioned to Malik.

"Abraham, take this and grab the stuff and come on out."

Malik handed me $200. I figured it was money from Phil Boogie and instantly I felt bad. I was a little angry because he knew how much I loved Michael Jordan. I had wanted a pair of his shoes forever. Now here I was about to spend blood money on my first pair. I considered walking out of the store and not getting them but when the cute salesgirl asked me, "Anything else?" she showed her pretty white teeth. I shook my head, "Nah, that's it," and walked toward the register.

"So how old are you?" she asked.

"Nineteen," I lied without remorse. "Why, how old are you?"

She couldn't stop grinning. "I'm twenty. You know you're kinda cute. You just look kinda young for your age. I bet you got a girl?"

"Nah," I was trying to sound cool. She was making it easy for me. "So you tryin' to gimme ya' number?"

She leaned over the counter. "We ain't supposed to meet niggas while we working, but the number to the store is on the receipt. As you can see, my name is Sondra." She pointed to her nametag. "Call me here before 9:00."

"That's what's up. I'ma do that." I looked at the receipt and turned to walk away when she came around the counter to walk me to the front of the store.

Sondra strolled up to me and whispered, "So you and your man got dough right?" I looked at her and she continued, "Because I got a homegirl who goes to NYU with me. I know he'll like her and we can hook up tonight. We just don't roll with no broke fools." I was shocked. I knew girls were materialistic but Sondra was brazen with hers. "A girl gots to have standards, right?"

I nodded and flashed her a smile. "No doubt. Yeah, we got dough. I'm gonna hit you up." I was almost out the door when she reminded me that I hadn't told her my name. "Abraham."

"Just like the president, huh?" she was laughing.

"That's me, Mr. President." I walked out to the sidewalk thinking about the nerve of Sondra. I imagined what it would be like to have enough money to buy a girl like her whatever she wanted.

When I walked out of the store, I saw Malik in the back seat of a Mazda MPV parked just in front of the store. "Come on, Abe." he yelled out. I headed over to the van a little uneasy. I didn't know the guy driving and wondered why we were rolling with him.

"Get in the front seat," Malik said.

I walked around the front of the van and climbed in. The big guy extended his hand, "What's up, youngster? I'm Carlos." I extended my hand but still showed the look of someone who didn't know what was going on.

"This is my fat cousin. I mean big cousin. He lives out in Queens. You remember when I used to go out to visit my cousins, Walt and Dean?"

"Oh yeah, back in the day."

"Yeah, well Los is their older brother. He was always away at college." Malik laughed out loud while he fumbled through a bag in the backseat as the van pulled out into traffic.

"Fuck you," Carlos responded with a chuckle, letting me know that the college he was at is also called jail.

I nodded and felt a little better. Though I had never heard of Carlos, if he was family then everything was cool. "Where we headed?" I asked.

"To handle some business," Carlos said as we drove across the Manhattan Bridge. Carlos sped through the Lower East Side onto the West Side Highway all the way up to 50th Street. He then hit Broadway headed uptown. When we reached 91st Street, he circled the block and found a parking spot just behind a dumpster in the alley.

I had been silent most of the drive. Carlos had a nice system in the MPV and had been blasting Fifty Cent's CD the whole way. "Is this the spot?" Malik asked from behind me.

"Yeah, this is it. You see the door right there, the basement apartment just below it?" Carlos asked. "I'm going to let you out and then I'll circle again. If he doesn't answer, then fuck it, just get the hell out of there and jump back in the van. If he's in there, run back over here to the alley as soon as you finish. When you see me, jump in the side door. Take the pizza container with you. You know how to do it." He even had a pizza warmer.

I didn't figure out what was happening until Malik handed me the sweatshirt he had paid for in the store. "Put this on and come on."

"Man, what?" This shit had bad move all over it. My heart started to race when I thought about what Malik might be about to do. I sensed he was ready to commit another crime and had dragged me into it.

"Listen. All I am going to do is go see if this guy has the money he owes my cousin. You got my back or not? If you don't, it's cool. I will go alone and you can circle the block with Carlos."

When I saw him standing there in the black hoodie looking like he might be headed for war, I felt like I had to be down with whatever he was doing. If I didn't have his back, I knew I wouldn't hear the end of it. Later, he would have given me the whole rundown on how he'd always had mine. And I'd have to admit that he always did.

Coming up, he used to take beatings from Lindsey for eating too much food when he was really sneaking it to me. Before my grandmother moved back to Brooklyn, I had many nights when there was no food in my house at all. Left up to my mother, I would have starved every other night, had it not been for Malik. He had always been there for me and now that we were older, I knew I'd always have to hold him down.

Malik held the empty Domino's box in his hand and banged on the door. At his instruction, I stood off to the side at the top of the steps. I was zoning out thinking about the tool he had just given me. I had held a gun before but I was far from being into gunplay. I had never carried one on the street. I almost didn't notice when the door swung open. "I have a delivery for George," Malik said. A balding man answered the door. His beard was long like an Arab.

The man answered, "There is no George here. You have the wrong address."

"This is 1448 West 91st, correct?" Malik asked.

"No, this is 1484."

"Oh, I'm sorry. Well in that case, let me…" Malik pulled his gun up from his pants and yelled, "Back your ass up from this door before I blow your brains all over the wall." The man was slow in moving back. "You heard me, mufucka, back up!" Malik yelled.

"Shit. Don't shoot, I am unarmed. I will give you whatever you want," I heard him say. Malik looked back at me and motioned for me to come down the steps into the apartment. "You can have whatever you want."

"Is there anyone in this crib with you?" Malik screamed on him. "If you lie, I swear I'll blast you." The man backed into his living room.

"No one is here. I'm alone," he said nervously.

Malik told him to sit on the couch then turned toward me, "Keep that gun on his ass. If he makes one wrong move, I want you to light his ass up." I looked at Malik with puzzlement. "Like the Fourth of July," he added. I was wondering who this crazy nigga was that I was with. Somebody had switched bodies with Malik. He had always had a little edge and even gotten into trouble at school, but he had changed overnight. I had no doubt that he was serious. "I'm going in the back to check shit out." He headed into the back of the apartment with his gun drawn like a cop in a movie.

Malik walked back into the living room. He walked up on the man, "You owe a certain someone some money. I am here to collect it. If you give it to me now, you can live. If you don't, then oh well."

"I have no idea what you are talking about. Who says I owe them? Perhaps you made a mistake in the address."

"The gentlemen I work for prefer that I don't use names. I will say this one more time. Where is the money?" Malik growled to him.

The man cracked a smile. "Aren't you two a little young to be enforcers?" Then he asked, "Who do you work for? He must be a coward to send you *boys* to handle his business."

I saw Malik's face tighten as he ran into the bedroom and came out with a pillow and put it around the pistol. He put the gun two feet from the man's face. The man flinched and tried to back away as if ducking would help if a bullet were coming. "Ten, nine, eight, seven, five, three, two...."

"No. No," he cried out. "Okay.... in my room, under the night stand is a hollowed out phone book..." Malik cut him off. "If you lying, you dying." He then went in the back and came back twenty seconds later. "Okay, now where's the rest? I know you have more."

"You greedy little bastard!" The man said a couple more curse words. BOOM! Malik shot him in the thigh and without hesitating, put the gun back to his face. The man was grimacing and moaning.

"Shut that fucking noise up before I give you something to cry about." He laughed at the man who was grabbing his thigh. "If I have to ask you again, I'm going to shoot you in the balls. I don't give a fuck." Malik placed the pistol next to the man's temple. "I want the product too."

"Okay. Okay. In the pantry, in the kitchen... the bag of sugar on the top shelf... that is all, I swear. Now please." I was in shock watching Malik look at the man. He went into the kitchen. He used a dishtowel to open the door to the pantry. He grabbed the sugar and poured it onto the table and saw two manila envelopes wrapped tightly into small packages.

Malik walked over to me and handed me the envelopes. "Put these in your pants. Don't mention it until I do." He looked into my eyes and then back at the man. "Are you up to it?" He paused. "Go ahead. Do him."

"No. I already gave you the money. Here take my watch." He was begging for his life.

I had no intention of killing the man. I didn't think I had what it took to do that unless my life or the life of someone I loved was in danger. I was about to admit that fact to Malik. Before I could though, the man lunged and grabbed the gun I was holding. I stumbled back and fell to the floor. He was on top of me. I didn't know where the gun was, but it was no longer in my hand. It had happened so quickly and now the man was on top of me reaching for the gun when Malik fired into the side of his head. BOOM!

"Oh shit! Oh shit!" I screamed. I looked and saw the side of the man's brains hanging out. I scurried to get him off of me. Malik was calm and looking at me as if I should have known better than to let the guy get the drop on me.

"Come on, we got to break up out of here." Malik pulled me up and picked up the gun I had dropped. He ran over to the door and looked outside. He opened the door and ran up the steps. I was on his heels. We crossed the street and made it to the alley and saw the van coming up the street.

I could barely make out any dialog between Malik and Carlos. I was riding with them but I wasn't there at the same time. I was now an accessory to murder and had a package of stolen money and drugs in my pants. My best friend was a cold-blooded murderer and I was sure he was going to get us both locked up for life. I started thinking about all of the things I would never be able to do. I wanted to graduate and get a good job. I had even thought about attending college. I wanted to sit courtside at a Knicks game next to Hova and Dame Dash, buy a car and pick up a girl for a date one day— maybe even a fine girl like Sondra.

My mind raced and I thought about her asking me about money. I was now sure that I had enough dough to get her to hang out, but if I had to do this to get paid, then girls like her weren't worth it. I daydreamed about her some more and began to wonder if Malik planned on sharing any of this money.

"We're here." The van pulled up at Penn Station and Malik got out. "Come on. Let's Roll." I jumped out and grabbed my shopping bag. "Take the sweatshirt off," Malik said. I noticed his was in the back on the floor. He slapped Carlos five. "Cuz, I'll call you in the morning about those guns."

"Okay, I should have them tonight. So just lay low until then and keep the one you have." Carlos looked over at me and smiled, "Stay up youngster. It ain't that serious. You are going to get money fooling around with Malik. He got heart."

I faked a smile and nodded and walked off. Malik walked by my side and we headed toward the subway. I thought about what Carlos had just said. How was I supposed to stay up when it was way serious? I wasn't sure how much money I was going to get fooling with Malik, but I knew there would be a lot of time waiting on me if we got busted. As far as heart, I wasn't sure if that was the word I would use to describe what he had. I had witnessed what Malik had done to Phil Boogie now firsthand. Two people in one week; at this pace, he was going to kill over a hundred people in a year. He had a gift and I wanted no part of it.

FIVE

Influence is power by a less imposing name. When it is used for good, influence can change and rebuild lives that would otherwise be lost. On the other hand, negative influence sidetracks and oftentimes demolishes the lives of all of those susceptible to its reaches. Leaders who are a good influence on their people will cause them all to prosper in some way or another. A leader who wrongly guides or directs those who follow him will cause suffering and eventual devastation to his clan.

I never wanted to have power over anyone until I got a taste of it. Realizing I knew what was best for those around me and that I might have to force it on them with an iron hand was not an appealing thought. Still, I had to come to grips with the fact that I was born to be a leader and protector of all those around me. There was a hell of a lot of responsibility placed on my shoulders. I would have to teach my mother to put her family first when no one had ever put her first in her entire life. Though she wasn't a hard-core crack addict, I was going to have to get Toni straightened out before she did something stupid and brought unwanted attention to all that I wanted to build.

It was hard to recognize the impact that I had on Abraham. As we rode the train back into Brooklyn, I watched him stare out the window with a far away look in his eyes. He was looking for something out of that window, hoping to find it the same way I had when I'd stared out of it a time or two before. Coming back from visits to the jail to see my grandfather and listening to him first open my eyes to the realities of life, I too had searched for my innocence. Abraham would have to learn that it wasn't something he could hold on to, not being a black man growing up in the projects.

My grandfather, Vincent Vaughn, was sentenced to 25 years to life in 1978 for killing a bank security guard who gunned down his partner in cold blood as they were in the midst of a get-a-way. I had heard stories when I visited my family uptown that he was one of the meanest men to ever walk the streets of Harlem. If there was a serious crime going down anywhere in the Wild 100's, he was in on it. He ran with the likes of the notorious Nikki Barnes, and Harlem Reds. He was rumored to have pimped more women, sold more dope, and robbed more banks in a fifteen-year span than most career criminals did in a lifetime. He stayed busy and banked money that was unheard of in the late sixties and seventies. He still owned two apartment buildings, a laundromat and a cleaners up in Harlem that my great Uncle Kelly runs to this day.

My grandmother had warned my mother to never let me go visit him, but when I hit ten years old, I started asking questions about my own father. My mother was so uncomfortable answering those questions that she called my Uncle Kelly and asked him to take me upstate to see my grandfather. I assume she figured that she could replace the guidance that I didn't get from my own father with some from a hardened criminal.

When I began to ask to see Vincent more often, she became concerned and confessed to my grandmother that she had allowed me to see him. It created a wedge between them and to appease my grandmother my mother cut off the visits.

By the time I hit thirteen, I was catching the bus and the train up to Harlem to see Uncle Kelly. It didn't take me long to convince him to begin taking me along with him on his visits. I grew closer to my granddad. He even told me to call him by his street name, Double V. He was the coolest old dude I ever met. When I came to visit, he would finish his visit with my uncle first then take me off into the courtyard or to a table in the back of the visiting room where we had the privacy to speak about life as I knew it and as he viewed it.

Last June on my seventeenth birthday, which happened to be Father's day, Double V professed me a man and began to drop his philosophy on me. It was amazing to me that as old as he was, he was still as imposing as any thug I had ever seen. He was 6'2" and built like he could have been a boxer back in the day. He wore a five o'clock shadow that was peppered with gray. His small afro was combed neatly to the back, never a hair out of place. He was handsome, even for a man who had lived hard on the outside and served over twenty years in a maximum-security house. His most noticeable features were his eyes. It was easy to see how he probably used them to hypnotize women that he turned into hoes and also to strike fear into the hearts of enemies who got close enough to see them. They were killer eyes. I wondered if he saw the same thing when he looked at me.

I gradually bought into everything Double V sold me. Through my visits with my grandfather, I lost my innocence long before I pulled the trigger in the laundry room.

"Malik, there are two kinds of people in this world. There are givers and takers. You have to decide which one you are going to be." He sat me down on the bench and laid it all out for me. "Son, I ain't saying there ain't a God, but you're taking a hell of a gamble if you betting on him taking care of you. You got to go out and get it yourself." He could tell I wasn't swallowing it all and went on. "If there is a God, then there has to be a heaven. In that case, the good givers will be the ones to reach it after they leave this Earth." He had paused and held me at attention while I waited for him to finish. "A good taker though... he has heaven every day and night, right here on Earth. He doesn't have to wait."

I remembered wondering about where I fit into the scheme. I had come to admire his wisdom. Double V had an answer for everything so I asked him what I wanted to know, "Which one do you think I am?"

He looked me in the eye, "You'll find out." Then a smile formed on his lips.

"When?" I asked as curious as a cat.

He turned back to me and said in an ice-cold voice, "As soon as a motherfucker tries to take something from you. You'll know then. C'mon, visit is over."

When we got off the bus on Atlantic Ave., Abraham told me he needed to use the phone. I asked him who he had to call and he explained the whole conversation with the hoochie in the shoe store. I smiled because it seemed like Abraham was alright. He was calm enough to think about getting some. I sat on the bench of the bus stop while he made the call.

He walked back up on me without hanging the phone up, "Malik, they tryin' to hook up. You down?"

I thought about what I had to do at home as far as getting my sister situated. I knew I had drama ahead from my mother. "Ask them if they driving to come scoop us around 10:00 tonight. Tell 'em we trying to get some grub and a room."

Abraham was headed back to the phone when I added, "If they ain't driving, tell them to meet us at the Days Inn on Marcy at 10:30."

Abraham came back to me smiling and told me that they would have a ride and were coming up. He told me that the girl, Sondra, and her friend, Aaliya, lived out in Jamaica. They were a step or two above real project chicks and I got the feeling that they were trying to find a couple of ballers to support them. He told me that they were both twenty and my mind began to fill with ideas on how I could use what they wanted to control them.

As we entered the courtyard, things were picking back up. There was more activity than had been seen since I had taken Phil out. I noticed that a few cats that hadn't shown their faces in the last year were out in the court trying to get money. Phil was a loose cannon and had scared most of the outsiders from stepping into Greenberg to hustle. He would rob a nigga and tell you that if you came back the next day, he would be there to take your shit again.

It was hard to believe that I had taken out one of the most feared men in our hood. There were a couple of men who held more respect for the way they did business as well as for the amount of money that they made. Cortez, rumored to have been a millionaire at twenty-five, was the king of heroin in our courts. If you weren't selling for him, then you weren't selling heroin in our court. Phil Boogie was his lieutenant and enforcer and he made sure of that. There was also Doc and Wendell who worked together to control everything else. They had the crack and weed hustle on lock in the courtyard and a couple of other strips within two blocks.

We made our way into the courtyard and I sent Abraham up to get Toni. I told him that I would meet him on the corner at 10:20 and to call the two chicks and tell them to be on time.

"You alright?" I asked my sister.

"I'm straight." I looked in her face. Her eyes were clear and she looked like she had been straight for a couple of days. "Abraham was cool. He treated me good."

"Not too good I hope," I said half joking and halfway serious.

Toni shook her head. "Gimme a break. I'm not hardly interested in your friend. I love him to death, but he's like a brother to me."

"Okay, just making sure." I smiled, breaking my all-business tone for a second and snapping right back into it. We were walking back towards our building. "I talked to Lindsey and you are coming back home." She was silent. "There ain't gonna be no drama either. I ain't having that no more. It's no good for Jade to grow up around all of that bullshit. Your baby either."

"Are you sure? She said I could come back?"

"No, I did." I stopped and looked at her. "Listen up. I'm only gonna tell you this one time."

"What is it?"

I asked Toni to take a look around and asked her if she really wanted more for herself, her baby, and for Jade. I told her that I had a plan to make sure that everyone I considered family would have a better life outside of the projects. She stood there smiling. While I left out the details, I outlined how I would come up with enough money to buy a house for us down in Georgia where our grandmother's family lived. I promised her the world and told her that she would never have to rely on another man other than me. Then I made her promise never to use drugs again, which meant that she wouldn't be able to see Quentin anymore. When she hesitated to promise not to see him, I pulled the gun out of my pants.

"For that baby in your stomach, I will do whatever is necessary. Now promise and mean that shit."

A whisper came, "I promise."

SIX

Lust for money, sex, power, or love all lead to the same road out in the middle of Hell. Once the desire for any of those things becomes the focal point of a man's existence, he then plots his destination for that very end. When he begins to find excitement on his journey, he quickens his pace. Some are fortunate enough to crash on the way and have the sense to turn back. Smart money says that right now, sitting in Purgatory are probably those who enjoyed such a smooth ride to self-destruction that the only thing that they will agree on is that they never once thought about turning back.

The second I saw Sondra pull up in her mom's BMW wagon, I knew she was going to be special. I was only seventeen and had seen a few lookers in my time, but when she got out of the driver's seat and walked around to give me a hug, I was mesmerized. She had on a pair of J-Lo jeans. My eyes caught her pelvic bones and I noticed that she had a belly ring. She looked ten times better than she looked when I had seen her in the store earlier. Her home girl stayed in the car talking on a cell phone. I looked at her face and could see that she was just as pretty as Sondra. "What up, Mr. President?" Sondra asked.

"Nuttin,'" I was giving her my hippest dialect. Before I could finish telling her that Malik was on the way down, he walked out between the two buildings. He was wearing a New York Jets hat with a stocking cap on underneath it. He had on a matching jersey and a fresh pair of Timberland boots. "Hey Sondra, this is my man, Malik." I didn't like the way she looked him up and down as if she was deciding which one of us she was going to choose.

"He was with you earlier when you came in the store, right?" I feared she remembered that he was the one who paid for the shoes. "Hey, Malik."

"What's good?" he mouthed and extended his balled up fist for her to give him a pound. I was surprised when she punched her fist softly against his. "Let's roll," he said.

We stepped to the car and Sondra told Aaliyah to get in the back when Malik interrupted. "Nah, stay up front. I need to talk to Abe anyway."

"Oh okay." I could tell she thought it was a strange request. Once we all got into the car, introductions were exchanged.

Aaliyah draped herself against the door and was trying to spark conversation and get up in our business. Malik kept her at bay like a veteran. I knew that this was my first time going out with some older honeys but from the way Malik was controlling the conversation, I thought that he had been holding back on some info. Malik gave Sondra the directions to the Soul Café on 9th Avenue.

While we rode to the restaurant, Malik gave me the rundown on what had happened when he went into the house with Toni. His grandmother had been there waiting and had questioned him about pulling a gun on his mother. I was shocked when he told me what had happened with his mom before we had hooked up in the morning. He said Lindsey had told her that she was scared for her life and that Malik was on his way to becoming as crazy as his grandfather. She had gotten hysterical and said that she wasn't going to stay under the same roof with him.

Within an hour, his grandmother had straightened everything out. Lindsey had even told Toni that she could stay with her for one year until she got on her feet with the baby. Malik said that he had given his mother $400 and apologized for the harsh stance that he had taken with her, but then warned her about getting out of line or treating Toni bad while she was pregnant. Then he leaned toward me and said, "This is for you. Put this in your sock and don't spend it." He handed me a wad of bills. I looked at it and saw a stack of hundreds. Then he whispered, "This right here is for you to blow tonight. Let these bitches see you spend it. Whenever I try to pay for something, cut me off and say that it's your treat. Got it?" I looked down and saw a thick wad of twenties and on the inside were a few fifty-dollar bills.

Instantly, I felt a sense of pride and happiness wash over me. I was excited about the opportunity to impress Sondra. "Yo, how much money did you just give me?" I didn't really care because whatever it was, it was more than I had ever had before.

"Three gees in the sock and one in your hand," he said like we had money like that on a regular.

"You got to be playing!" I yelled out. The girls looked to the back to see what all the excitement was about. "Are you for real?" He nodded and I could have shit on myself right there in the backseat. I took a deep breath and slumped back into my seat.

As instructed, I had paid for dinner, sprung for valet parking, and bought flowers for both girls from the Mexican guy walking around the restaurant. Malik was playing the back for some reason and letting me shine. I had to admit that I was loving the way both girls were hanging on my every word. I was telling them all types of fictitious plans that I had. I had them believing that I was about to open a barbershop, a nightclub, a carryout, and maybe a rim shop. Malik was co-signing right on cue without overdoing it.

When dinner was over, Malik went to the payphone to make sure all of the arrangements were made. He came back and told the girls that we were heading over to the Days Inn. "I understand if you have to get the car back home. You don't have to stay the night." They looked at one another trying to compare signals. "I have a couple bottles of Cristal on ice if you just want to have a quick drink." Then Aaliyah nodded her head.

"I'm game," Sondra said.

"Well alright then," I added in.

When we got to the lobby, Malik walked to the desk and returned with a key. "Come on, ladies, fifth floor." When we got to the room, Malik told them to pop one of the bottles and pulled me into the hallway. "Come here."

"Where we going?" I asked anxious to get back to the room.

He held up another key. "Listen, you can't trust these hoes. We don't know them from jack. This is our other room. Come on and put that loot away. He walked into the bathroom and put something into the septic tank on the toilet. He waved toward the television. "Leave $300 and some change right next to the TV. If someone breaks in here, they will think that is all the money we have. Let's go."

That was good thinking on his part. He had turned into a criminal mastermind in the last week. And here I was becoming his faithful sidekick. We walked out and up the hall back to the room where the girls were. When we walked into the room, everything that I had worried about had left my mind. Aaliyah was taking the bottle to her head and Sondra was dancing to B2K's remix of *I Need a Girlfriend* with nothing but her panties and bra on. Her ass was jingling as she spun in a circle revealing her pink thong underwear.

"C'mon, Mr. President," she mouthed and finger motioned for me to come towards her. I obliged and she pushed me into the chair and climbed on me like she was giving me a lap dance.

Aaliyah was still drinking and Malik popped opened the other bottle and poured me a glass. It was the first time I had ever drank champagne and it tasted horrible, but I swallowed like it was my favorite. Sondra was still on top of me in the chair grinding and I was getting hard underneath her. She knew what she was doing. I looked out of the corner of my eye and saw Malik take Aaliyah into the bathroom. A few seconds later, the shower cut on and he stepped out of the bathroom butt naked and hit the light switch. Sondra stood me up and began to undress me. I was a little nervous because of her aggressiveness, but when she took hold of my penis and said slowly "niiiice," I relaxed a bit. Once my clothes were off, she quickly came out of her panties and bra.

Within seconds, we were in the bed kissing. Sondra had taken the scrungie off of her ponytail and let her sandy brown hair flow across the pillow. I was reaching through my pockets on the floor trying to grab a condom when she said, "Don't worry about it. I'm on the pill." With my next move, I immediately tried to put it in. "Hold on, Abraham." She looked up at me like I was a maniac. "You got to lick it to stick it."

"Huh?" I was trying to process her request.

"C'mon, Abe. You got to get it wet first. I like that," she said while pulling on my earlobe with her lips. I contemplated for a second and then I went down to do what I had never done. Erica, the one serious girl that I had dated, had never asked me to do that even if she wanted it. But Sondra was a grown woman and if I planned on seeing her again, then I had to please her.

I had expected a funny smell, but there wasn't one and relief set it. I begin kissing her hips and thighs in an effort to stall but that seemed to turn her on. When I finally headed for her center, she grabbed the back of my head and pushed my face into her. My mouth opened and my tongue began to taste and massage her. "That's it, Abraham. Don't stop." I was surprised that I was doing a good job. I remembered what I had seen the men in x-rated videos do and tried to copy them. "Oh. Oh. Ooooohhhhh." she started panting and I really started to get into it. I locked onto her thighs with my hands and licked her middle like an ice cream cone. "Got damn, boy." Her back was arching off of the mattress and she was bucking against my face. "Oh shit. I'm cumming." Her body jerked and she fell back onto the bed. She pushed my head away. "Baby, you are so good. Are you sure you're only nineteen? I've been with men twice your age who haven't licked it like that. You got skills."

I was smiling and eating up her every word. I climbed on top of her. She put her legs up on my shoulders and began rocking away underneath me. She felt perfect on the inside. I was hoping that I would get to have her on a regular basis. Her arms were around my neck and she was staring right into my face. "Oh, Sondra, it feels so good inside of you."

"You like it, baby?"

"I love it." I was humping away. "Turn over."

"Oh, you want it from the back." She flipped over and put her ass up in the air. "Come on. It's all yours, daddy." She looked back at me with a devilish look on her face.

I eased back into her and wondered if she meant that. She was the bomb and I had already crowned her my queen if she wanted the role. I was grinding my hips against her until I felt myself about to explode. My breathing quickened and within a few seconds my insides began pouring into her. She let out a moan and collapsed with me on top of her.

We were lying still in the dark and noticed that the shower was no longer running. We could clearly make out the sounds of Malik fucking Aaliyah. She was screaming his name and we could hear items being knocked off of the counter. They went at it for three or four minutes and then the sink began to run. The toilet flushed and then the door opened. "Hey, girrrrrl," Aaliyah walked out smiling. Her body was tight. They had left the bathroom light on and I could make out each detail and curve. Her breasts were bigger than Sondra's and she had hips like a grown woman. I noticed that her pubic hair was shaved into a little box. She was caramel-colored like Malik and was the perfect height for him. He didn't like his women too tall. He was 5'9" and preferred to have five to six inches on a girl.

I had no hang-ups about height. I was an inch or two taller than Malik and had liked a couple of women who were taller than I was. "I heard you in there A.J. Cuz must have been hitting that spot."

"A.J.?" Malik asked.

"Aaliyah Jarvis," she replied.

"Oh."

She then went back to Sondra's comment. "Yeah, Malik was putting it down up in there. How about Mr. President, right here?"

"Oh Abe has mad tongue game." She wriggled her body thinking about it. I saw Malik's eyebrows raise up.

"You licked that coochie, boy?" he started laughing. "Don't tell me you got my man open like that already."

We laughed and talked shit for a little while. A.J. and Malik were in the bed closest to the door and were sleeping like babies. I was thinking about my money in the other room. I was the last to fall asleep as I was wondering where Malik was getting all of this game from and when and if it would stop.

I felt her hands massaging my dick and I was getting hard. I looked over at the clock; it was 4:00 a.m. Before I could turn over, I heard Malik's bed squeaking and then her moaning in pleasure. It made me rock hard and I wanted to sneak a peak. When I turned over, I saw Aaliyah's face in front of me. Her eyes were closed and she was still rubbing me. I couldn't believe my eyes when I looked over in the other bed and saw my queen on top of Malik, riding him like a pony. My heart sank for a second. She had gone from a potential girlfriend to an around-the-way hooker in a matter of less than one night. I watched and wondered if she was enjoying Malik more than she had me. My thoughts were interrupted when A.J.'s mouth found my hardness and began to suck me.

A few moments later and I was thoroughly enjoying the swap. Aaliyah was riding me and she felt even better than Sondra. She screamed out and came and I came right behind her. This time, I had put on a condom and A.J. took it off and went to the bathroom to flush it. It had been a wild night, a wild week for that matter. Malik was pulling me into whatever hole he was sinking into and what scared me the most was that it was starting to feel good.

"Here, take this $10 and go get the car. Tip the valet. We'll be down in a second. We have a few stops to make."

"Malik, I really need to get my mother's car home."

"I thought you two wanted to go shopping."

They looked at one another. "We do, but we just don't want my moms to start tripping about her car." A.J. frowned at Sondra.

"Well, I'm going to stay with them. I'll pick out something for you," A.J. said.

"Hell no, bitch. If I leave, then you are coming with me." There was dissension in the ranks. Sondra looked like she was ready to protect her discovery—us.

"Look, just run us back to Brooklyn." He tapped my shoulder. "What you holdin'?" He pointed at my pocket. I pulled out a roll of money. He took it out of my hand and put aside $200 for me and counted out the rest, giving half to Sondra and half to Aaliyah.

They both said, "Thanks," in unison. He had given them $300 apiece. "Be outside when we come down," he demanded and left the room. I knew where he was headed but they didn't ask.

When I walked into the room, I saw Malik looking through a light blue duffle bag. "What's that?" I asked.

"This is about a hundred years if we get caught with it," he said before pulling out three boxes. He popped the lid and tossed it to me. "This one, I ordered special for you. It's a Taurus Pro PT 145. Ten in the clip and one in the chamber."

He pointed to a box on the bed. "Speer Gold Dot. Hollow tips, they will rip a hole in a nigga big enough to see through." I picked it up and studied it quickly. "Check these out." He showed me a Glock and a Desert Eagle. Then he reached in the bag and pulled out two tiny guns that could fit in any front pants pocket. "I got ankle holsters for these."

I watched as he pulled out what looked like a machine gun. "What the..." I was wondering what war he was preparing for.

"Mac 11. It's ten years old and never been shot. These are all clean." He laughed, "Until we make 'em dirty." He reached on the side of the bed and handed me a smaller Old Navy backpack. He began packing up the guns and the ammo. Before I could ask he answered my question. "Carlos brought all of this stuff up here. He's the one who got the rooms and the drinks too. He'll get whatever we need."

"Need?"

"For my plan." In the next breath he said, "You need to look in that pack and know what you are holding." I peeped in and saw a couple boxes that had cell phones and in the bottom I saw a portable scale, two knives, binoculars, and a couple of holsters. "Let's roll."

Malik filled me in on his plan as we moved toward the elevator. I thought he was dreaming but didn't say so. If it worked as he described, I would welcome the day we could leave the Greenberg Towers rich. We both had loaded guns on us. He looked at me and warned me that we could not allow ourselves to be stopped with what we had on us by the police. His demeanor told me that I might as well be prepared to use the guns if it came down to it. I already knew he was.

When we reached the front of the hotel, the girls were parked outside in front of the hotel behind the area that the valet had blocked off. When we approached them, I noticed that Aaliyah wasn't in the car. She was standing on the curb talking to a guy in a Yankees cap. The guy had the kind of hungry look a man gets when he already knows what he plans to do with a woman. Malik handed me the bag he was carrying and motioned for me to put them in the car. "Get in, I'll be right there." He then walked over to A.J. "Get your ass in the car." The guy looked at Malik and when A.J. started to walk away, he grabbed at her hand. In an instant, I saw Malik haul back and hit him with an open-handed slap. A.J. screamed when she saw a red line open on the man's face followed by a stream of blood that began to flow. The man saw the horror in A.J.'s eyes before he felt the sting of the cut Malik had given him. He instinctively grabbed his face and saw the blood on his hands. He screamed out and tried to lunge at Malik but Malik's foot was already in flight toward his midsection. Malik had kicked him square in the balls and his Yankee cap fell off as he hit the ground. Malik quickly grabbed Aaliyah by the back of her neck and ushered her to the car. She was looking back at the man and Malik gave her a smack in the face as well but without the razor. "Bitch, get in the car. Sondra, move it."

Sondra had a smile on her face. She was actually enjoying the drama. She whipped the wagon out into traffic and hit the corner headed for the Westside Highway. "Y'all niggas is some straight thugs, huh?" She looked like she had found the man of her dreams when she looked back at Malik. A.J. on the other hand was pouting and looked pissed at being slapped. Sondra turned the radio up and Malik leaned his head back and closed his eyes as he bobbed his head to the beat. He seemed to be drifting off, not to sleep but somewhere else.

I was looking at Aaliyah while I tried to make conversation that would take her mind off of what had happened. When we made it home, Malik jumped out of the car and walked around to Sondra and began talking to her. Since some type of unofficial switch had taken place, I walked around to A.J.'s side and handed her another hundred and whispered, "Shit happens, don't take it personal. Malik just gets off the hook sometimes."

The hundred had made her forget and she was smiling. "Oh I ain't tripping. It was my bad for even talking to the guy." She gave me her number and said, "So I guess it's me and you." And then she laughed because Malik and Sondra were kissing like two old lovers.

"We out," Malik said as he walked around the front of the car. I moved away from the car. Malik looked over at Aaliyah. "Don't ever disrespect me or my man again or I will open that face up for you. Understand me?" She nodded her head and looked like she had seen a ghost. She had.

The Malik I had known all my life was dead, but yet he was still walking right in front of me with a nasty attitude and a bag full of guns.

SEVEN

Construction starts with destruction. Nothing can be built without something being torn apart. Even with thoughts and dreams, everything that discourages and causes self-doubt, must be eliminated before the building begins. Just like the forest must give way to the cities. victory is never built up until the walls of fear crumble. It is most important to remain constant in construction or one becomes the victim of destruction. It's as complicated as building a new empire after destroying a faulty one, yet simple as watching life destroy the innocence of a child to create an adult.

I walked into my apartment and greeted my grandmother, who was in the kitchen cooking lunch for Jade. She spoke to me, "Hey, baby."

"Hey, Grand." I hugged her. "Where's Toni?"

"She and your mother went over to Stanley Avenue Beauty School to register her. Toni said she wants to become a beautician."

"She went with Lindsey?" I asked sounding shocked.

"Sure did. After you left, they sat up half the night talking. Your mother does love you all. She might not show it, but she does." My grandmother could tell I wasn't buying that. "Lindsey always had a hard time showing her feelings, even as a child."

I nodded out of respect and went to my room after kissing Jade. I locked the door and reached into my bag. I started going through all the stuff that I had gotten from Carlos. The first thing I did was put the new lock on my door that he had gotten me. I loaded all of the guns and put them on the shelf, except for the Desert Eagle. I put that one in the holster and put it into the back of my jeans. I took the scale out and placed it on my dresser. I then took the red tops out of the shoes in my closet and opened up the package I had taken from the caper. I was surprised when I saw it was heroin and not cocaine. I weighed it and came to two and a half ounces. Wholesale that would cop me another $7,000. I had taken $9,000 from the envelope, three of which I had given to Abraham. I had given Carlos the twelve grand from the phone book. In exchange, he had given me $3,000 of it back plus the guns, ammo and equipment in the backpacks. He was also taking Abraham and me down to MVA to get two sets of fake IDs and a passport. My grandfather had always suggested I have a false ID on me at all times whether I was committing crimes or not.

I called a kid I knew named, Black Sidney, who lived over on Marcy Ave. Black Sid used to go to school with me and I knew I could trust him a little bit. I asked him to come scoop me so we could talk about a few things.

The sun was starting to set at 7:00 when he arrived. I had him drive towards The Piers. While we rode, I told him that I had some product that I wanted to get rid of. He laughed and said, "Not you. You finally gettin' in the game, huh?"

"Not in the traditional sense," I responded.

"What you talking about then?" We were cruising across town in his Escalade. Black Sid was getting a few dollars. He had the luxury of older brothers who had connects and had put him on when he was a youngster.

"I'm talking about taking shit over not slinging drugs. If niggas want to hustle in my courts, then they gonna have to pay me daily. I'm talking about diversifying my hustles, a little of this and a little of that."

Black Sid started laughing. "Nigga, is you crazy? How you gonna take over something? Why the fuck would a nigga give you anything?" He rolled down his window and spit his gum out. "I mean, where you comin' from with all this?"

I looked straight ahead. I reached behind me and pulled the pearl-handled chrome pistol out of my pants and slammed it on his dash. "Do you know who my grandfather is?" He had a look on his face as if he was riding with a stranger. He was. He shook his head no. "My grandfather is Double V., Vincent Vaughn from Harlem. Ran with Nikki Barnes and the likes of them."

"Yeah, I heard of him. He was big time back in the seventies, right?"

"Yeah. He owned the fucking city and he took whatever the fuck he wanted." I looked right at Black Sid. "I'm going to do the same thing. Anybody who got a problem with that is a problem and this here..." I waved the gun, "this is the problem solver." When we reached the pier, it was dark and I had him park while I ran to the rail and tossed the gun I had used on Phil Boogie and the foreigner uptown. I got back in the car.

"What did you toss?"

"A nine." He didn't have to ask. He knew I wouldn't have tossed it without a good reason, meaning a murder or two was attached to it. "Listen, I want you to move this in your hood. A one-time deal."

He took the package and looked at it. "Why can't you move it in your hood?"

"I ain't a drug dealer. You are. It's two and half ounces, worth seven thou wholesale. Give me back five. I'll pick it up in a week."

"Man, what am I supposed to tell my brothers? I move product for them."

"Are your brothers gonna give you a price like that? No, they aren't," I answered emphatically for him. "Work that shit in with theirs but just make sure you have my money." We drove back towards Brooklyn.

"I don't know about this," he said as we pulled back up in my complex.

"Sid, everything is going to be cool. You have a chance to make some extra dough. Don't be stupid." I handed him my cell number. "Hit me when you have my money." I turned and was about to walk away and then I stopped and called him before he could pull off. I was at his door. "Listen. There will be more product coming at ridiculous prices. You will be the only one I hook up so make sure you do a good job." I explained that it wasn't personal and that his brothers could get on too if they cooperated. Then I warned him, "I haven't been down to your hood since the street ball tournament that Jigga held for the kids a couple of years back." He nodded. "If I have to come down there to get my money or because you tell me that you got robbed, I won't be shooting baskets when I roll through. You got me?"

Black Sid looked at me and nodded with a nervous smirk on his face. He pulled off. I thought back on how I used to be afraid of making him angry as a kid. He would have beaten me down if I had gotten out of line back then. After junior high when he started getting money, he had a reputation to live up to and did a good job of it. He was definitely respected.

But what had happened on our little ride was another indication of what was to come. I had struck fear in his heart with my brazen approach. All of what he knew about me as a kid had gone out of the window. He recognized that he was in the presence of a soldier that would end his life if he got out of line. The power that he had before had been taken away with the tone of my voice and wave of my pistol. It was a beautiful thing and it was only the beginning.

Before heading into the house, I stopped at the corner store to grab a Code Red Mountain Dew and a bag of sunflower seeds. When I walked out of the store, I saw Cortez and two of his runners crossing the street heading back into the courts. Cortez was seldom seen inside of the Courtyard. He was a kingpin and knew that if the feds came close to photographing him near drug transactions, it would give them wet dreams. I ripped open the bag and watched the three of them head towards the northern entrance into the courtyard. I didn't think twice about it until I saw three guys climb out of a PT Cruiser just up the block. They each had scarves tied over their mouths and though I couldn't make out what types of guns they were carrying, I could see they were all strapped. It didn't take a detective to figure out that either a robbery or a hit was about to take place. I stepped out farther and moved toward the cars parked on the street. I wasn't looking behind me when I felt someone walk right into the back of me.

"Get the fuck out of the way, nigga," the voice said. Then I felt a hand the size of Shaquille O'Neal's, palm the side of my head and push me into the telephone pole. When I regained my balance, I looked up and saw that this was a big boy. He was wearing a mask and had a sawed-off shotgun at his hip as he and the guy walking with him moved toward the other three gunmen. They stopped briefly at the entrance and talked for about ten seconds and I noticed that a couple of them cocked weapons and then they turned towards the courts.

My adrenaline began to pump. I began to visualize what was about to happen and I wondered if Cortez was going to make it. It was obvious that they weren't bringing five guns to rob one of his runners. Pure nosiness led me to creep slowly toward the entrance and as I was walking, I saw Aaliyah jump out of a cab. When she noticed me, she waved. "Yo, Malik, is Abraham with you?" The cab hadn't pulled off and she asked me to come over. "Abraham was supposed to meet me down here to pay for this cab."

As soon as she said that Abraham might be in the courtyard, I ran off towards his building. I could hear her yelling my name as I ran full speed toward the courtyard. Abraham would not have made it to the cab if the guns were putting in work. I slowed as I reached the corner and stuck my head around it slowly. I looked off to the left and witnessed the first pistol crack followed by several screams. I saw Abraham and a cat named Terrell both on their knees in front of Abraham's building. There was one kid with a gun pointed at Abraham while the second one was going through Terrell's pockets. Out of all the dealers, Terrell was one of the only ones that we associated with. We played ball together and had been in a few classes together at Garvey. Unlike most of the other guys out there, Terrell was truly hustling to feed his family. His moms was an addict and his dad was disabled. They had seven people living in a two-bedroom apartment and he had grown tired of seeing his siblings going to bed hungry.

It was ironic that the two people that I needed to save were right next to one another. I didn't waste anytime because

I remembered Double V saying to me, "He who hesitates is lost". I pulled my Glock from my belt and ran toward Abraham with it drawn and cocked.

The second robber was pulling a knot of money from Abraham's pocket when he looked up and saw me coming. It was too late. He yelled out, "Sonny, watch out!" As Sonny began to turn around everything slowed down for me like a scene from *The Matrix*. When Sonny's eyes met mine, I felt a sense of euphoria wash over me. It was like Michael Jordan with the ball, trailing by one with ten seconds left. Everyone in the building knows he's going to shoot it. The question is: can he be stopped? I honestly thought this scenario through in my mind as I glided toward Sonny like a tiger closing in on its prey.

I heard two shots fired in my direction but I didn't slow down. I saw Sonny's gun as he began raising it. He never got the barrel fully pointed in my direction. The effects of the gun recoiling shook my forearm and rose through my shoulder. I saw the effect of the impact as the first bullet struck him in the stomach. I kept firing and the second, third, and fourth shots hit him in the neck, shoulder and eye. Before his body hit the ground, Abraham and Terrell had turned and grabbed his stunned accomplice. I saw Terrell's arms wrap around his throat and was surprised when I saw Abraham's boot begin to stomp the gunman's body. "Get down!" I yelled out when I saw fire coming from the barrels of two pistols headed my way.

"Over there, dog!" Terrell pointed toward the playground.

"Kill them niggas!" said the big one who had shoved me into the pole minutes earlier. Instantly, a chorus of fire erupted from behind the sliding board. I saw the big guy with his sawed-off yelling at Cortez telling him to walk or get blasted.

Cortez tried to resist and in the next moment I heard him scream out in pain. I ducked back around the corner. I could see Abraham behind the steps. He and Terrell had beaten the second gunman unconscious and dragged him behind the steps.

I yelled over to them, "Terrell, you strapped?"

"Nah."

"Damn," I responded. "Yo, is that nigga dead?"

"Damn near if he ain't!" Terrell shouted back.

"Terrell." I could see him looking toward me. "Run over and grab the other gun off of the one out there. I need you to cover me."

"Come on, let's just go out of the back gate," he answered back.

"So them niggas will come back tomorrow and dust you off while you hustling by yourself? Get that gun before I start firing over there at your ass!"

To my surprise, I saw Abraham dart out from behind the steps and creep toward the lifeless body. The guy, Sonny, was dead as a doorknob but was still holding his pistol and Abraham had to give it a yank to pull it from his hands. Abraham didn't see him, but one of the gunmen had slipped over near his building and had a clear shot at him. When Abraham turned to run back towards the steps, the third gunman, who was wearing a Raiders Jersey, jumped out toward Abraham and fired two shots. He must have been nervous because he missed both shots and on the third attempt his gun jammed. I was already headed toward Abraham when I saw my best friend do the unthinkable. Instead of firing, he charged the gunman and threw a punch that landed flush on his temple. It was as pretty a punch as I have ever seen and the gun dropped like a board, face slamming into the pavement.

"Finish him, Abe." He looked at me. I raised my gun and put it to Abraham's face. "This muthafucka just tried to blow you away. If you don't have enough heart to shoot him, then I might as well kill you where you stand, dog, because you already dead."

Abraham took a deep look in my eyes trying to decipher if I was serious or not. At that point, I was so hyped up on adrenaline that I wasn't sure if I was or not. Faster than a Roy Jones Jr. jab, Abraham turned his gun in my direction and fired until I lost my sight for a second. My eardrums were ringing so loud, they felt like they were bleeding. He kept firing and I fell to the ground as my head felt like it was bursting. I lost count of the shots. Seven, eight, nine and suddenly he stopped and looked at the gunman who was coming to. He took two steps and on the third step he placed his foot on the waking man's chest.

I was shaking off the shock of what he had done and then realized why he had shot so many times and not hit me once. As I crawled to my feet, I saw the fourth gunman, the one who had walked in with the big Shaquille O'Neal look-a-like, sprawled out behind the bench with blood pouring from the four holes Abraham had put into his torso. Terrell ran over to us at the same time I heard police sirens going off. "So what you gonna do?" Terrell asked.

Abraham nudged the body beneath him and the dude just looked up at him. There were now three guns on him and he knew his life was over. Abraham put the gun to his head and I stopped him. "Nah." The joker looked up at me as if I was his savior.

"Thank you, man." He began panting as his words came out, "I swear I will bring you big money for this..." He was thanking me for sparing his life when I cut him off.

"No, I need to know where the money is. If it ain't where you say it is, then you die." I had every intention of killing him anyway.

"It's in my crib." He reached into his pockets and pulled out keys. "We robbed some Dominicans uptown last weekend. I got fourteen in cash in my closet. It's taped inside of the left arm of a Sean John jean jacket." He was rambling on, spilling his guts. He went as far as to write down his address and directions to his crib in the Bronx on a receipt he had in his pocket. "I do have a pit bull though." He was concerned about us getting bitten only because he thought that us getting the money safely was his ticket to survival.

"Okay, let me see that pen." I took it from him. "What about the rest of your crew?"

He shook his head. "I don't know them all that well, except for Easy and Frank." He pointed at Frank who was dead behind the bench. "I don't know where they keep their loot."

I nodded approval. "Okay that's cool. Any last request?"

"Huh?" he said. I grabbed him by his Afro and in one motion, I swung the pen that I had taken from him and jammed it right into his eye. He screamed out. Sounded like it hurt bad. I laughed. "Terrell, your hands are still clean. Get 'em dirty."

Terrell looked at the guy rocking back in forth in pain and looked at me in disbelief. I had always been just a regular kid from the hood. My transformation into a ghetto warrior had him off balance. "But...I thought..."

"Do or die, nigga." I aimed my pistol at Terrell. If it came down to it, Terrell wasn't family and I needed him in on this crime. Instantly, Terrell fired twice into the top of his head. It looked like a watermelon being dropped on the sidewalk. The sirens grew louder and began to disappear. They hardly ever came through even after the twenty or thirty shots that had been fired in the last fifteen minutes.

"Give me that gun, Terrell." I took the gun that he had just used before he could wipe his prints off. "Abraham, that girl A.J. was out there waiting on you. Go find her and make sure she's alright. Terrell, meet me at the corner store... that is if you want to go get some of this money. I need to go get some more ammo."

"Bet." He took off and headed for the store. He never thought that I was going to go keep the gun for safekeeping. If someone had to go to the pen for this, it wouldn't be me. I headed off toward my building to stash the gun. On the way back, I saw Cortez being dragged out of the building next to mine. Shaquille had him by the ankles. He was handcuffed and he looked like he'd had the shit knocked out of him.

I crouched down against the side of the building and moved as quietly as I could. "Why you tryin' to make this shit harder than it has to be?" The big fella kicked Cortez in the ribs. In the next instant, he was on his phone. "Pull the car around to the entrance across from the gas station." He tightened his grip and jerked Cortez. "I got this nigga." The person on the other end must have said something the big guy didn't like because I heard him say, "Shut the hell up and just bring the car around. If they ain't there when you pull up, then we leavin' 'em. Fuck it."

Just then, the big guy swung to the ground and punched Cortez three times and it looked like he was out because in the next instant, he slung Cortez up over his shoulder and walked to the end of the alley. I didn't care much about Cortez at all or any drug dealers for that matter. I was about to turn and head to the corner store to meet Terrell when a conversation that I had had with my grandfather entered my head. "Share your talents with those around you and you will grow richer."

I stopped and paused to think about how Cortez could use my talents right now. As a matter of fact his life and the life of his family and children were all in my hands. The same went for Shaquille. As I moved toward the alley, I remembered him putting his hands on me earlier not knowing that I would hold the power to change his destiny. I couldn't have been more than fifteen steps behind him when the PT Cruiser pulled up. "Get out and open the damned door."

At Shaquille's demand, the driver jumped out and quickly ran around the car to open the door. As soon as I could see him clearly, I moved in. Once the traffic on Lafayette Avenue thinned out, I completed what would be known as the Greenberg Towers Massacre. I raised my Desert Eagle and opened fire on the driver first. The first shot missed him and hit the side of the car with a loud crash. The second shot hit him in the shoulder and knocked him off of his feet. The big guy dropped Cortez and instinctively got low. He tried to return fire with the sawed off but he moved to slow. I took aim at the huge target and slaughtered him right there with six shots to the mid-section. I could smell the gunpowder coming from the barrel and walked up on him to see him still breathing, but barely. Cortez looked up at me. "Who sent you?"

"Your fairy godmother." I released another shot into the forehead of the driver. Blood exploded onto Cortez's white sweat suit. The big guy was looking up at me and blood was coming out of his mouth. "You remember pushing me into the phone pole on the way in, you fat muthafucka?" He was shaking his head, no, but his eyes gave him away. "You didn't think your caper would turn out like this, huh?" He was looking, trying to talk but he was choking on his own blood. I laughed. "I killed every last one of them. Every nigga you brought with you is dead so when you get to Hell make sure you tell 'em who sent ya'." BOOM! Cortez flinched as the gun erupted.

I now had made a habit of going through the pockets of people I killed. "Don't do that," I heard Cortez say.

"What?" I couldn't believe he had tried to give me an order. I continued. I pulled out some money and the keys to the handcuffs. "You need these?" I tossed them to Cortez.

"It's undignified to steal from a dead man. Bad Karma," Cortez said as he used the keys to unlock the cuffs.

"Undignified. Whatever. He damned sure can't use the money." I got up and turned to walk up the street. Within the next few moments, the cops would arrive and wouldn't see me at the scene or around the Towers for a couple of days at least.

"Hold up. Who are you?" He stood and tried to dust himself off. "I've seen you around. I didn't know you were in the game though."

"I'm Malik. And I am not in the game, per se."

"I can't tell, the way you handle that steel. What you do then?"

I took a look back up the alley into the courtyard and then I paused. I realized that I was talking to one of the biggest H dealers in Brooklyn and that the Greenberg Towers had been one of his most lucrative money-making strips for years but it didn't stop me from looking him in the eye as I spoke to him, "I run these Towers."

"Say what?"

"You heard me. I run these towers and the courtyard too. I take a piece of whatever is made around here. The way I see it..." I pointed at the two bodies, "you died tonight. You know it and so do I. The only reason why you are breathing and they aren't is right in front of you." He had the strangest look on his face. It was as if he had never been spoken to in such a manner. He was a kingpin after all. Even after nearly being kidnapped and taken to his death, he still wanted his respect. His had to come second to mine though and I went on. "I will run the details down to you another time, but I won't bend.   I will kill anything moving in these Courts if I don't get mine."

"ESPN Zone, Times Square tomorrow at 1:00 p.m.," he said as I walked away.

"See you then." I took off and by the time I reached the corner store, Terrell was out front talking to grown man who was thin as a bean pole and a little kid who looked like he could have been Old Dirty Bastard's bastard.   The little kid was talking shit and had Terrell and the grown man laughing hysterically.

"Let's roll." I tapped him and began walking. "Where is Abraham?"

"He said he was going to hang out with some chick. He seemed a little shook by the events of the evening."   Terrell laughed. We crossed the street and headed down the block. "So we gonna do this or what?"

"Yeah we are, but we need a car." When we were a few blocks away from the Towers, I called Carlos and asked him for a ride up to the Bronx.   Carlos took ten minutes to pick us up.

In less than an hour, I had walked into an empty apartment, killed a pit bull with one shot, and collected fourteen grand and a brand new Smith and Wesson with the halogen laser scope.   I gave Carlos two grand for the ride up and Terrell two grand for riding with me. I had five grand set aside in one pocket for Abe. He was my partner even though he hadn't rode on this quick heist. I was proud of how he held it down tonight and fired to protect my back when I had gotten a little careless. In 'Do or Die' time, he had done and died at the same time. Strange as it sounded, he had killed the last of his innocence when he pulled that trigger tonight and there was no turning back.

EIGHT

Discovery is what comes at the end of each voyage. Every man, whether he knows it or not, is on a series of voyages. Sometimes the voyage is planned out and attacked like a quest brought forth through intuition. Other times a man is swept along carelessly at the mercy of whatever life reveals to him. The discoveries all add up ultimately to one thing. The one thing is true knowledge of self. The voyages may be rough just as often as they are enjoyable, and the knowledge may come at a price that sometimes feels too costly. Ultimately though, the hardest part of finding that truth or knowledge of self, isn't paying for it, but rather accepting it. Most people can't.

"**Why** can't you sleep? You've been staring up at that ceiling since we layed down," Aaliyah said as she lay on her side staring at me.

"I'm okay. I'm just a little wound up," I lied. When I'd left the courtyard, I called A.J. and found out that she had taken the cab over to her aunt's house. Her aunt was only twenty-six and didn't mind me coming over. Once I arrived, A.J. asked if we could sleep in the spare bedroom. Her aunt granted the request and had thrown us a couple blankets and pillows to make a pallet on the floor since there wasn't a mattress in there.

I wanted to confess and tell her what I had done, but common sense prevailed. I was now afraid that I would be caught and sent up the river for certain. We had lit the courtyard up like the Fourth of July. I had lost track of all the bodies that were left in the Courtyard. I began to sweat when I replayed my part in the whole thing. I wondered what would have happened if I had come out of the house two minutes earlier.

A.J. felt my tension and began to rub my back. I wasn't in the mood for sex, but it felt good being rubbed and when I turned onto my stomach, she began to massage me and then jumped up. "Be right back." She was out the door and then back again in an instant with some baby oil and a candle in the other hand. I looked up at her and thought to myself how comfortable she was making me feel. She flipped on the radio and began to sing along as *Officially Missing You* played. She lit the candle and I had no choice but to relax as she began rubbing me down with the baby oil.

"That's nice," I managed to get out as I felt the tension being rubbed out of my shoulders. Her hands danced down my back and I felt more oil being poured all over my butt and thighs. She massaged my ass and worked her hands down my thighs. I'd never had a woman give me such a thorough massage. Her thumbs kneaded the muscles in my hamstrings and loosened me up. She poured more oil into her palms and proceeded to massage and caress my feet. She then sat on my back. I could feel her nakedness and her bush touching me. I heard her let out a soft moan as she started grinding herself against me. The fan was blowing across the floor and I felt a cold spot on my back from where her wetness had dripped onto me. Her fingers were running through my fro'. Then she took two fingers and began to press against my temples and ran them down my face and up behind my ears. By the time she had her thumbs on the back of my neck, I was totally loose and turned on by her attention. She rolled me onto my back and straddled me, taking my hands to extend my arms.

"Damn, girl," I whispered as she rubbed my arms up and down before massaging my hands to perfection. "You are trying to make me fall for you, huh?"

"Trying?" She smiled. I was looking up at her. She still had on a bra which I quickly reached up and unhooked. I watched as her breasts fell slightly.

"Nah, you're succeeding." My erection had grown underneath her. She was oiled up and shining like a chocolate bar. I wanted a bite.

"Make love to me."

I rolled on top of her and gave her just what she wanted and what I wanted too. I had always longed for a girl that I could make love to on a regular basis. Aaliyah seemed as if she was always going to be eager and willing to give it to me as much as I wanted. She was built like she could have been a track star except that her breasts were too full. I was glad that I had ended up with her instead of Sondra. Her body was tight and so were her insides.

My body slid down hers and I tasted her for the first time. I had eaten Sondra the night we met and was surprised that she had chosen Malik. But the way I was prepared to lick A.J. up and down, I had no doubt that she would be on lock when I finished.

"Got damn, boy. Got damn," she cried out. I was wasting no time. I made short circles with my tongue while my fingers massaged the skin in between her vagina and her ass. "Don't tease me baby."

I started pulling her lips with mine and flicking my tongue across her clit. She was crying out, lifting her ass off the floor. I could barely get two fingers inside of her, but when she began to shiver, I jammed four of them inside her and she erupted like a volcano. I didn't stop licking until she began kicking her legs fighting to get away.

In an instant, I was on top of her and pulled her legs up on my shoulders. She was moaning but trying to keep her voice down at the same time. I ground my pelvis into her slowly for five minutes while she stared into my eyes. "Turn over," I said.

I was looking down at her and watching her chocolate ass jiggle as I slammed into her. Between the moonlight that crept through the window and the television that was still on, I could make out a tattoo on her backside. It was a busted cherry with the name Rico on it. Whoever the cat named Rico was, I had to take my hat off to him because this was the third girl I had seen with his name tattooed on her ass or titties this year. I smacked her right on the tattoo and she cried out to let me know that it excited her and she began to talk nasty to me as she came. She pulled away and flipped onto her back again. "Come on, Abe."

She had her hand spreading and rubbing her clit while I moved in and out of her. She could sense that I was ready to cum and she quickened her pace. I lost control and began to bang violently into her as I released and then collapsed on top of her.

I was still and panting and I thought that she was breathing hard but when I rolled off of her, I noticed that she had tears running down her cheeks. "What's wrong? Did I hurt you?" I leaned up.

No answer. She just stared for a moment and I stared back. "No, you didn't do anything wrong."

"Well then why are you crying?"

"Because..." she wiped her tears away one cheek at a time, "... you did everything right."

I didn't understand that one so I just held her tight and kissed her on the cheek. She leaned back and gave me her tongue for a moment and then she curled up against me and we both settled down together and apart at the same time. She held on to her pain and pleasure and I fought back the scenes of the demons in my mind until I could take it no longer. I was now one of the demons that I fought in my dreams and prayers. I was no different than any of the others. I thought back on how I used to dream of having a church of my own. Someplace where the little kids could come to be safe and learn about Jesus. Someplace where I could help people and teach them about the Word. Now I had drifted further than ever. I was no longer a Slayer of Dragons. I was a Slayer of Men.

When Aaliyah woke up, she saw me on my knees in front of the window praying. I was praying so deeply that I didn't see that she was awake. I was praying myself to freedom. My conversations with GOD were always incredible and this time was no different. He had told me that I was now walking in the wilderness and that I wouldn't make it out alone. He told me that if I were going to make it out, that I would have to bring many souls with me. He had forgiven me for murdering already.

I wanted to know if I would have to kill again, but I knew better than to contemplate sin while in conversation with my father. I prayed for everyone around me and I opened my eyes. When I did, I looked at A.J. and smiled. I felt light. That lasted for about five seconds.

"Oh shit. Look, that's your neighborhood," she said pointing at the set.

The newscaster said, "*A deadly night in Brooklyn as eight men are killed in a shoot out*". I sat up. Seven. I started counting trying to match up the numbers. One for me, one for Terrell. I didn't think there was any way he could have killed six people... "*Lets go to Kenny Campbell who is live in the Greenberg Towers Housing Complex.*"

Kenny was standing right in the middle of the courtyard, a few feet from where I had blasted the guy. "*Thanks Angela... Yes indeed. A deadly night here in Brooklyn's Greenberg Towers Housing Complex. There are no suspects and only a few residents are even admitting to hearing gunfire. Police have very few clues as to what happened here except the identities of two of the victims. One is Perry Winters, 21 from the Bronx and the other Frank Lyons of Harlem. It is believed to have been part of a gang war or a possible vendetta. Police did find several shell casings but found no drugs, cash or weapons at the scene.*"

Angela chimed in, "*Can you tell us if the police have received any valuable leads or how people who are afraid can get in touch with investigators.*"

"*Absolutely. Anyone with information is urged to call...*" I clicked the set off.

"I need to run," I said and began to slip on my clothes.

"Why? You don't think Malik was..."

"No. Hell no. But I need to talk to him," I lied. It had just dawned on me that I never spoke with Malik last night.

After I got dressed, A.J. walked me to the front door. "I ain't trying to act all mushy but can I see you later? I will still be here." She sensed my unwillingness to commit. "It doesn't matter what time." She smiled and kissed me on the neck.

"Yeah, that'll be good." I turned to head out the door.

"Oh, Abraham." I looked back at her. "I wouldn't mind going to the mall to pick up something sexy to wear for you tonight. Got dough?" she said imitating the *Got Milk* ads.

I laughed to myself and reached into my pockets. The kid had robbed me of $700 and I had robbed him right back plus an extra $400. I gave $300 to Aaliyah, kissed her on the forehead, and headed out the door.

I headed up the street and called Malik. He was fine and mentioned that he had seen the news last night. He seemed calm about it. In fact, he called it 'old news' and told me to meet him at the basketball courts in Jefferson Park in an hour. I bounced up Flatbush with the sun shining on my face, but noticed a dark cloud in the sky looking like it was headed my way.

When I reached the courts, Malik was seated at the bench with Terrell, Carlos, a thirteen-year-old kid from the Courtyard named Ferris, and two other guys that I had seen hanging around the Towers from time to time but didn't know personally. There were two large McDonald's bags and everyone was grabbing food out of them. As I moved through the gates, I looked back when I saw a young brother come running pass me with three guys chasing him.

Laughter erupted when one of the teens tackled him like Ray Lewis sacking a quarterback and began beating him. The other two joined in and I heard him screaming for help. The ballers had slowed the game down and were watching the beat down. Malik began to shout my name, "Yo Abe, you ain't gonna save that nigga?" He was joking but the thought ran across my mind as I looked back and saw that the crew was still punching the boy. I was trying to listen as the two bigger boys were yelling at the victim and spitting in his face.

I felt for the guy and wondered why the city soldiers were so cold. Why they were so willing to watch an unfair fight all of the time. I turned around and walked back out of the gate and violated one of the most widely known rules of the hood. "Mind your business, nigga," one of the teens said to me as I walked up to them.

"Yo, let the shorty go." I stepped in between the boys and put my hand on the biggest one's arm.

"You want some of this, nigga?" one of them asked me.

"Motherfucker, are you trying to get yourself killed?" the second one said.

I nodded toward my crew on the bench. "We roll a little too deep for that, my friend. I just don't want to see you fellas catch a murder beef out here. Take what you gonna take from shorty and roll." I looked into the biggest one's eyes. He was a little shorter than me but much skinnier. I knew that I could break him in half if need be but I was just trying to end the beat down.

"We ain't robbin' this clown. We beatin' him down 'cause he thinks he's motherfuckin' P. Diddy or some shit."

"What?" I said looking at the kid. His eye was going to be swollen shut and blood was pouring from his nose and mouth.

He spoke out. "I rap and make beats. These dudes hatin' on me because I won't *give* them some beats." He wiped his face. "They not even from 'round here. They came around here because some chicken-head told them that I was selling beats. She called me to come around her house and told me these clowns wanted to talk business."

One of them yelled out, "Yeah, it was business!"

"Business means you coming with cash. Y'all motherfuckers ain't come with no money. Fuck that." Just then, the biggest one leaned in and swung, trying to hit him and punched me instead. I turned and swung, throwing two jabs and a right cross. Each punch landed flush to his jaw. He hit the ground landing between the curb and a car. One of his partners then took a weak swing at me. The kid I'd saved came from around me and began firing punches at him. I watched as the two of them began exchanging blows. The rapper quickly took him down and continued to pepper him on the side of his head with blows until he had taken all of his anger out on him. The third kid stood by and watched not wanting to mix it up with either of us.

"That's enough. C'mon." I grabbed the rapper and pulled him off the kid. I watched as the two got up off the ground embarrassed and angry.

"We'll be back."

I pulled the Taurus out of my pants and pointed at them. They froze. "Maybe." I pointed it into each of their faces. "Go home and thank God I didn't blast you out here today. As a matter of fact, you all need to get up and go to church tomorrow." They were staring at me like I was crazy. "What's your name, boy?" I was pointing at the big one.

The rapper was behind me. "His name is Omar," the rapper said. "That's Tye, and the one whose ass I just kicked, his name is Reese."

"Yeah well Omar, Tye, and Reese, this block ain't for suckers. Stay off of it." I waved my gun and shooed them. "Don't forget. Church for y'all." They turned and ran off. I heard one of them call me crazy.

"Thanks, man," the rapper said.

"Yeah, it's all good. That's foul what they did. You might want to go to the emergency room, kid." I pointed at his face.

"Nah, I'm a soldier. That chump, Reese, needs some medical attention." He put his fist up. "I'm Bing."

"Abraham." He told me he had just moved into a brownstone up the way with his mother and sister. He told me that I might know his sister if I saw her because she doing big things. I laughed and then he went on to promise me that he would repay me one day because he knew that I had put my ass on the line for him without even knowing who he was. "Not necessary. We sort of from the same hood," I mentioned as we parted ways and I headed over to the benches where Malik was sitting with all of the fellas while they grubbed.

Malik gave me a pound and introduced me to the two guys from around the way. "This is my partner, Saint Abraham." He started laughing. "You see how he saves niggas just for fun."

"What up?" I said. Then he introduced them as Wheeler and Casper. Wheeler had plaits in his hair and sunglasses that made him look like a rock star. He had on a platinum chain, or a silver one pretending that is was platinum and a diamond encrusted charm of Jesus on the cross on it. I wondered if it meant anything at all to him as I shook his hand. Casper was dressed like a college kid except for the white doo-rag he wore. He had on a pair of khaki pants and a polo shirt. He also had on a pair of frames that you might imagine a Wall Street broker would wear.

Just then, Carlos walked up to me and gave me a hug like we had known each other for years. "I see you nice with those hands, son." He laughed out and punched the air imitating my combination. "You knocked that nigga out like you was Tyson or some shit."

"Yeah, but you pulled that thing out and didn't squeeze it," Malik joined in. "That's bad luck."

I looked over at him. "Man, those niggas wasn't worth the bullets or the charge."

"Then don't pull it out," Malik said with a serious look and then repeated. "If you ain't squeezing that trigger, don't show it." I focused on what he said for a moment and then moved on. I told him all about the beef that Bing had with the boys.

He nodded and proceeded. "Listen up," he went on with his plan for the afternoon. He started off like he was a general mapping out a secret mission. When he finished, he told each person sitting there why he had included them. Once he had addressed everyone he said, "If you don't think you man enough to roll with *my* clique from here to the finish line, let me know now so I can kill you right here." He paused and reached behind his back and pulled out his newest weapon. Everyone looked at one another and wondered if he was serious. He didn't smile while he cocked the Smith and Wesson. "What?" he said. "Y'all niggas looking all dumbfounded. I'm serious."

In that moment, everyone realized that they were in with Malik to the finish line unless they wanted the finish line to be right there. I had stopped wondering if he was serious about threatening to kill one of us. It didn't even matter what he was willing to do anymore. It was what I had discovered about what I was willing to do. Saving Bing had felt good. I had also taken pleasure in what I had done to the crew who had attacked him and I came to grips with the fact that the violence was beginning to bother me less and less.

NINE

Attack is often confused to mean the same thing as a fight, a battle or a war. That is a victim's way of thinking. Victims most often think that they are being attacked only once they are under some form of duress. What most people fail to understand is that the attack starts with the planning before the duress. Attack is a part of business, life, and love. Every minute of every day, in every part of the world, people are planning attacks and being attacked simultaneously. The reason why people are so often taken off guard is because they don't understand that the enemy is always planning against them. The only way to keep from being attacked is to plan for it constantly and to embrace each attack as an opportunity to crush those who have planned against you.

At 12:30, I watched as Cortez walked into the ESPN Zone and was escorted to a seat. Two minutes behind him were Doc and Wendell accompanied by Wild Steve. Wild Steve was Doc and Wendell's bodyguard. He was respected all over the city. I respected him but I didn't fear him. It was strange because a month or two earlier and I would have probably left if I had seen Wild Steve come in for a meeting. I took it now as a sign of respect. These niggas were here to talk about my taking over the Towers.

I sat in my booth watching them as they got comfortable. I even ordered a burger and fries as I waited for the time to tick down. It was obvious that they knew the hostess as she kept coming in to give them updates every five minutes, probably letting them know that I hadn't arrived. At five after one, I paid my bill and walked over to their table.

"What's good, Cortez?" He looked startled as I walked up behind him.

"Hey," he said recognizing my voice and face. I could see in his eyes that he was wondering how I had made it past the hostess. "Have a seat." He introduced me to Doc and Wendell and then he pointed at Wild Steve whose face was into his food. "Him right there, you don't want to know him," he burst into laughter.

"Steve, right?" Wild Steve looked up wondering how I had known him. He nodded.

"So you want something to eat? I got you." He slid his menu to me.

"Nah, I'm stuffed."

The waitress came back over to check on us. When she left, Cortez started in, "So why don't you tell my colleagues what you shared with me last night."

"So now these are your colleagues?" I asked. Wendell put his glass down.

He stared at Cortez and then asked him, "What does he mean by that?"

I cut in. "I'm right here. You can ask me what I mean." I paused. Wendell was a big guy. He looked like my man, Kenyon Martin, the pro baller. "What I mean is this. You all might have shared the Courts because you all sell different product, but now since I'm taking over…"

Doc interrupted me, "Little nigga, you ain't taking over shit." He looked at Cortez. "Cortez, I can't believe you brought me down here for this shit. This is the nigga that saved your ass?" He paused and shook his head in disgust.

"You may as well had let Bear kidnap and kill you last night. I understand you scared and all, but look at this *boy* you ready to bow down to."

"Hey, look. Don't give..." Cortez got out before I stopped him.

"Hey, listen up. Maybe you don't understand what I am trying to do, Doc. I don't want to sell product in the Courts or the Towers. I just want to be paid daily... *me and my crew* for keeping your workers safe. The way I see it is this... Just like them niggas came for Cortez last night, they gonna come for you and Wendell." Wendell took a sip of something he was drinking and put his glass back down. "They definitely gonna come around and rob the shit out of your work."

Doc's eyes were squinted and Wild Steve was just sitting there trying to look interested in his wings. I knew he was ready to pull his tool out and blast me on demand. Cortez looked across the table. "I've seen you work, so I am already impressed with you, but they don't know shit about you. You know though, you are being very bold and borderline disrespectful to everyone here with your request."

"Cortez, with all due respect..." I took my gun out and put it on the table and slid it to him, "... I don't give a fuck about that. This is business. Now if I was one gun deep, I wouldn't have a chance, right?" I reached into my jacket and pulled out another gun and put it on the table next to Doc. "Now when I take the last gun that I have on me out from my ankle, guess what?" I said looking right into Doc's eyes.

"Yeah, what?" he said looking back into mine.

"I'm still going to have twenty loaded guns aiming for this table." I nodded my head to the table on the right. There were two girls and a guy in a suit. The guy in the suit was Casper. I whistled and he pulled his suit jacket back to reveal a nickel-plated Beretta. I pointed to the balcony and Abraham was seated with Aaliyah. Without looking down he slid his pants leg up to reveal a nine-millimeter strapped to his leg.

Just then, Ferris walked by the table and lifted his sweatshirt to reveal a .357 on the way to the bathroom. "I could do this all day." I casually grabbed my guns and pulled them off of the table as I saw the waitress coming back.

I knew that I had impressed them because Doc's face was tighter than a virgin's booty. Wendell was breathing loudly through his nose while biting his bottom lip. Wild Steve had a smile on his face. He was a killer and a sick part of him was showing admiration. Cortez simply leaned back into his seat and looked at the three of them saying *I told you so* without words.

"So what are you looking for?" Cortez asked. He looked at his counterparts. "Let's just hear him out."

"I know that you all take at least thirty grand out of the Courtyard and another ten from the Towers in the hallways. Bump that up by fifty percent on the weekends and that's about one point three mill a month for you. You keep the mill and I'll take the three hundred grand that's left over—every month. That's ten gees a day, paid daily. I will tell you where to send the money. And it won't be in the projects either. Now an alternative would be to pay a month in advance and then you don't have to worry about using manpower to make the drops."

"You are out of your fucking mind!" Doc yelled out. Wild Steve laughed. I looked over at Cortez.

"Is that how you feel, Cortez?" Then I looked at Wendell.

"We are going to have to discuss this."

"What exactly are you going to do in order to earn this money?" Wendell asked.

Doc was playing with his fork, stabbing the table. "Nah. The question is, what are you going to do if we don't pay you shit? Because I ain't paying nothin'." He tapped Wild Steve on the shoulder. "Go get the car."

"No. I wouldn't move out of that seat, Steve, if I was you." Wild Steve looked at me. "They are instructed to only allow me to leave the table first. Anybody else leaves first and we all make CNN." He knew I was dead serious, and still stood. "Cortez, if he doesn't sit in five seconds, everyone at this table is a dead man, and I am assuming I am too but that shouldn't comfort you."

"Sit the fuck down." Cortez looked at Doc. He ordered Steve to sit.

"Unfortunately, there is no time for you to think it over. You all have twelve workers in the courts and six in the towers including two lieutenants on post right now. If you don't agree, they will all be dead before you can make it out of this restaurant. The same will happen tomorrow, next week, and the week after that, even if you are able to kill me. Don't get it twisted, my organization is the future of the Towers. We are not into dealing. We are into protection amongst other things."

"Your organization?" he asked. "What are you, part of a crew?"

"Yeah, I guess you could call it that if you like."

"What crew is that?" Wild Steve spoke for the first time and it came to me as I looked him in the eyes.

"Do or Die," I said and Wild Steve nodded his head in approval.

"So who is Do or Die protecting us from?" Wendell asked.

"Mostly us. But there are crews all over Brooklyn who are watching the Towers and believe me, the word is out that Phil Boogie is dead and every crew within ten blocks around is gonna be plottin' to come in and take over the Towers and the Courtyard."

There was silence as they looked at each other. I stood up. "Deal or no deal, I need ten a day. A penny less and I shut shit down like Bin Laden." There was silence.

"Can I speak with you?" Cortez asked.

"If only the meeting wasn't over you could." I glanced at my watch. "I am assuming we have a deal. I will call you at 7:00 to make the first pick-up."

Cortez lowered his head. "Listen, I expect a lot for my money. There better not be as much as one robbery in the Towers. I also want to know who set that robbery up last night."

"I'm already on it." I glanced over at Doc. "I hope you don't make this harder than it has to be." Looking over at Wendell, I said, "Talk some sense into him or you will need a new partner."

"Fuck you, little nigga." He stood up and Wheeler put a red dot on his forehead from four tables away. I pointed to it and Wild Steve pulled him into his seat.

Wild Steve spoke up again, "Be careful, Doc. Shorty is for real." Then he started snickering. "He reminds me of myself back in the day—only smarter." Then he winked at me.

I looked at Wendell. "Deal?"

"For now."

"Yeah, for now." I put my chair underneath the table. "Before you all leave, make sure you wait at least ten minutes. Any earlier wouldn't be good." I turned and walked out of the restaurant like the second coming of Tony Montana.

As I hit the corner, I immediately began planning the murders of Doc and Wendell. I hoped that I wouldn't have to do it, but I was going to map it out because I knew that they would soon be planning mine.

"I was beginning to think that you weren't going to call me."

"How could you think that? Plus as fine as you are, I know you weren't worried about me calling you." Angel was blushing when I said that.

"Actually, I was thinking a lot about you. You really made an impression on me when we met. Not many people would do what you did." She stirred her soda with her straw. "I was able to get my niece some summer clothes with that money."

I felt good and bad in the same instant. I had killed her father and bought her clothes as a trade-off. "Listen, I want to do more for her." I realized that I didn't know her name so I asked.

"Her name is Gemini. She is so sweet." Angel smiled and her one dimple melted me. "She is nothing like her father."

"Now that ain't nice."

"Hell, it's the truth. Everyone knows that my brother was a stone- cold killer. You were at the funeral. Everybody feared him. He hardly had any real friends, even if I include you, I can count them on one hand." She shrugged her shoulders. "Live by the gun…"

"That's true in a perfect world, but not necessarily in the hood." We changed the subject while we finished eating. Talking to Angel made me feel calm. I wanted to know all about her. She told me that she never knew her father, because he was killed hustling in the streets and that Phil's father was doing time. We ordered dessert and continued sharing life stories with each other. She said that she wanted to go to college in a couple of years and that she wanted to go to a historically black school like Hampton or Howard. She was interested in becoming a therapist for children with debilitating illnesses. I was impressed.

"So what's up with that boyfriend you told me about?" I was a little disappointed when her eyes lit up.

"Well, his name is Kirk Fullwood. You may have heard of him. He used to play point for De Witt Clinton. They won the city championship a few years back." I had never heard of him and shook my head no. "He won't be home until Christmas."

"What's he in for?" I asked being nosey.

"Distribution and assault," she said almost proudly as if he was away at college getting an education.

"So do you love this cat?" If she said yes my whole game plan was going to change.

"I guess. I will say that I really care about him. He was really good to me before he went away. We had a lot in common and spent a lot of time together."

"You don't seem like the type to go for a drug dealer. I guess I had you wrong." I was disappointed. What she had said to me was that he spent a lot of cash on her and they did a lot of fucking.

"No, you don't. I never approved of that life for him or my brother. I simply meant that Kirk and I did enjoy a lot of the same interests, like movies, books, and old music. And we talked a lot. We were open with each other about all types of things. I even got him to go back and finish school." She laughed. "He says that he was going to go to college with me."

"Oh." I sipped my lemonade. "So you aren't in love."

"I'm not sure if I even know what love is at this point in my life." She pushed her sundae toward the middle of the table.

"Maybe if you're lucky, you'll learn." I waved to the waitress to bring the check. The bill was $25 and I left a fifty. I saw Angel's eyes widen as I stood to leave. "You ready?"

"Aren't you going to get some change?" I took her hand and said, "Not from the waitress," and we made our way out of TGI Fridays and headed to the movies.

We checked out *Biker Boyz* and walked around Times Square. We looked inside of Tower Records and I bought her a few CD's. She wanted to replace her Maxwell, *Now* CD. She also grabbed Marvin Gaye's, *Live at the Palladium* and *Barry White's Greatest Hits*. I picked up *Miss E*, the *Biker Boyz Soundtrack*, and Fabulous' new joint.

As we rode home, I told her that I wanted to see her one day the upcoming week after school. She smiled and said, "Of course."

"I want you to pick up a couple more things for Gemini and grab a few outfits in a girl's size 7." Her eyes showed puzzlement when I peeled off a stack of twenties. "My little sister needs some summer gear too." I handed her $600. "Oh and I almost forgot, make sure you grab something for yourself too." I gave her another $200 and a grin slid across her face. I had never had money before, but I acted as if I had been old friends with it. I was giving it out freely because I knew that I would only make more if I shared what I had with other folks.

When the cab stopped in front of her building, she leaned over and gave me a long, soft kiss. I opened my mouth and I felt her tongue slip in between my lips. She was a good kisser and I felt my dick getting hard. "Goodnight," I said as she pulled away and exited the cab. I watched her make her way up the steps. She was a dime piece for sure and even if she didn't know it, she was going to be mine.

"Where to?" the cabbie asked.

"The Econolodge on Westfield Ave. in Queens." Sondra was waiting on me. I handed the cabbie another twenty and said, "Step on it."

"No problem, Boss."

I thought to myself. *Boss*. Then I whispered to myself, "You damned right."

TEN

Affluence once acquired, brings about two changes in lives of men. Inwardly he changes as he gains a sense of self-worth that he should have had from the start. Outwardly, the world he encounters changes as he is now deemed both credible and outstanding by those who are aware of his affluence. With wealth, even the slightest of men is given a voice that commands respect. For there is a widely accepted notion that only the wise or smart become rich. There also is an underlying belief that simply by listening to an affluent man, others can follow the same path to riches. This belief is a mistake and often proves to be the very thinking that keeps the affluent perpetually rich and the poor perpetually poor.

I was listening to the pastor as he began to shout to the congregation, "God made a covenant with Abraham. It was a blood covenant that as long as he believed, he would indeed have great wealth. In addition, all of Abraham's seeds would be entitled as well." I knew that my name was biblical, but I had never heard the story of this covenant. I was moved as he went on. "You see, people, we are all the seeds of Abraham and *we* are all entitled to prosperity… as long as we keep the covenant."

I was being educated and moved at the same time, mostly because he kept saying the name, Abraham. I knew what he was saying, but I kept feeling that the message had a special meaning for me. I started not to even come to church, but my grandmother had insisted. Not that I didn't want to come, it was just that I had been up until 3:00 in the morning with Malik watching the Courtyard along with the rest of Do or Die. My grandmother was screaming hallelujahs as the pastor was proclaiming and prophesying riches for all of the poor people.

He ended with, "Remember, you have to believe. Wait on GOD and in the perfect moment, he will move the wealth where it needs to go. Some of you might receive it today, others fifty years from now. Some of you have been waiting a long time and your patience will pay off." I looked at my grandmother and saw her move her lips and mouth the words, "*I believe.*" In that moment, as I looked at her and to the rest of the congregation, I knew why I was getting money. I had a plan of my own and was about to do whatever to make it happen.

The sun was shining and the Courtyard was full. I was sitting on the steps of Malik's building as he instructed. Terrell was armed like Rambo, sitting on the merry-go-round on the playground with Ferris. Malik was over near the Towers with Wheeler and the crew of guns that they had hired. For a hundred dollars a day, Malik had gotten a small army of niggas to hang on his every word. They seemed as though they would have busted their guns for free, but now that they were on the Do or Die payroll, they were feeling real extra.

It was hard to believe that a few weeks back, Malik and I were just a couple of young cats trying to avoid the drama and mayhem that this type of life brought. Now here I was his lieutenant, ready to do whatever to keep that money coming in.

I didn't hide the fact that it was beginning to get boring watching the same thing every day. The steady drug traffic moved in and out of the Courtyard day in and day out. The same fiends copped daily, all day. Most of the white folks who came through copped enough for a day so that they wouldn't have to come up here after dark. It always bothered me, but now that I was forced to watch it to earn my pay, I was hit with the reality of its hopelessness. I started fantasizing about what it would be like to have the playground enclosed in bulletproof glass so that the kids could play safely. I was startled when my phone rang. "What's up?'

"You haven't forgotten about your girl have you?" It was Aaliyah.

"Nah, never that."

"What's up for the night?" she asked.

"I'm handling some business 'til late."

"You up for seeing me?" I paused while I thought about it. I needed to get up for school. I had finals coming up and I was trying to pass. I didn't want to let her know that I was still in high school. Malik had all but stopped going. He said that he had been drafted into the game right out of high school like LeBron James. He had joked that he had a nicer shot than Lebron.

"How about tomorrow? We can go get something to eat. What about hitting Macy's? They have a sale and you could use a few nice things." She was getting really forward about asking for cash, but since I was hooked on her sex, it was getting really easy for her to get money out of me.

"Okay whatever. I'm gonna need some loving with that."

She laughed. "Okay, big daddy. You got it." We said good-bye and I got back to work—sitting there watching.

It was almost 10:00 when I saw a guy in a mechanic suit walking into the Courtyard. I didn't recognize him when he walked through the buildings, so I pulled my pistol out and told him, "If you looking, you have to go back out and come in through the main entrance. If you live here, I need some ID." Malik had changed the direction of all the drug traffic. All of the customers for the Towers and Courtyard were forced to enter one way, the main entrance off of Atlantic Avenue only. The only people that were allowed to walk into the complex from between the buildings were women and children.

There had almost been some static when Wendell had tried to enter from the alley. Three of Malik's gunmen had met him before he could make it completely through. Wendell, irritated, explained who he was and when Malik came over, he had explained that the rules he had set were for everyone except for Do or Die lieutenants and whoever accompanied them. Twenty minutes later, Wendell had shown up with Doc and Wild Steve.

"Listen man, I don't give a fuck if you bring Mayor Bloomberg down this motherfucker. I told y'all that nobody enters, except through the main gate." Words were exchanged for about ten minutes. Malik pointed out that there had been no robbery attempts and that only workers with their product were making money. Any renegades who tried to move their own product on the outskirts of the complex were unable to catch the customers because they had learned to come through the main entrance.

In all actuality, the set-up simply made it easier for Malik to police what was happening and we all knew to draw our guns if intruders tried to flank us through any other inlet. Doc had tried to calm Wendell down for ten minutes straight before Wendell decided to do the unthinkable and curse his own partner out for bowing to Malik. Doc had simply walked off and told him to deal with it his way then, and as his chest swelled up, he saw Wild Steve walking off behind Doc. Realizing that he would be signing his own death warrant that night, he walked off talking shit, but never tried to enter that route again.

"Grandma."

"Yeah baby," she said while in the kitchen frying chicken and listening to her *WOW Gospel* CD.

I walked to the door and leaned in. "Where would you go if you had the money to leave here?"

"Oh, I don't know."

"Seriously. Think about it."

She paused and closed her eyes. "Do you really want to know?"

"I wouldn't have asked," I said laughing. "Tell me."

"I would move down to Fort Lauderdale where my sister lives and get me a nice apartment with a good air conditioner and take those $99 Bingo cruises she brags about taking every month."

"That sounds nice. How much money do you think you would need to do that?"

"A lot more than I have. Her husband left her in good shape when they split. When your grandfather passed, all he left were bills."

I nodded and began to walk away without my answer but changed my mind. "Yeah, but how much would it take?"

"Probably $30,000, but I'm happy here with you. The Lord has provided all I need."

"Yeah, but you are promised everything you want. If you believe... gotta believe." She smiled. "One day I will give you enough money to go on down there."

She gave me a quick hug and replied, "I believe. I believe in you."

I jumped when I felt my phone vibrating. I walked into my room and answered. I had a date with Aaliyah and I figured that she was being impatient. I didn't bother looking to see who it was. "Hello."

"Come to my house quick." Malik hung up the phone without letting me know what was up so I shot out of my room and told my grandmother not to worry about my dinner. I heard her fussing as I ran out the door. I sprinted with my hand on the trigger. I was getting really used to carrying the weapon on me. It made me feel safe.

When I reached Malik's door, I heard shouting on the other side. I twisted the knob without knocking and when it turned I entered—slowly. Once I was inside, I saw that the apartment was a mess. Malik was in the living room sitting on the couch with a wet towel rapped around his left hand. I looked on the floor in front of the TV and saw the Jamaican who had gotten Toni pregnant, laid out on the floor. Malik was still shouting insults and threats at him.

"What happened in here?" I asked imagining from the looks of the apartment. If Lindsey walked in with it looking like it did, she was going to go ballistic.

"You ain't gonna believe this shit," Malik said. "I'm in the room counting up some money and I hear this cocksucker banging on the door like he's the got damned police. So I go out to check to see who it is and here this mufucka is at my door, cussing and fussing, asking for his bitch."

I looked at Quentin, who was lying completely still on the floor, and couldn't believe that Malik had taken him out without shooting. He had three inches and probably twenty pounds on Malik. "So what happened?"

"I told him to hold on while I got his bitch." He reached down next to the coffee table and picked up one of those old-school, black cast-iron frying pans. "I let that fool in and swung this pan into his grill like Sammy Sosa swinging for the fences at Wrigley. I'm positive that I broke his nose with the shot, but this jackass kept coming and that's how the apartment got trashed."

"So you called me to help you clean up before your mother gets home? Man stuff never changes, huh?" I laughed.

"Oh it's a little more serious than that." Malik got up and went to the room and came back out with a roll of duct tape. "Strap his legs and hands together. After that, I want you to go and get Terrell, even if he's clocking. Tell him to come with work on him."

I did as Malik instructed. Terrell asked twenty questions on the way back up, none of which I knew the answers to. "What he want?" Next there was, "Was he mad?"

"I don't know just come on." I had answered as best I could.

Terrell was the only member of our crew who was allowed to sling dope. Malik figured that it was good to have a man fully in the game on our crew, plus Terrell was good at it. He was the only one in the Courtyard selling product that didn't belong to Cortez, Doc, or Wendell. He got his product from who ever Malik robbed.

Malik had made it a point to rob enough to keep a nice supply for Terrell and to keep balance in the game. Addicts feed off citizens, dealers feed off addicts, and stick-up boys feed off of dealers—the top of the food chain. All the kingpins knew that there were some stick-up boys that were so good at what they did and so ruthless, that the most they could hope for was to survive their attacks. Cortez, Doc and Wendell all knew this, which is why they came to grips with what Malik was providing them.

In the three weeks that Malik had been the reigning protector of the Greenberg Projects there hadn't been one successful robbery. The only attempt had ended with two crackheads having their skulls bashed in by three members of Do or Die. Malik had watched the would-be robbers from the moment they entered the Towers from the stairs above. When they pulled out their pistols, Malik simply called outside on his walkie-talkies and had them met at the door. He had made sure that all of the hustlers working for Cortez, and especially those working for Doc and Wendell saw the type of street justice he executed.

A couple of their workers even quit the next day after witnessing how Malik demanded the fatal beating. It had been hard enough watching the two men get beat with bats and poles, but when Wheeler, who was fast becoming as feared as Malik joined in, a couple of the dealers had vomited. Wheeler had created a weapon from a simple two by four. He had the blade from a circular saw attached to the end of it and nails protruding from the opposite side of it. The electric tape on the bottom end provided the grip and an opponent was fucked no matter which side he hit them with. Their faces were nothing but a bloody pulp when he'd finished and the word spread throughout Brooklyn that robbing in the Greenberg Towers wasn't taken lightly.

We made it back to Malik's apartment and began to knock on the door. When there was no answer, I began to fear something had gone wrong until I heard Malik calling me from up the hall. "Yo come on."

We headed over to the steps where Malik had dragged Quentin, who was now awake but wasn't able to scream or run because he was all taped up. "Yo what the fuck you doin' with this clown?" Terrell asked.

"We're about to carry this fool up to the roof so he can get really high," Malik said. Quentin started squirming and trying to mumble through the duct tape. Malik pulled a chrome Berretta nine out of his pants and pointed it at Quentin. "I'm gonna tell you what, you dirty baby fucker. I will blow your balls off right here, one nut at a time, if you give me any shit." Malik looked like he was about to go off. "Can y'all believe this mofo got my sister pregnant? Look at his nasty ass. He looks like he's forty-five." Malik motioned for us to grab him and Terrell was all over it.

I was leery because I knew that nothing good was about to happen, and as we climbed the steps, I found myself deep in prayer. We carried him to the roof and I noticed that Quentin wasn't even kicking.

We walked across the roof, dragging Quentin along. "Set his ass right there. Terrell, pull out four bags of heroin and two bags of coke." Terrell did as instructed. Malik handed him a lighter and a spoon. "Fire that shit up." Terrell put the powder onto the spoon and put the flame to the bottom of it. It began to melt into liquid and bubble from the heat. Then Malik pulled out a syringe and carefully put the tip into the liquid on the spoon.

I watched as Malik filled the needle up with what I suspected was a lethal dose of heroin. I was still praying, giving the man his last rites when Malik ordered me to hold his head still as Terrell held his body. I tightened my grip and he squirmed wildly and tried to yell out as Malik stabbed him in the neck repeatedly. When a vein appeared, Malik jammed the needle into it and emptied the drugs into him.

I stepped back when I felt his body go limp. "Do it again, Terrell." Malik ordered Terrell to fry up some more heroin. "This time, mix the coke in with it."

All in all, Malik shot enough drugs into Quentin to kill a rhino. I stood there and looked at him with foam coming out of his mouth and said a short prayer. Malik reached down and wiped his prints from the needle and inspected the ground for any evidence. Malik laughed as we walked away. I wanted to cry because my best friend was gone. The Malik that I had grown up with was now a monster—a dragon to be exact.

ELEVEN

Drive, not talent, is what separates nine percent of the world's population from the other ninety. Everyone has enough talent to achieve a level of excellence that would bring them the perfect amount of sustenance. The telling fact is that some just don't have enough of a hunger to use that talent to make something extraordinary happen. Understanding that a million dollars is a dream for one man, comfortable for another, and yet broke to the next man, is key to taking the action necessary to bring dreams to fruition. Being comfortable in any position leads to complacency, and most people would rather be complacent than hungry. Make the simple decision to satisfy that hunger and pursue a dream and divinely the world will allow one to go from the ninety percent complacent into the nine percent driven. As for the other one percent... some people are just plain lucky.

I didn't really to go to war with Black Sid and his brothers over $5,000. It had been a month and a half since I had left him with the stolen drugs and I hadn't seen nor heard from him. I'd honestly believed that he would respect what I had offered him. I didn't even need the money. I had collected close to $400,000 from Cortez, Doc and Wendell. After paying the crew of Do or Die I was left with almost half of that.

I had made some major moves since taking over the Greenberg projects at the direction of my grandfather. My uncle had gotten me an apartment in New Jersey and had purchased two cars for me in his name. One was a used Toyota Camry that I drove around in with the intention to stay inconspicuous. The other I treated myself to for my eighteenth birthday. It was a silver 2002 Mercedes CLK 430 convertible. Double V had schooled me on what to wear and how to act when I drove it in order to reduce the attention from police. I had a fake Columbia University student ID that matched my fake driver's license. If I was ever pulled over, I was Malik Sharpton, son of Reverend Al and a law student at Columbia. This meant bad news for any officers trying that racial profiling shit or trying to do an illegal search.

"So you understand why you have to bring this cat a move? It's the principal." Double V explained, talking about Black Sid.

"Yeah, Grandad, but things are going so smoothly. Once I go around there starting this war over five grand... I mean these guys aren't chumps."

His eyes seemed to burn into me as he said, "Listen up. If you are afraid of war, then tuck your tail and get out of town. You are already at war, even if you don't know it. If not this very minute, then later on today one of your enemies will be plotting to take you out, and odds are that someone in your camp wants you dead so that they can have your spot. Think about it." He leaned back and folded his arm, "Let me add this, son-son... you can also count on some bitch crossing your path who will be part of a set-up."

"Damn," was all I came up with before he went on.

"The last thing I'm going to warn you about is your moms and sisters."

"What about them?"

He gave a smirk that asked if I was really as green as I appeared. "Nothing now, but if you don't move your family out of the Towers, they'll all be dead before the summer is out. That includes the baby." He saw my face drop. "Charge it to the game, kid, but make moves two steps ahead of your enemy."

"I thought I had been doing that."

"You have and believe me, that's what's brought you so far so fast. But you can't stop there though." He sipped his water. "For example, tell me the one person you can count on."

"That's easy. Abraham."

"What if you couldn't? What if he flipped and wanted your spot? What if he decided what you are doing is so easy that he could do it without you?'

"What you sayin'?"

"You know what I'm saying."

"Nah, fuck that. Abraham wouldn't ever do me wrong."

"Would you bet your life on it?"

"I'd bet mine and yours on it," I said in a tone letting him know that I didn't appreciate him trying to plant seeds of doubt about my brother.

He nodded his head and then a smile crossed his face. "Would you kill for him?"

"No doubt."

"Do time for him?"

"Life."

"Die for him?"

"I ain't dying for nobody but Jade."

"That's deep, son-son."

"That's real, pop." And so the conversation went. More education. More names and people to meet that would help me with my plan.   More murderous pep talks and criminal direction.

When I left there, I knew that I had to get money plus retribution from Black Sid. I also needed to move into the next phase of my plan. I had already laid the foundation and established the income. It was time to hide the money and build my *Underground Railroad* out of the projects.

I flew down 95 back into the city and took the Cross Bronx Expressway and headed for Harlem. I stopped at my Uncle Kelly's and picked up a package that I would need in the morning. I then called Cortez and told him where to meet me for the drop-off. As usual, he was instructed to come alone and he always did ride alone or at least appeared to.

I suspected that he would have tried to have someone follow me after the drop to find out where I was taking the money. It was obvious that he didn't fear me trying to take him out. He knew that he was worth more to me alive than dead, which is why I would have him followed almost everyday. I had learned enough about him to rob him and his connect blind, but that wasn't my goal.

For instance, I knew that before he came to see me, he always went to a brownstone in Fort Greene to pick up the money from the day's earnings. The money only stayed there for a few hours. After that, a tow truck would come and tow the same minivan out to Freeport. On Wednesdays, Cortez would show up in a green Ford Explorer and ride with his money to Kennedy Airport. He would wear a yellow hardhat and drive into the construction entrance, which let me know someone had been paid off. The woman riding with him would take the suitcases and head straight for the Caribbean without so much as one security checkpoint. Cortez's program was tight, but too easy to pick up on for someone truly trying. I couldn't believe that the stick-up crew that I murdered had been too lazy to do some simple surveillance. They could have easily found out the same info that I had and robbed Cortez with very little effort. The money and power had made Cortez sloppy. Doc and Wendell were another issue.

Usually on alternating days, the very same van would show up around the Towers around 6:00 to make a drop or collect, I wasn't sure which, but I had people on it. I had no intention of robbing any of them. I just thrived on having the most information possible and on making sure that they had little on me.

Papaya's had a bit of a line when I arrived, but I still went in to grab a seventy-five-cent frank and juice while waiting for Cortez. I was sweating as soon as I walked back out of the door because it was humid out even at dusk, plus I had started wearing a bulletproof vest.

Cortez pulled up in his E Class and the window slid down. I didn't budge because I never walked up on cars—too easy to get yanked into. Instead, I nodded my head for him to come into Papaya's. He parked across the street and got out of his car with a backpack in his hand. He passed me and went to the counter and grabbed a couple of dogs for himself.

We grabbed a table. "Look, everything is going smooth," he said. "As a matter of fact, since you have been doing your thing, I'm making more money than ever."

I was surprised at what he said. "Oh yeah?"

"No doubt. What we are paying you is a drop in the bucket." He took a huge bite. "But don't even think about asking for more money. That would be extremely unethical and I think that you and Wendell would go to war over it. So …" he bit again, "…leave well enough alone."

"So why bother telling me?"

"Because I happen to think you have a future in these streets." He slid the backpack underneath the table. "I convinced them to ante up. You now owe us your services thru the month of July."

I was surprised. "I can't believe you got that damned Wendell to come up off some cash. That's whoa."

"Yeah and there's an extra hundred in there, but you have to do me a favor."

There was nothing free in life even when it appeared to be. If he was willing to pay me a hundred, it had to be worth three to him. "I have a little situation with a former co-defendant." He sipped his drink and looked out of the window. It just dawned on me that I was seated in a vulnerable position. Wheeler was outside watching the whole time in case anything strange went down, so I felt safe. "You see, I am out on bond. Very few people know that."

I nodded my head, "Okay."

"What I need is for this co-defendant not to testify. My trial is in three weeks."

"What's the catch? Why the hundred grand?"

"My co-defendant is a former NYPD. He also happens to be on house arrest and is being guarded by armed security."

"How much time you looking at?"

"A shit-load."

"Are you positive about the address? Absolutely positive?"

"I am certain."

"How so?"

"His security is on my payroll." He grinned and laughed.

I laughed too. "I'll do it. I need another fifty grand up front and then another hundred and fifty gees after. I trust you." I stood up. "That's non-negotiable." I looked down at him. "Would you like the extra hundred you gave me back?"

He waved his hand like a blackjack player passing on a hit and told me to wait. I looked at him as he ran across the street to his car and then back into the restaurant. "Here's the fifty and here's the address." This time he got up and headed out first. When we got to the outside of the restaurant, he turned to me and said, "I need this done ASAP so that I can start sleeping again."

I gave my best impersonation of an Italian mobster and said, "Fuggedaboutit."

He didn't laugh but just headed off to his car.

As I pulled off, it dawned on me that I was holding $450,000 in cash. I had enough money to leave town and never come back. I imagined what it would be like for a second. Then I saw myself coming back to Brooklyn broke in five years and being hunted down like a dog.

I hooked an illegal U and pulled up next to Wheeler who had crossed the street after ensuring that everything had gone smoothly.

"Change in plans." I dropped a hundred dollar bill out of the window as he moved toward me. "Get a cab back and I will catch you in the courtyard."

He had a puzzled look on his face. I didn't care. There was no way his ass was riding next to me with that kind of cash on me. I would have killed him over less—way less—so I had to figure that he would have done the same to me.

I left the village and headed towards midtown and purposely rode into the thick traffic at Times Square. Once I passed the Theatre District, I turned around and headed for Grand Central. Once I made it there I pulled out my cell and made the call. At the 43rd Street entrance, I saw Abraham on the corner waiting. I am sure the people behind me thought I was tripping when I put the car in park and jumped out of it and headed into the station. Like clockwork, Abraham jumped in and headed back to Brooklyn.

I had gotten used to giving misdirection to anyone who may have been following me. I switched trains four times before I wound up in Harlem at Reche's Monthly Parking Garage. At my request, Sondra had left her mother's car with the key under the mat. She had then taken the train into Jersey and would be waiting at the Sheraton in the Meadowlands for me when I got there. I would of course take the money to my apartment in Teaneck first.

No one other than my landlord knew that I lived there. Hopefully the only person that would ever know about the Gibraltar TL-30X6 would be the Armenian technician who installed it. He ensured me that the safe was the best money could buy and that it could be hit by a bomb and still wouldn't open. I came to this apartment with as little as possible. I didn't have much in the apartment except for a few changes of clothes, a bed, couch, television and plenty of guns. The only reason why I had furnished it at all was to give the appearance that I lived in it.

Most other nights, I was in a hotel remaining hard to be tracked, patterned, and most of all followed. I had finally convinced Abraham to do the same thing. He didn't have an apartment, but I kept his money for him anyway. He had been instructed to visit my grandfather if anything happened to me. Double V would then give him any instructions he needed to handle business and to retrieve the money. It hadn't been necessary for him to know where the money was. I trusted him with my life, but I had my doubts about how he would hold up under torture. Torture would have to be expected if he was ever kidnapped. There were some sick cats out there who did things that most people thought only happened in books and movies.

It was 1:00 a.m. when I finished counting the money. It came up to $449,820… and nine counterfeit twenties. I had no problem with that, assuming it was an error. Adding my portion to what I had saved, I was getting close to the money I would need to implement my plan. It took money to make money and broke to stay a joke.

After shutting the safe, I took a hot shower and sat on the bed air-drying. I was lying back looking up at the ceiling and it finally hit me. I had become a criminal and crime was paying like a motherfucker. In less than three months, I had amassed a small fortune worth almost $300,000. I had been forced into the game by my surroundings and was becoming a top-notch thug. Keeping my sister from being raped had pushed me to use everything my grandfather had taught me from the first time I visited with him and it appeared that all of the knowledge he had given me was more than enough to stay ahead of the streets. I reflected on the killing and wondered why I felt no remorse. I reasoned that even though it was real life, it was a game that we all chose to play. Everyone knew that the rules were made up as we went along, but that one thing never changed: If you lost, you either died or went to prison. I never once remembered hearing a prosecutor say that they felt remorse for someone being sent to prison so why should I cry for the dead? We were all holding court and all of the sentences were justifiable to the judges.

I used the key and walked into the room with my Glock drawn. The TV was on but Sondra was sleep. "Yo, wake up."

She came out of her sleep instantly. "Damn, Malik, look what time it is. I told you my mother wanted her car in by one. It's almost two now."

"She'll be a'ight," I said. "Come on. Grab your shit."

"So you ready to go? We don't ever spend any time together," she was complaining and I didn't feel like hearing it.

"Okay... you right. I just don't want you to get in trouble. I am going to need you again next weekend." I motioned for her to give me a hug. She did and I put my lips on her neck. She got hot for me so easily. I dropped my pants and fell back onto the bed.

"Oh, baby. I love licking you. You smell so good," she said. I wasn't trying to go all night with her so I pulled her away.

She unbuttoned her shirt and unfastened her shorts. "Bend over," I said as her shorts fell to her ankles. I rolled a condom on and dove into her from the back. She started making sounds like I was going too fast or being too rough. I slowed down and started to make sure she would enjoy it. I knew that she loved it when I pulled her back into me.

"Got daaaammmmmnn, Malik. I love it. I love it from the back. Hit it. Hit." She was bouncing back against me trying to get her nut. "Fuck me. Fuck me." Her pussy was making slurping sounds. She was into it and didn't notice that I wasn't. As she began to cum, I was watching Blind Date on Fox.

I could tell she was about to reach an orgasm, so I chimed in. "Baby yes. Yes, I'm coming. Come with me."

"Oh yeah... yes I am." She shook violently and collapsed onto the bed.

A few moments later, she wanted to speak on how good the sex always was. While it was decent, she didn't know that I didn't want her for sex or even really want to have sex with her. She was an unwitting soldier in my army. I always made sure that she was with me because she was chasing dollars. That way I would have no remorse if things went bad and she became a casualty.

I called the valet to bring her mother's car up and told her that I would call her in the a.m. "Here, tip the valet... the parking is already paid for."
She was in the bathroom washing her booty as I was heading out of the door.

"Where you headed? You ain't gonna walk downstairs with me?"

"Don't question me and don't get brand new. Have I ever walked you downstairs?" I handed her $500. "Here, take this. Drive safe."

I was halfway out of the door and heard her say, "I love you, Malik." I kept walking and hit the elevator.

I rode the elevator up four floors to the eleventh and headed for my room and went through the whole drill with my gun again. "You up?"

"Hell yeah, Boo. I was waiting for you." Angel said showing that dimple. She had candles lit and had some soft music playing.

"You look good."

"Good enough to eat?"

"All night." We kissed. "That music is tight. Who is that?"

"Yazarah. She's new. That shit is banging right?"

"No doubt." I started to undress. "Let me take a shower. As a matter of fact, get in with me."

"I guess I could do that."

We showered and kissed like the young lovers that we were. She had played hard to get for a couple of weeks but she couldn't resist my persistence. Plus the word was on the streets that I was the man. It was either she slid with me or watched some other chicken head try her hand.

I respected the fact that she had made me wait a month before she opened her legs to me. However, in the last month, she had proven that she knew how to be the First Lady to the new Street Ambassador. She didn't appear to be into sexing as a sport, but she took to it like a fish to water. Once I began financing her, it didn't take long for her to decide to keep me by any means necessary.

She was going home only to get clothes and to spend time with her niece. Kirk had to have been missing his visits and was definitely missing his phone time. I figured that there could be problems when he made it home because his girl had been drafted and I had to admit I was catching feelings.

"I love making love to you, Malik."

"Yeah? Why?"

"Don't make me say it."

"Say it." She started giggling. "Say it."

"Alright. You just want me to pump your head up." I stared at her. She stared back. "I love making love to you because you make me feel like a woman and not a little girl. When you touch me, it doesn't feel dirty. I don't feel used."

"That's good, because I'm not using you."

"I know." She paused. "It feels like you are making up for all of the bad that has ever been done to me. I feel like I am on the verge of starting the life I'm gonna have. It's so beautiful."

I thought about the power of her words and how she communicated. "You mean a lot to me. I hope you don't let me down."

"Never would I do that." She smiled and kicked the covers off of her. "Oh and there is another thing I like about making love with you."

"What's that?"

"You got a big-ass dick and you know how to work that magic stick." Then we both laughed as she climbed on top of me and we made love again like a scene from a movie. As I stared up into her eyes, I thought about including her in my future and hoped that we could have a happy ending.

TWELVE

Religion has almost nothing at all to do with faith. Those who believe that there is a GOD bestowing undeserved mercy on mankind as the end of this world draws near, maintain Faith. Contrary to what most experts on theology understand, there is a religion that is widely accepted across the globe that transcends ethnicity, race, or gender. That religion has more followers than Christianity, Islam, Buddhism, and Judaism combined. That is the religion of Self-Indulgence. It is widely accepted because human beings are programmed to try this religion of comfort first. Nearly all humans try a religion based on faith at some point because they feel the sickening void that Self-Indulgence never satisfies. However, in the end, they almost always come back to practicing Self-Indulgence. In the end, whatever people choose to love most eventually becomes their religion... money, power, sex, fame, cars, and drugs all become the idols that drive men to their graves.

Malik and I took a day off from Do or Die. Terrell was left in charge and we were only a phone call away. We rode out to Yonkers at 7 a.m. and met with a middle-aged white woman at her real estate office. When we got there, the door was still locked and we noticed her as she pulled up next to us. She was pushing a Lexus SUV and had on a big pink hat looking like she was going to church. She looked over at us two young black men sitting in a convertible Benz and a grin slid across her face.

Getting out of her car, she hit the alarm to lock it and said, "Hello, boys. You must be Malik." He nodded. "And you are?"

"Abraham," I said smiling.

"Well come on in, fellas." Looking back at Malik, she said, "You know, I see a definite resemblance to your grandfather."

She had him going because he loved being compared to Double V. I was wondering how she knew his grandfather. "Nice office," I said as we stepped inside.

"Thank you. Make yourselves comfortable." She fumbled through a stack of papers on a desk and then said, "Oh that's right. Hold up, fellas, I need to grab your folders out of the back." Malik had mentioned that we had business to attend to today but I hadn't pressed him about the nature. She headed into an office in the back and when she reappeared, she was holding two manila folders. "Okay, this is the deal. I am able to get the tickets in any name you need and one apartment in Camden for $950 a month. It's a decent neighborhood but if you aren't dead set on the Philly area, then you might consider a couple of other locations."

"Like where?"

"Towson, Maryland, essentially Baltimore, and there is also Newport News."

"That's near Virginia Beach, right?" Malik asked.

"Thirty miles or so, but in the general area."

"How much for the one in Baltimore?"

"You're looking at about $900 for the one in Baltimore. It's a duplex with three bedrooms."

"And the one in Newport News?"

She flipped a page. "I believe that one is $650 a month. It's only two bedrooms though."

Malik nodded. "Okay, I'll take the one in B-More." Malik got up and walked out to the car and grabbed a backpack from the trunk. When he walked back in he added, "I want the spot in Camden too, but I only need it for six months."

She nodded approvingly. "So is this the gentleman you wanted the other place in Fort Lauderdale for?" she said motioning toward me.

"Yeah, is that taken care of?"

"Well yes and no," she replied taking a sip of her coffee. "I am going to need the signatures and the rest of the info for that one since you want to actually buy it."

"No problem. We'll have everything to you nice and neat." He motioned for me to come over. "You are going to have to get your grandmother to fill out this application."

I looked at the paper. It was a scholarship questionnaire for the University of Rhode Island. "What's this?

The white woman answered, "That is the paperwork that a guardian fills out in order to secure a student loan for a potential student. You simply need to tell your grandmother that you have an opportunity to go to school on scholarship and that she needs to fill this form out."

I had a puzzled look on my face. Then she went on, "Your grandmother would be in favor of you going to college, right?"

"Of course she would," Malik chimed in on my behalf.

"Well then Abraham, once she fills out this info, my associates will have all of the info we need to process the paperwork for the house that you are buying her. We can easily have her signature duplicated for the deeds and insurance info." She folded her arms. "She'll have that house in no time."

Malik talked to her for a few more moments before he took the folders and two sets of keys from her. She said something about going to visit Vincent and gave Malik a hug as he was about to head out. When I stood to leave, I noticed that Malik had left a stack of money in rubber bands on her desk. I nodded and said goodbye as well and headed out the door.

While we cruised back into the city, Malik explained that we needed to get our families out of the projects. He already knew how he was going to get Lindsey out of the place where she had lived for ten years, but he was worried about my grandmother. We both knew that there was no way that she would take blood money to live on even if it meant her getting a home down in Fort Lauderdale where her sister lived.

He came up with one idea that seemed like it might work. The only problem was that it would involve bribing the pastor at my grandmother's church. If that didn't work, he was going to attempt to strong-arm the situation until something gave.

We got off of the Major Deegan in the Bronx and hit Jerome Avenue. The sun was beaming and we had the top down even though it was 9:00 in the morning. Malik was blasting a DJ KaySlay's mix CD featuring Tasha Robb. We pulled into the Amoco. "You want anything?" I asked as I went inside to grab a bottle of grape juice.

"A root beer and some Pringles. Go ahead and put twenty on pump five."

"So what's up for the day?" I asked as I handed him his breakfast.

"There are only two things I need to take care of today." He popped open the can. "The rest of the day we can do whatever you like. As a matter of fact, you're driving."

"Man, I don't have a license and you know it'll be just my luck to get pulled over driving this pretty mufucka."

Malik looked at me all strange. "Man, do you hear yourself? Cursing like that, that ain't like you." He started laughing. "Look in that folder on the side of the seat."

I slid into the car and pulled out the folder. My mouth dropped when I saw a driver's license with my face on it. There was also a NYU student ID card, a passport and a registration for a Nissan Maxima, all with the name Thomas Cochran Jr. on them. I looked back at Malik for an explanation. "What's all this?"

"If you get pulled over, you are Johnnie Cochran's nephew. Let that be the first thing out of your mouth. Then start talking about lawsuits for racial profiling." He smiled. "That shit will work. I swear to you."

"What's up with this registration?"

"Oh, I forgot to tell you. I bought you a car. We are going to pick it up on Monday."

I couldn't believe it. "The money is that good? So you've graduated from buying me Jordan's to buying cars for me." I reached out and slapped him five.

"A 2003 no less, my nigga."

"That's big. So what color is my joint?"

"That I don't know yet. My uncle knows a guy who gets cars for like seventy percent off the sticker." My eyebrows rose a little. "They do some tricky shit with serial numbers, but it's all good. The registration is legit and even if they run the serial number the cars never come up stolen."

I was amazed at all the crooked people Malik had become connected to. We stopped off at Carlos' house to drop money off for a few items that Malik said he needed. By noon, we were headed up to Harlem to meet Sondra and Aaliyah at Sylvia's for some lunch.

The entire ride up, Malik talked about Angel and how much he liked her. He went as far as saying that if everything went well he might even marry her. It was strange to hear him talk like that. Malik had always liked girls, even when we were kids, but he was always more serious about basketball, video games, and even school at some points than he was about having a serious girlfriend.

There was a girl, Marcella, who Malik had a crush on in seventh grade. In the ninth grade he finally worked up the nerve to try to get with her. She told him that she had a crush on him from the first time she laid eyes on him and they decided to become an item. Two weeks later, her mom's boyfriend was killed by an undercover officer, and without so much as a goodbye, Marcella and her mother moved away. Malik was crushed. He never said anything, but I knew he was. Those seemed to be the best two weeks of his life and I never heard him speak fondly of another woman until now.

We walked up in Sylvia's and saw the girls standing outside waiting. There were some guys standing around, but they weren't paying Sondra and A.J. any attention. I secretly wondered if they had tried their hand and been warned. A.J. looked scared to death. I wouldn't have allowed Malik to hurt her though. Even though he described them as "our little hookers", I had gained some respect for Aaliyah. She had been through a few things in her life and I wasn't into judging.

"What's up, ladies?"

"Hey, Abe," Sondra said as A.J. grabbed me and gave me a hug.

"What's up with y'all?" Malik said as he allowed Sondra to give him a hug. We turned to walk into the restaurant.

"Mmmm, youngin' your bitch is tight. That's your lady?" I heard one of the fellas say while we were walking in.

In the next second, I heard a familiar tone. "Aw shit, here we go," I said to myself.

It was Malik's voice as he said, "What?" He turned and headed back out the door. I tried to grab him, but he moved out onto the sidewalk. "You talkin' to me, nigga? I know the fuck you didn't say nothing about my bitch?"

The guy who Malik was talking to pointed to another brother who was leaning on a parking meter, "That was him."

Malik walked over to the guy. "You got something you want to say about my bitch?"

The guy didn't say a word at first. He just smiled and stood up straight. "I was complimenting you on your lady." I walked up to Malik's side. I noticed the teardrops tattooed under his eye. He had the look of a killer if he wasn't one. "You might want to leave it at that, youngin'."

"Nigga, you don't tell me. I tell you. I'm sensing disrespect coming from you. I can see you all swole up, and I see the tats for your work. I see you done had your day and done a bid."

"Well then recognize, little nigga, 'cause I don't do too much talking."

"Yeah well neither do I, but I'll tell you what. This is your lucky day. I'm gonna let you live as long as you get off this block. 'Cause if you still out here when I finish eating, I'm gonna end you."

He smiled again. "I believe you'd try, little man, so this is your lucky day. Since all these police are out here, I'm gonna step off. But the next time you see me, we can dance." He tapped his waist then cracked his knuckles. "Any way you want to get down." Then he turned and walked up the block.

I looked at Malik and said, "Man I ain't even gonna lie. That nigga had me a little shook."

Malik started laughing. "You? I wasn't even trying to get into it with that nigga. Did you see how big that mufucka was? He would have squashed me like a grape. The only thing I could have done was shoot his ass in broad daylight surrounded by all these cops, and got thirty fucking years."

"So why the hell did you run up on him?"

Malik nodded toward the crowd. "Streets is always watching. Remember that." He shook his head. "You never let a man disrespect you or take from you in public. You must address it or you open the gates."

I nodded. We went into the restaurant and the girls were waiting to be seated. I had calmed down and was ready to get my grub on. "I don't know why black men are so disrespectful," Sondra said to Malik. "He just don't know, he almost got dealt with, huh, baby?"

"For sure," Malik said. Sondra was on Malik. The way she looked at him, I could tell she would do anything for him. She was hypnotized by the power of his presence. She was proud to be in the company of a killer and clung to his side like Hillary to Bill.

We were seated and had ordered enough food for a Thanksgiving dinner. When it came, I noticed that Malik didn't eat like usual. I on the other hand was a soul food junkie and Sylvia's was one of my favorite places to eat.

"So are you going to go over to the fair with us?" Sondra asked.

"What fair?" I asked.

"The Harlem Book Fair. They have it every year. That's why the streets are so crowded today."

"Man, I ain't going to no book fair," Malik answered.

"Well we goin'," A.J. said. "It is a really nice event. Plus you get to meet a lot of the authors."

"Big fucking deal," Malik answered while chewing.

"It is to me. I want to go see Darren Coleman and Eric Jerome Dickey."

"What did they write?" I asked.

"Darren has a book out called, *Before I Let Go*. Let me tell you that joint is off the hook. He has some crazy sex scenes and drama in that book. Plus he ain't a bad looking brother either." She sipped her fruit punch. "And Dickey, he has plenty of books out. But I want to get a copy of his latest, *The Other Woman*."

Malik joined in, "I don't like that relationship shit. The only authors I want to read are Donald Goines and Iceberg Slim. My grandfather turned me on to those. That's some real street shit."

Sondra tapped Malik, "No, baby, there are some new street joints out that are just as good as Donald Goines."

"Like what?" he asked.

"If you like a good street story, you absolutely have to read *No Way Out* and *Lost and Turned Out* by this new author, Zachary Tate. Zachary's shit is fire."

"Yeah, where's he from?" I asked.

"The Bronx."

"Yeah, well I ain't going to no book fair. Bring me back a few books though." He slid a hundred dollar bill to Sondra. "If I don't like the books, I want my money back."

We talked a little more and A.J. massaged me under the table until I was rock hard. When we got up to leave, I gave her the money for a hotel and told her I would see her tonight. Oddly, she gave the money back and said that we could stay at her aunt's for free since she was going to baby-sit tonight.

It wasn't like her to turn down money, but I was definitely cool with it. We walked towards the door and I wondered if the big guy would be out front waiting. I breathed a sigh of relief when he wasn't there and an even bigger one when we hit the FDR and headed out of Harlem.

Malik hit the CD changer and the first Lauren Hill CD came on. "That was the joint right there," I said.

"Yeah, you know Lauren is my baby mama. That's why she ain't been comin' out with any new joints lately."

I laughed. "Oh you keepin' her busy raisin' your babies, huh?"

"No doubt," he laughed.

"In your dreams, fool."

"Maybe. But with paper, anything is possible," he said and reclined his seat.

I digested his words and it hit me like a ton of bricks. Money, not love made the world go 'round. I was starting to see how life changed with money. I looked at myself. I had on a $400 jersey and $200 dollar tennis shoes. My shades were $300 Gucci frames and I was wearing a David Yurman bracelet with a matching watch. Now I never dressed like this in the hood, but Malik had told me to floss a little today and I had run with the opportunity.

I loved the way I looked in the nice things that I had bought. I also loved the way that A.J. treated me as if I had been a big wheel all my life. Biggest of all though, was the fact that Malik had assured me that my grandmother was going to get a house and a better life out of all this. The fact that he claimed there would be enough left over for me to buy a small church down south somewhere added to my excitement for this life.

I had even entertained the idea of taking my mother along. If I could find her and hold her interest long enough to tell her what I was doing, it might have been possible. The bottom line was that it was all about my grandmother and my church. The story behind it all was that I had become willing to do anything in order to get all that I wanted. I knew that one day, I would have to answer for that.

THIRTEEN

Sanity is overrated. Nearly every great mind and figure in history has prospered directly from his own insanity, or has thrived in spite of it. Does anyone bother to question the sanity of a man who prepares his body to be launched from the earth to walk on the moon when no one else has done it before him? Isn't it just as insane that an Austrian born white supremacist of average intelligence can come dangerously close to taking over the entire free world. If a college drop-out can come up with an idea that few believe makes sense, and then surpass every oil baron, sultan, king, and real estate tycoon to become the richest man on earth, why can't a fatherless child from the projects of America use wits, guns and guts to build an empire?

"**Baby**, why can't you stay in with me tonight?" Angel asked. She was lying in the bed naked looking extremely sexy.

We had just finished making love for over an hour. "You haven't had enough?" I laughed. "Plus you'll be sleep in fifteen minutes. Don't front."

"Maybe I will, but why can't you go to sleep with me for once? A girl likes to be held every once in a while." She rolled over and I had to take my eyes off of her ass. She was looking good enough to eat a second time.

"I will be back as soon as possible. You just be ready." I put on my G-shock and checked the time. Carlos was picking me up in twenty minutes and I had a short jog.

She stood up on her knees and wrapped herself in the sheets. "Kiss me before you go."

I sang out as I kissed her, *"Just in case I don't make it home tonight..."*

"That ain't funny, Malik."

"Damn, it's just a song. I thought you liked Jahiem."

"Yeah, but my brother used to sing that song to his baby's mother..." She shook her head and looked real sad. I felt sick. I wanted to tell her. There just was no way to say it, *"I'm sorry, but I had to kill your brother".* Even though it was true, the most I could do for her was to embrace her and tell her that everything would be alright.

I kissed her again before I left the room. "I don't have a room key with me. If I don't come back tonight, go to your mom's in the morning. Take this key with you and I'll let you know what to do with it. Once you are at your mother's, keep the line clear and ..." Her eyes were focused looking right through me. "I'll see you in a little bit."

I left the hotel lobby in jeans and a T-shirt. When I hit the street, I began a slow jog up toward Paramus Mall. When I reached the parking lot, I saw Carlos hit the high beams and start rolling towards me.

"What's up, cuz?" he said.

"You ready to do this?" I said all business.

"I stay ready," he said. "Who brought you into the game?"

"Not you."

"Whatever."

"Right. So let me see what my money got me and do I have any change?"

He nodded his head. "Right there under the blanket. And I spent what you gave me plus ten more. So you owe me."

"You spent seventeen? Come on now. Don't bullshit me."

"You said you wanted to make shit easy, right?"

"Yeah I do, but shit."

"Quit complaining until you see what I got." He pulled over into the McDonald's parking lot. We got out and opened the door. When he pulled the blanket back, I almost fell out. He had two rocket launchers, two big containers of gasoline, and some high-tech looking Molotov cocktails. There were also two assault rifles and plenty of ammo. I pointed to a box on the floor.

"What's in those?"

"Those are paint guns. I'm going to a paintball tournament tomorrow. You want to come? We battlin' some white boys out in Long Island."

"You are a big-ass kid."

"Look who's talking, the Playstation King."

I nodded and smiled because he was right. Then I said, "Hey, you did good. You went all out. Better safe than sorry."

"Exactly. So who's coming with us tonight?"

"Ferris."

"That little nigga?"

"Yeah, it's time to let him put in some major work. Believe it or not, he's the future of Do or Die."

"Man, you tripping."

"Shorty is live. You'll see."

We headed through the Lincoln Tunnel and hit the West Side Highway headed for Brooklyn. I directed Carlos to a gas station on Tilery Street. We were parked there for ten minutes when Ferris pulled up in a Black Dodge Durango. "Perfect," I said under my breath. I had told him to get something non-descript and he had done just that. "Come on."

I made sure that everyone had on their latex gloves as I got into the driver's seat. Carlos was in the back and Ferris was in the front. "So everything went smooth, lil' man?"

He nodded like he had done this a hundred times. "Yeah, everything was just like you said. I didn't have to hurt anybody to get this joint. I pulled up on this white guy real slow, stocking over my head and all. He was leaving the bar and was drunk, just like you said. I led him across the street and handcuffed his ass to the dumpster. I duct taped him so he couldn't yell. I took his wallet and told him if he reported this joint stolen before the morning, that I would come to his house to pay his family a visit." Ferris chuckled. "He was scaaaaaared than a motherfucker." Then he burst out laughing again.

"Yo, who is this, Malik Jr.? Shorty is sick wit it."

"I even got his cell phone, but I didn't call nobody."

I gave him a stern look. "Are you sure?"

"You said don't. This ain't no game. One mistake and you go to jail and I go to the state until my eighteenth. I ain't goin' out like that." He looked at me. "Plus I know you'd kill over some dumb shit like that. So would I."

"Good job," I said as I pulled onto the BQE. "Change your clothes." I had slipped on all black and wanted him to do the same. We drove out to Queens and wound up on Hollis Avenue just up the street from where Russell Simmons was raised. The street was quiet, but not completely dead as I hoped so we drove up the street to the White Castle and I decided to chill for an hour or so before we made a move.

I looked at the paper that Cortez had given me. He had described the house down to the chimes and red furniture on the front porch. Just as he said, there was an unmarked police car in front of the house. Cortez had told me to wait for one of the guards to go on break to make it look better, but he had been unable to give me the exact time.

I looked down at my watch. It was 1:15 a.m. At 2:30, this nigga's life was going to end. I decided that time for no reason at all. It just sounded right.

We sat in the car kicking it for a little while, fighting sleep and listening to the radio, when a news flash came on Hot 97. A seventy-five-year-old woman had been beaten to death on Myrtle Avenue in an apparent robbery attempt.

"Now that shit don't make no sense," I said sounding disgusted. "Why the hell would someone do that to an old woman?"

"True," Carlos said.

"I mean if a nigga need money that bad, get a fucking job flipping burgers. If he's a junkie, steal a damned DVD player. I gots no tolerance for dumb shit like that."

Ferris joined in sounding like a man with a boy's voice, "Yeah, his ass needs to get the death penalty for that shit."

"You right about that," I said. "You know what?" I asked and then went on, "I am going to find out who did that shit and kill his ass dead in the streets for that shit."

Ferris and Carlos fell out laughing. "Man, you crazy."

"Nah, I'm serious." And I was. "I might even chop his fucking head off and stick it on the Brooklyn Bridge. You know they used to do shit like that back in the day."

"Nigga, you been watching too much TV," Ferris said.

"Yeah, that's some Mel Gibson, *Braveheart* shit," Carlos said. "I love that movie."

Then out of the blue, Carlos asked, "Hey, if you could kill anybody, who would you kill?"

I thought about it. "That's some hard shit right there. How about my top five?"

"Yeah that's cool. Your top five."

"Let me see. Not necessarily in this order but first off let me see... Osama Bin Laden, George Bush, the judge who gave my grandfather all those fucking years, Shamar Moore for being a fucked-up host on Soul Train..." Everybody started laughing. "What? I'm serious." More laughter, "... Oh and my last kill would be whoever the nigga was that killed Biggie Smalls. I would get that nigga."

"Yeah, I loved Biggie. *Baby Babaay,*" Carlos hit his Biggie imitation.

"Yeah, who would you kill?"

"Oh gosh, let me see." He changed his voice up like I had asked him a question on Jeopardy. "I would take out Osama as well. To hell with America, he came too close to Brooklyn," he chuckled. "I wouldn't kill George Bush... that white boy got balls... I like him. I would kill Sadaam though for being so fucking cruel to the women in his country and for fucking with the oil supply... I would kill my fifth grade teacher, Mr. Morgan, for telling me that I was dumb... I never forgot that shit. The whole class laughed at me. I don't think I cried again after that day. How 'bout that senator, the one who had to resign...Trent Lott ... yeah him too. I would kill Rush Limbaugh's ass quick too. He's a dumb fuck trying to dog McNabb."

We laughed and then I looked at Ferris. "What about you?"

He looked back at me. "I don't really want to kill anybody unless money is involved. The only person I want to kill is dying already."

We were silent and my eyes showed my question.

"My dad is a junkie and an undercover faggot and he gave my mom HIV. Lord knows if he wasn't already suffering from his disease, I would blow his damned head clean off of his shoulders. That's why I'm tryna' get money. That fucking medicine is expensive and I want my mom to have that shit. Fuck a pair of Jordans."

More silence. The game was over.

Ferris looked like a miniature ninja all dressed in black as he crept back to the car. "Three of 'em in there. One on the couch, two playing cards in the kitchen."

"These niggas don't want to sleep, huh?" I instructed him to take one of the guns and cover me as I took one of the gas containers and crept to the back door. I proceeded to douse the house with gasoline, making sure that every exit to the house was saturated.

I thought about it. Three hundred grand for one life. The other two were casualties of war. I was giving Ferris and Carlos $10,000 each. After hearing Ferris' story, I decided to double his payment. I made it back to the car with the container empty. "Okay, this is the plan. Ferris, take this and wait in the back. Anybody coming out of the back door... light 'em up and cut 'em down. But stand back. Put these on." I gave him a headset and made sure it was working. "Don't speak into it. The only thing you are going to hear is the word 'roll'. That means you got fifteen seconds to get to the car." Carlos, on my move, launch your rocket. Aim for the window in the living room." He headed across the street with one of the rocket launchers. I waited for Ferris to get into position and then I took the cell phone and dialed the number to the house. I positioned myself in front of the house as if I belonged there.

"Hello."

"Yes, sorry to disturb you, but this is Raul from the House of Pleasure. I was calling to see if my ladies made it out there yet."

"Pardon me?"

"I'm sorry. Is David Webster in?"

"Who did you say this was?'

"Raul. David made a call for a girl."

"Hold on."

I looked over and watched through the window as one of the officers walked from the kitchen to the couch. I knew then that the mark was on the couch.

"Who the hell is this? Stan is this you?" I took careful aim as I unlocked the safety and pressed the button. I felt like a soldier in Iraq as the kick from the rocket launcher knocked me flat on my back. I was still down when I heard the explosion. Three seconds later, there was a second explosion as Carlos launched his bomb as well. I pulled myself from the ground and watched in amazement as the house went up in flames. There would be no need for Ferris to shoot anyone because there was no way anyone was coming out of that house.

"Roll!" I yelled to Ferris, but he was already coming around the corner.

"Ain't nobody in there alive," Ferris said as we took off for the car. As soon as we cleared the front yard, I heard a crash. A window blew out from upstairs. The next moment, a body engulfed in flames came out of the same window. The body rolled off onto the roof above the porch and then to the lawn. I watched in amazement. It looked like a scene from a Jason Vorhees flick. I glanced over in time to see Ferris running up on the body with the assault rifle. He opened fire and must have shot twenty times.

"Come on." We headed for the car. Carlos was already in the driver's seat. We were almost in the car when two shots hit the back of the truck. I turned to see another unmarked car headed our way with an officer firing out of the window. Ferris fired back with the assault rifle. I grabbed mine and joined him. As the tires blew on the car, I heard the screeching sound as it slammed into a parked car. I was about to run up on the car when Carlos yelled, "Get back!"

He slung a cocktail at the policemen and the whole street lit up like a bonfire. The car was swallowed in flames as I crouched back from the brightness. Ferris fired a couple of shots to make sure that they were both dead.

We were doing about a hundred out of Queens headed back to Brooklyn. I was looking back the whole time waiting for more police. We had done it now. I was thinking that it wouldn't be fair for me to keep the entire $250,000 that would be left over after if I gave Ferris and Carlos twenty each. I added what I spent on the guns and it was still close to a quarter of a million dollars.

Then I figured, fuck it. I am the mastermind behind all of this shit. Carlos should have been on top, he was damned near thirty and Ferris was still a kid. He had time left to earn. This was my deal and they were lucky to make what they did. Some niggas in the hood made twenty grand for a year's work not a night.

The streets seemed empty as we rolled onto Tilery. "I got this, you go 'head and drop Ferris off. I'll square up with you both in the morning."

"The Penitentiary is full of niggas who trusted others to get rid of their dirt." That's what Double V told me. I drove to the industrial site over on Gold Street. It was deserted.

There was Sondra sitting there in my Camry just as I'd instructed. She didn't see me when I drove past her and parked the Durango around the corner. I emptied the other container into the truck and poured a small trail of gasoline to give me a little leeway. With the remaining cocktails left in that truck, I knew that it was going to blow sky high.

I dropped the match and watched the fire hit the gas I poured on the ground. I jumped away from the truck and took off like a runaway slave. I had gotten thirty yards away when the explosions hit back to back. I glanced back to see the car still burning. I was hoping the owner had his insurance paid up.

I tapped on the window and Sondra jumped. "Oh shit," she said.

"Move over." She climbed into the passenger seat. "I'm taking you home."

"Why?"

"First, I told you not to question me. Second, because I have work to do."

"Fuck it then, Malik." She folded her arms and pouted. "I'm getting tired of your shit. It's always all about you."

"Listen." I wanted to calm her down. I needed her for a few more months at best so I told her the best lie that I could, "See, now you're going to mess up my surprise, acting like a little bitch."

"No you didn't just disrespect me like that."

"Shut up and listen for a second." I reached into my jeans. "I wanted us to do this real romantic like, but you keep getting this attitude with me." I held out the ring that I had gotten for Angel. "I got some business to handle in these streets, but, baby girl, I intend for you and me to be together... forever."

Her mouth dropped and she put her hands on her chest. "Oh my God. No, Malik, are you serious?"

I nodded my head yes. It hurt me because I had that ring designed for Angel. But without Sondra's help my plan would never work. I could never trust a guy other than Abraham to be wherever I needed, whenever I needed them. Sondra was like an extra set of hands.

It was 4:00 in the morning when I walked into the Greenberg Towers through the alley. I waited and heard a "who dat?" come from the roof. If I hadn't heard it, then I would know that my crew was slipping. I identified myself and made my rounds. When I reached the playground, I saw Cortez walking towards me.

"Malik, you are a man of honor. I value you and respect you. Even more so than Phil Boogie, but I must ask you... why?" He paused and sat on the bench. "Why did you kill the officers?"

I stared into Cortez's eyes. I looked deep and realized that he had survived in the game for so long for one reason only. It wasn't because he was brilliant. Nor was he imposing. I doubt seriously that his workers feared him. He wasn't even particularly driven or talented as far as I could tell. I looked at this brother who had sold more horse in Brooklyn than almost every dealer in history and I realized why he was still free and breathing. Plain and simple—he was lucky. Then I answered him, "You really shouldn't be questioning me after I saved your life for the second time in three months. Instead, you should be apologizing for the misinformation you gave me."

"Huh?"

"The fact that the officers never left the house and the fact that two more were in the vicinity, means you either didn't do your homework or you were trying to set me up to fail." I put my hand to my waistline. "That, my friend, is grounds for termination of your life."

He said nothing for a few moments. "Malik, you know that I did not set you up, right?"

"The only thing I know for sure is that if you did try to set me up, it didn't work. The rest doesn't really matter much in the scheme of things." I turned to walk off. "I will talk to you in afternoon about the rest of my money."

"I can give it to you now if you like." He sounded like he was trying to appease me.

"I'm not prepared tonight so tomorrow will do. Besides, I have another stop to make before I go in. But you might want to smooth things over with me for everything your lack of preparation took me through."

"To the tune of ... how much?" he asked.

"I will let you make a gentleman's offer. If I don't like it, then don't expect me to be a gentleman about it."

I headed back to my car and out of the Towers. I contacted Do or Die's members via Nextel as I left and everyone was in position. I ran a tight ship. I smiled thinking that my grandfather would have been proud to see me as I headed out onto the street. I had killed five men tonight and the only thing on my mind was getting back to the hotel to be with Angel. I imagined getting caught by the authorities in the life that I was living and having to plead insanity. I wondered if it would actually work and then I thought about all that I had done, and for a moment, wondered if it was true.

FOURTEEN

Fear is the most primal instinct known to man. Baby animals without any experience of death, cling to their parents because they know for some reason that it is the smart thing to do. The adult animal naturally knows what can happen and guards its young out of fear of extinction. The laws of nature program animals to respond to fear naturally by fight or flight. Animals only fight when confronting a natural enemy that their instincts tell them they can defeat or if flight is not possible. A seal will never attack a shark just as a gazelle will never attack a lion. Humans are the only animals who attempt to face their fears for the sake of what they may gain from victory. Most find out that they had that fear for a good reason but by then it's often too late.

I wasn't to say a word. I was only there to make sure nothing went wrong. Tears and terror were expected, almost necessary. Malik's words were plain and simple. "One hair harmed on any head in that house and everyone involved dies." I believed that whole-heartedly.

I almost cringed when I heard the words come out of Terrell's mouth, "Bitch, shut your fucking mouth and if you don't shut that little girl's mouth, I'm gonna shut it for good."

Casper was ransacking the place to make it appear as if he were searching for something. Acting disgusted, he exited the bedroom that belonged to Malik, though he hadn't slept in it in two months. "Bitch, where is the money?"

"I don't know what you're talking about."

Casper threw the Ziploc bag filled with baking soda on the table. "There's the fuckin' coke. I know he has some money too." He cocked his pistol and put it to Lindsey's head. "Don't make me do it. Tell me where the money is."

Toni was crying while Ferris tied her wrists behind her back. "You all should be ashamed of yourselves," Malik's grandmother said sternly. "Let my babies go. I will get you some money, just leave them alone."

"You ain't got enough money, now sit your old ass down before you have a heart attack," Casper said and I raised my pistol at her and motioned for her to have a seat. "I need you to call Malik and have him come up here."

"Why, so you can kill him?" Toni asked.

"No, so we don't kill you," Ferris chimed in. "He's in the game. He knows what time it is."

Casper shook his head. Ferris was a baby gangster and he loved watching him work. Then Casper added, "He should have known better than to leave y'all in these projects."

Lindsey shouted, "Okay, give me the phone. I will call him. Just don't hurt my babies. Matter of fact, let them go and I will stay."

"No, Ma. Don't, they will kill him."

"Better him than us. We ain't ask for this shit."

His grandmother was shaking her head calling out Jesus. "Lord the boy is going to get us all killed. I told you about letting him see that damned Vincent. Malik was such a good boy."

Lindsey dialed Malik. "Maaaalik. They got…" Casper snatched the phone.

"Look here, dog. I got your peeps and I need some major loot or they all dead." I knew Malik was directing Casper on what to say. "Okay, if that's how you want it... No, we want twenty gees. You got twenty minutes before somebody dies." Casper paused and then finished with, "You better be alone and at that door unarmed. As a matter of fact, be butt-ass naked with nothing but the money."

"What? What did he say?" Lindsey asked.

"He said he is gonna bring the money. Lucky for you." He waved his gun, "Go sit your ass down over there and don't move. Yo, Rocky, you watch 'em," he said to me.

Fifteen minutes later, there was a knock on the door. "Yo, Rocky, get that." I moved to the door and looked out the peephole. I then opened the door to see Malik standing there buck-naked with a paper bag. I almost laughed at him. This guy was a nut, but I admired his professionalism.

"Okay, step inside," Casper said. "You alone, right?" Malik nodded. "You better be. 'Cause if anyone jumps out at me before I get to my car, she gets it in the head." He pointed to Jade. "I make it to the car and she'll be outside waiting. Don't come out for five minutes. He'll be watching." He pointed at Ferris. "Take care of the phone lines and Rocky, grab the kid."

Toni screamed, "Noooo," as I grabbed Jade and scooped her up. Lindsey tried to jump up and Ferris put his gun to her mouth. Malik grabbed her and wrestled her back to the couch. Ferris yanked the phone lines from the wall and slammed every phone in the house up against the wall shattering them all.

We exited the apartment and I heard Lindsey cursing Malik, threatening to kill him if something happened to her baby. Malik wouldn't let anyone leave the apartment. He convinced them that Jade would die if they did. He put some clothes on and headed out the door five minutes later.

I sent Jade over to him when I saw him come out the door. I pulled off my mask and headed up the alley. I heard Jade's cries die out as her big brother embraced her and took her in his arms.

Ten minutes later, I was on the roof working for Do or Die. I was looking down on the courtyard as the sun was setting on the projects. Sitting on a stack of milk crates, I read a few pages of the book, *No Way Out,* that A.J. had purchased for me at the book fair. I got pulled in quickly because it was a real page-turner and I was actually a little startled when Malik came through the door.

"Thanks, man," he said. "Y'all did good."

"They alright?" I was really worried about Toni.

"Yeah, they gonna be fine. I gave them ten minutes to pack what they absolutely had to have now."

"How did that go over?"

"My grandmother wanted to call the police. Lindsey wants me to go to jail. I shut them both up when I told them that I had $100,000 and a place for them down in Maryland."

He went on to say that they were in disbelief, but when he explained to them they couldn't sleep another night in the projects because those niggas would be back, they agreed to leave for Jade's sake. His grandmother had suggested Harlem but Malik had told them that it would be best if they left the city until he caught the culprits. He never intended for them to come back.

He was leaving for Baltimore in ten minutes. It was amazing how his plan had worked. He had scared them so bad that they were leaving their home taking nothing more than a few outfits and photo albums. He had even convinced his mother to use the false ID he was going to send them. To seal the deal, he had promised Lindsey that in addition to the $100,000, he would give her the money to start a business.

He hugged me and thanked me again. "Tomorrow we take care of your grandmother." I nodded.

"Yo, man, I want to ask you this."

He folded his arms. "Yeah what?"

"Don't you feel the least bit ashamed for taking your peeps through that? Your sister was in there begging for your life." I shook my head when I thought about it. "I mean, you had niggas cursing your grandmother and moms."

"They believed that shit was real though, didn't they?" He stared back.

"Yeah, they did."

"Then it was the right thing to do." He extended his fist and I gave him a pound. "Don't worry. This other thing is going to work and we won't have to do your grandma like that. I promise you."

That was what I wanted to hear. "Bet." I sat back down and started to read some more.

"Look alive and keep that headset on. One of them jokers should relieve you in a couple of hours." And just like that, he was headed south with everyone he cared about in tow. Almost everyone.

Malik was sitting patiently while I did my best to convince the pastor to help me out. "Son, I don't know how you expect me to justify lying to your grandmother. If she is in danger, then we need to let her know and let the authorities know. Whatever it is that you did, you need to turn yourself in to the authorities."

"You aren't really understanding." Malik finally cut me off.

He moved up next to the desk from the couch that he was sitting on in the pastor's office. "Listen up, man, nobody is turning themselves in. We are trying to give you a chance to help your church out and at the same time save a life."

"This is ridiculous. You young men..."

"No, hear me out Rev," Pastor Watkins leaned forward in his chair. "I didn't even want to ask you this but you forced my hand."

"Uh huh."

"Do you think it's okay to kill sometimes?"

"What?"

"You heard me. Do you agree that it's alright to kill... sometimes?"

"The bible says, *Thou shalt not kill.*"

"What about in the case of defending your family? Would you kill to protect your family?"

"Where are you going with all of this?"

"Where I am going is here..." I saw Malik reaching for his waist.

"Hold up!" I shouted. "Malik, I need you to step for a second. This is a house of God."

Malik gritted his teeth and stared the pastor down as he walked out the door. "I'll be in the car."

"I apologize for that," I said. "It's just that this is a critical matter."

"Hanging around with people like him, son, will be your ruination." He flipped his bible open and pointed to 1 Corinthians 15:33, "Read this." *Bad associations spoil good character.* "Do you understand what that means?" he asked after I read it.

"Yeah, I do. And I agree now more than ever. But I am in a bind. However, I have a solution."

"Well, I am all ears."

"The spoils of the wicked will be used to uplift the righteous." I pointed to another scripture and slid the bible back across the desk. He nodded his head.

"Go on."

"Our apartment is about to catch fire and she will lose everything. She will need a place and will take it as a sign if you make an offer."

"What kind of offer?"

"I am buying my grandmother a home in Florida. The condo is going to cost $110,000." He was listening attentively. "I need you to tell her that the church owns several properties and that you would like, in exchange for all of her faithful service to the church, for her to have the one you purchased in Fort Lauderdale, especially in light of her situation. In return for that, I will give you $50,000 to do whatever you decide. Use it for the church, the youth center or whatever."

"Where am I supposed to tell your grandmother this money is coming from? And how will I keep this from the rest of the congregation?"

"Tell her that God told you to do it for her because she has always been a faithful servant to him. Tell her that she must not cause dissention amongst those left behind. When she tells you that she couldn't possibly take the gift, present her with the deed and the keys and tell her that it is a done deal. Give her a few thousand in cash and tell her that you took up an offering for her. I will leave you the cash for that."

"Son, I really don't see how I can do that."

"Pastor, do you listen to the signs that God gives you?"

"All the time."

"Could your church use fifty grand?"

"Of course, but..."

"Make no mistake about it. This is a sign. The young man who just left out of here *will* kill you without so much as a blink and won't lose a minute's rest behind it. And if he doesn't do it himself, he has ten crazy counterparts that will do it at his command." I paused while he thought. "Those are your two options. Remember that you are more valuable to this community alive with fifty grand at your disposal..."

Just then, Malik walked back in and finished my sentence, "...than found dead in your office with a note saying that you were killed by a choir boy who you molested ten years ago."

"In the name of Jesus!" he shouted out.

"Exactly," Malik said and threw $25,000 onto his desk. "In the name of Jesus, be smart." Then he walked back out.

I watched the pastor as he fumbled with the money on his desk. I could see he was impressed by it. "The apartment burns tomorrow...I'll bring the deed over on Friday. As soon as you give it to her, you get the other twenty-five."

I stared. He stared back. He reluctantly gave me a nod. Then I left.

Malik and I were headed over to see Black Sid. We were in the Benz because he wanted to show him that the money wasn't the issue. We cruised up the side street and pulled over to where the basketball court was. It was packed and I saw Sid's Escalade parked and we pulled in right next to it.

"Look, I don't really want to go to war. Hopefully, he will be sensible and we can settle this without bloodshed," Malik said and I was surprised to hear him say something that was that sensible.

"Good. I got your back though." I thought about the money we had been making and asked. "How much money are we down here for again?"

"Five or six grand…I can't even remember. The point is he owes a bill. He has to make retribution."

I nodded and we sat and chilled and talked for a while. His family had been in Baltimore for a few days and they loved it. I was nervous about how my grandmother was going to take me falling asleep smoking when she didn't even know I smoked, which I didn't. It would be easy to fake and I was going to let the fire burn just enough, but not out of control, I hoped.

We kicked it for about a half an hour before Sid started walking around the corner. He had five guys with him, but he still looked like he was going to shit his shorts when he saw Malik sitting in the Benz. It wasn't impossible, but highly unlikely that they were armed from the way that they were dressed. The guns were probably in the truck. "Sit on the trunk, Abe, and make sure no one comes up from behind us," he said.

"I got that." I took a look at Sid and didn't say a word.

"So what's the deal, Sid? Are you doing so bad that you have to try and hold out on an old friend?"

Sid tried to regain his composure. "We ain't friends, nigga."

"Sid, what's up with this clown?" A dude even darker than Sid asked.

"You might want to watch your mouth unless that little print in your shorts is a pistol." I laughed and everyone else got quiet.

"This is Malik, the dude I told you about who gave me the red-tops to move."

"Oh, okay," the guy said. "My apologies, Malik. I'm Sid's older brother, Levi." He extended his hand.

Malik said, "What's up?" Then he reached out and shook his hand.

"I thought we would have heard from you sooner."

"Yeah, well, I been busy."

He looked at the Benz, which was now sitting on chrome 22's. "I see, I see. Well listen, I have to tell you that was very disrespectful what you did. But since you are a youngster in the game and I know of your grandfather, I decided to cut you a break."

"Oh, really?"

"Yeah, for sho. You see, my pops is doing time up there with Double V and they have a decent relationship, I'm surprised your pops didn't tell you. Marty Shaw, that's my dad." He sipped his Gatorade and kept on talking, "So when Sid told me what went down, I came up with a solution."

"What was that?"

"Well I took the work and put it up for you. When you didn't come for it after a month, I figured that you had gotten too big or were scared so I sold it. Now Sid here, he took a beating for accepting that package from you. That was disloyal on his part. If he'd been a bonafide worker in my camp and not my little brother, he would have been killed behind this shit. If you were a friend of his, you would have never asked him to do that."

Malik was silent, and for a minute, it sounded like he was talking to his grandfather. Then he said, "So what's up now?"

"What's up now is this. I will give you the money myself since he fucked up and took it from you."

"Okay that's fine…six gees."

He nodded to one of his homeys and he pulled a knot out of his sock. He threw it to Malik. "Now everything is settled between you and Sid, correct?"

"Yeah, I'm straight."

"Okay. Now what are you going to do to make things right with me?"

"Say what?"

"You heard me. You got to make it right, here and now. I'm the boss of this here so it comes down to you and me. I know you got guns and appear to have the jump, but look around. There is only one way out of here and even if you got off a few shots, do you think that there would be any way in hell you could go screeching out of here?" Malik eyeballed the crew by the exit to the parking lot. "There won't be any gunplay unless you force it, but there will be justice." He paused and appeared as cool as a cucumber. Then he added, "Now I could beat you down out here the same way I beat Sid, or I could end you and let your homey take your body back over to Greenberg in a bag. Or you could come up with a gentlemen's offer."

Malik showed no fear and I watched a smile come across his face. "A gentlemen's offer, huh." It probably reminded him of the terms his grandfather used: *"Son when you are wrong in these streets, sometimes you gotta be humble and graceful and own up. Make a gentleman's offer to smooth shit out."* "Okay, you right." I watched Malik count the money. Out of the six grand, he counted out $1,000 and gave it to Sid. "I never thought about it in this manner, Sid, but I have to admit that me asking you to bite the hand that feeds you, wasn't looking out at all. My bad, Sid, for causing you trouble." He then turned to me and gave me $1,000. "I shouldn't have brought you over here. It was all my foolishness." He then turned to Levi and gave $3,000 to him.

"The last thousand, I keep for my time and anguish. Fair enough?"

"I accept your offer." He gave Malik a pound before turning to Sid and saying, "See, if you had gave me a few gees, I wouldn't have had to whoop that ass."

Sid just frowned up and said, "Fuck you," under his breath.

"Y'all want to run some ball?" Levi asked.

"I would, but I got too much work to do."

"I can respect that. Stay up."

"No doubt," Malik answered as we got into the car and rolled out.

Malik never ceased to amaze me.

FIFTEEN

Incarceration in the physical sense is necessary to separate those who prey on society at-large or who refuse to obey the laws set forth by a governing authority. When a guilty man faces incarceration, he must decide whether he is as lowly as his deed or if in fact he is better than his mistake. A man who realizes that his worth is greater than the tag of 'criminal' that society places upon him, will find within him the dignity and desire to become free from mental incarceration. At this point, a new wealth of thought will make him even more dangerous to those who have designed the system that thrives on a pattern of over-incarceration. The man who can accomplish that feat is gifted and will never be imprisoned again, mentally or physically.

"Son-son." Double V gave me an embrace filled with love and pride. "It's good to see you. How was the drive?"

I had raced up I-87 to see him. My Uncle Kelly had told me that he wanted to see me immediately. It was October and the weather was starting to cool off. "It was nice. The leaves changing colors and what not, shit you don't pay attention to in the city."

"Yeah, I can dig it. How's family?"

"They're fine. It took a little while for them to get used to being down south, but now Lindsey loves it. She opened up a hair salon last week. Grandma is there everyday decorating and answering the phones, just having a ball. You'd think there wasn't a decent hair salon in Baltimore as quick they found all the stylist to come work there. They are at maximum capacity."

"Oh yeah? What's your cut?"

"Oh nah. I didn't ask for that. It was just about them moving. It only cost $18,000 to open it."

"Fuck that. Business is business, family or not." He took out his handkerchief and blew his nose. "A fool and his money are soon parted. It won't hurt them to give you a couple hundred a month from what they make, even if you put it in a mutual fund. Do you know that $2,400 a year in the right fund could be worth almost one hundred and fifty grand in twenty years? That measly $200 might not mean much to you now, but if you get locked up, it becomes a king's ransom."

"So you telling me that you're still collecting from folks you helped out back in the day?"

"Now you getting all up in my business. Just take the advice or don't, it's all up to you. But if I haven't steered you wrong yet…"

I nodded because I wanted to move on to the business at hand and not dwell on me charging my family for the money I gave them. It made a lot of sense though. "So what was it you needed to see me about?"

"Come on let's walk." Double V led me past the vending machines and rest rooms toward the courtyard. We stopped off on the patio and took a seat at one of the tables. "It's getting cool out," he said. I had on an Eddie Bauer Jacket with Gore-Tex lining, so I was fine. "For what we need to discuss, we can't be too close to anyone. For all I know, the feds could have the room wired for sound trying to catch someone else and fuck around and pick up our conversation."

I was amazed that he was so adept at thought. "Cool, I understand."

"Yeah, so listen. How much money do you have saved?"

"How much do I need to have?" I asked trying to seem uncomfortable disclosing all of my business. He always told me, *"Trust no one."* Now although I did trust him fully, I knew he would be upset at me for going against his teachings.

He laughed. "You are going to need $350,000 to do this right."

"I had that last month."

"Are you sleeping well at night?" He sneezed. "I mean, that's a lot of cash for a young man. You aren't worried to death at night about someone coming to get it?"

"I sleep decent enough. I never sleep hard and I never sleep in the same spot as that money. So if they catch me, they don't get the money unless I take them to it, and that ain't happening."

"So you understand that you could die for that money. It's always good to keep your perspective."

"I understand. But that really ain't enough to die for," I shot back.

"How much is enough to die for?"

"Ten million."

"Is that enough to hide out from the feds for a lifetime? You know that if you steal that kind of money, they are gonna look for you forever." He cracked a smile.

I had no answer to that. Money is great, but having to look over your shoulder forever didn't sound too appealing. I had enough money now to disappear and start a good life somewhere. Six months earlier, I was living off of what I made on weekends at the Gardens selling sodas at the Knicks' games. Now here I was holding almost $450,000 in a safe in my apartment in Jersey. I had gotten my family and Abraham's grandmother out of the projects. I could have decided to quit now and called it a career except for one thing: crime was in my blood.

Double V and I sat and talked for another two hours. Once he was convinced that my heart was into the plan, he went over every detail of what I would need to do day by day. He went as far as to get a pencil and paper from the guard to outline each critical step. "Memorize this and destroy this paper by tomorrow," he said.

My grandfather didn't embrace me when I left. Instead, he grabbed my hand and gave me the hardest and firmest shake I had ever had. Then he said, "I'm proud of you, son. You are conducting yourself like a true professional and warrior in those streets, and the streets is all people like you and I have. Society makes no room for us to get rich in the corporate world. Our strength isn't respected on Wall Street, but it's the same strength this country has relied on while we pilfered and raped other countries of their riches since we became a superpower. So don't look back and don't feel any remorse. Remember that $350,000 ain't shit. That is an insult to the wealthy." He paused as we began to head back into the visiting room to exit. Then he went on, "If all you wanted to do was be 'nigga rich', then you could stop now and do this petty crime until some youngsta' comes along and puts three in your body...or you can have the American Dream."

"What's that?" I was wondering if he was referring to a house, a wife, two kids and a dog.

"The American Dream is becoming the ultimate capitalist. Making something big out of next to nothing and making something humongous out of something big.

Basically, it's never stopping, just repeating the process until you're shitting hundreds and wiping your ass with twenties."

I smiled at the thought. "I think I'll stick to the Charmin."

He whispered into my ear, "You know the next time I see you will be on the other side. Stay up, stay strong, and stay smart." I nodded and heard him whisper under his breath as I walked off, "I love you, son-son."

Angel looked good driving my car. When I walked out of the Greyhound Station, she was parked right out front. I caught the southern boys stealing glimpses of my sweetheart, but I knew that was all they could get from her. When I reached for the handle, she unlocked the door and showed her million dollar smile. "Hey, love," I said and reached over to kiss her. I caught a taste of her tongue. "Mmmm."

"You missed me on that bus ride down?" she said as she pulled out on to Fayette Street. We were in downtown Baltimore and I was trying to make sure we were headed the right way.

"No doubt. How was the drive?" A smile was her answer. "I see you looking real comfortable behind the wheel over there."

"You know I'm feeling this joint. But you could have had something other than rap in the CD changer."

"What else did you need? I specifically picked those classics for you. Nas', *Illmatic;* Biggie's, *Life after Death;* Jay's, *Reasonable Doubt;* AZ's, *Pieces of a Man;* and Dre's, *The Chronic.* You needed to hear those hits."

"What happened to the R. Kelly and Jahiem you play when you trying to climb all up in this?" she said giggling.

"A time and a place for everything."

"Well you better be glad you didn't leave any cash in here 'cause a sistah would have stopped at Best Buy and revamped your collection."

"Oh snap, I thought I left a few dollars in here for you." I opened the glove compartment. When I didn't see any money, I pulled the visor on the passenger side and an envelope containing five hundred fell into my lap.

"I looked in the glove compartment for that… where you said it would be. It's a good thing I had fifty bucks on me. Gas and tolls took most of that."

"Sorry, Angel. I'll make it up to you tonight. We are going to have a good time tonight."

"You better," she said laughing.

We pulled into the housing complex where my family had moved. It was a far cry from the projects where they had come from. The playground had wood chips and there was thick dark green grass in the small yards. There were no broken down cars or junkies walking around. It looked like it was safe enough to raise a family. I wondered how Jade was enjoying her new surroundings and if she was playing outside with new friends.

I rang the doorbell and waited a second before taking out my key. Before I could, Lindsey opened the door. She looked good. I could still see the wear and tear from her life but there was a look that I couldn't place. It was almost as if she'd been renewed. She said, "Hey Malik," and then she did something that she hadn't done in years. She hugged me real tight. "It's good to see you. In that minute, I knew that had done the right thing getting my family out of New York. "So you must be Angel. I have heard some good things about you."

Angel was all smiles. "Thanks, it's nice to finally meet you. I see where Malik gets his good looks from." She extended her hand and Lindsey reached out and pulled her in for a hug as well.

They exchanged pleasantries and went through the female posturing gestures. When they finished, we had taken a seat and were relaxing eating some cookies that my grandmother had baked. Within moments, Toni, Jade, and my grandmother came through the door.

It had been a couple of months and Toni had swelled up. She was due to bring her fatherless child into the world any day now. She asked if I had seen Quentin in the hood and I told her the truth, that he wasn't living *there* any more and that nobody had seen him for a while. It had to be a cold feeling knowing that your child would never know his or her father, but if that was the worse life offered her baby, then it'd be fine.

"So, baby, how was your trip?" my grandmother asked.

I looked at Angel as I answered, "It was fine. We cruised right down with no traffic." She looked a little puzzled, but she didn't need to know why I didn't ride down with her. Truth be told, I had almost every penny that I had made in the gym bag that I had carried down.

"That's nice."

"So is the guy coming tomorrow to do the patio?"

"Yes, as far as I know. He said that you called him three times to make sure that he knew you'd be here to oversee him. What, you don't think I can tell him what we want done?" Lindsey asked.

"No, not at all. I just don't want to do anything that violates the lease on this house. It is a real steal."

"That's understandable." my grandmother added. "We really like it here. Don't we, Jade?"

Jade nodded yes and then said sweetly, "Malik, I thought you were bringing me something."

"I did, pumpkin. Believe it, I did."

It was 3:00 in the morning when I climbed up off the sofa bed with Angel and started upstairs. "Baby, where you going?" she asked while I pulled on my sweatshirt.

"Go back to sleep. I got to do something." She rolled over and went back to sleep. She always listened, seldom questioned and that meant the world to me.

I went upstairs and out to the backyard. As instructed, Lindsey had had a six-foot wooden fence put up. I went to the shed where my packages from UPS had been delivered. I opened the box with the shovel inside of it. In the pitch-black dark, I began digging. An hour later, I was satisfied with the three-foot-deep hole I had created.

Instead of trekking through the house with dirty boots on, I decided to walk around the back of the row of townhouses to get to my trunk. Once I reached my trunk, I popped it and grabbed the safe out of it. I threw the safe into the trashcan that I had in the trunk as well and hurried to the backyard.

"Hey, what are you doing?" I heard a voice call as I was reentering the gate.

I turned and saw a figure, but couldn't make out a face. I reached for my waist and remembered that I didn't have a pistol. "I live here. Who the hell are you?" I saw a porch light come on.

"You do not live there. I'm calling the police," the voice answered. My heart started to jump out of my chest. I was going to have to kill this person with my shovel. I grabbed the shovel and started off in the direction of the stranger.

I felt a sense of panic come over me, realizing that I couldn't kill my mother's neighbor. I couldn't figure out what in the hell he was doing up at 4:00 in the morning anyway. "Hey, Mister, listen there's no need for you to do that. This is my mother's house. I am down here visiting from New York. I can go get her if you like."

I could see he stepped off of his porch. "Are you Lindsey's brother?" I got closer and saw that he had on a security uniform with a flashlight on his belt. He looked like he was at least eighty.

"Nah, I'm her son. I came down from New York to visit for the weekend."

He looked me over. "What's the shovel for?"

I imagined myself swinging it and knocking him out cold. "I'm cleaning out the shed. We're having some work done to the house in the morning."

"Why are you working in the dark, son?"

"No reason," I answered then shot back, "So who are you?"

"I am the head of the Neighborhood Watch Program. I been in charge for ten years and we haven't had a successful robbery here in nine years, and that one happened when I was on vacation."

It didn't take me long to figure out that the old man was a little senile. I talked to him for about five minutes before his wife came to the door. "Lucius, get in this house. I told you about wandering out." He headed back toward his door without saying so much as good-bye. His wife didn't see me and when she asked what he was doing outside, his reason wasn't received well. "Okay, sure you were investigating."

I was so relieved that the whole incident turned out to be nothing. I hurried back to work. In ten minutes, I had the money, which I had shrink-wrapped inside the safe and the safe was inside the trashcan. I sealed it tight and put electric tape all over it before dropping it into the hole. It was 5:00 a.m. when I had completely packed the dirt into the hole and took a break to wait for the contractors to arrive.

"That looks so nice," Lindsey said looking at her new patio. "I can't wait to put the grill out there. I know just what type of furniture I want to put out there." I had sat out there all morning and into the early afternoon. I took a piss at 7:00 that morning when they arrived, and didn't so much as move or take my eyes off of them until they headed for their trucks at noon.

My money was buried underground or most of it at least. And now I had four inches of cement over top of it. This wasn't part of the plan that Double V had designed. This I had come up with on my own. Instead of using my own money to pull off the operation, like any good business man, I figured that I could use someone else's. Just in case things didn't go as planned, instead of being ass out, I could come back here and collect and make another move.

The cement would be completely dry in 48 hours and then I would leave. "Ma, I want you to work on getting your credit straight so you can buy this place. Even if you outgrow it, Toni can keep it for her and the baby."

"I didn't know that it was for sale."

"Anything is for sale. Just do what you gotta do. But promise me you will keep this house. I picked it out just for you. It means a lot that I was able to get it for you."

"I promise you, baby." She shook her head. "I can't believe how you have grown up." She pointed at me and added, "Don't get me wrong. I don't approve of you being in the streets, but I always told any nigga this... If you are going to be out there, then be the best or close to it."

I nodded my head and felt my cell phone vibrating. It was Sondra.

"Hey, Malik. Where you at?"

"I told you..."

She cut me off. "I know, I know... don't question you. But listen, I need to talk to you." I was on the couch and I got up to excuse myself.

"Ma, I got to get something out the car." She waved me off. I only had a few minutes because Angel was in the shower getting ready for us to go out for lunch. I was taking her down to Mo's Fisherman's Wharf for some seafood. Toni had told me that they had the best seafood in Baltimore. I stepped out the front door into the beaming sun. It was seventy degrees at least. For October, that was mad warm. I took a seat on the hood of my car. "So what's up?" I asked.

"Malik, please don't get mad."

"What the fuck did you do?"

"What did *I* do? Malik, I'm pregnant."

"So that means that you have been fucking around with someone else because I've never nutted inside you without a rubber."

"No, I haven't been fucking around on you. I wouldn't do that."

"So explain."

"Well, I'm four and a half months pregnant."

"Well, why the fuck are you just telling me this now?"

"Malik, I didn't know. I came on my period every month. I went for a physical and my doctor noticed that my weight was creeping up. I'm surprised you didn't, but then again, you only see me in the dark and aren't really paying me any *real* attention." She sighed deeply. "I know that you aren't the father." There was a moment of silence. "I got pregnant that first night with Abraham."

SIXTEEN

Dreams are the most mysterious part of the human psyche. People work hard to put themselves in the best positions imaginable, but even when they achieve what is perceived to be the ultimate that life has to offer, most still dream of much more. There is a line where a euphoric reality actually crosses over into fantasy, and just across that line is where the senses are overloaded with thoughts of pleasure, feelings, and sensations that can't be captured by reality. There is also a dark space where dreams gone wrong lie in wait. They are born from the pangs of anxiety, fear, guilt, self-hate and evil. Those dreams bring about a terror that rips through the being of children and men alike. Those dreams become nightmares so frightening that even waking up isn't enough to stop the effect.

I tried to stop myself from crying, but the pain was too severe. I never hurt so bad, never felt so alone in my life. I was a child again, remembering the day that I woke up in the apartment my grandmother had once lived in, but left for me and my mother. Back then, my mother dated a man who lived three blocks away. While the word dated is a bit of an exaggeration, she did spend time with him.

I was four years old and my mother had been making a habit of leaving me alone overnight. This wasn't the first time, but it was the last. It was certainly the worst. I remembered lying in my bed in the dark, when I felt my room being invaded. I tried to wake up, but I couldn't open my eyes. It was incredibly difficult to breathe and I was cold from the sweat that had drenched my body and sheets.

My bed shook even more violently on its own than my shivers and movements caused. It was the devil coming for me. He actually called out to me and told me to give up the fight. He told me that this was the best life would ever offer me. He promised that I would be alone and scared always. I tried to fight, but the air was escaping my lungs and I was getting too cold and weak to fight. The devil promised me warmth for all my days. He told me that I would never be cold or hungry again.

I was still fighting to open my eyes as I refused him with all that I had. The next thing I knew, I felt a warmth wash over me that was comfortable. I heard a voice call out to the devil, *You must go. He has refused you. He has chosen death over you, and for that, he shall be protected by me.* I remember being able to open my eyes suddenly and seeing nothing but light, *He belongs to me for all his days.* The voice commanded my freedom and all of the darkness and coldness left me.

Although I could see nothing clearly, the *light* was with me in that bed and in that room until the morning came. I never remembered climbing out of the bed and walking into my mother's room to use the only phone nor to my recollection had I ever been educated on the process of dialing 911. When the paramedics arrived, I had been in the bed for a day and a half. At the hospital, the doctors discovered that I had suffered multiple seizures and should have been dead for all practical purposes.

I remembered a nurse coming to sit with me every day and praying over me. My mother was hiding from social services and never came to the hospital. A week later, Child Welfare took me from her and made me a ward of the state until my grandmother got wind of what was going on.

Three months later, my mother showed up at my grandmother's house, saying that she wanted me back. I was terrified that my grandmother was going to let her take me and I began clinging to her leg. When my mother reached for me, I witnessed my first act of violence. My grandmother beat my mother to the ground and picked her back up only to continue whooping her. She went as far as to get an extension cord and beat my mother, who was twenty at the time. It was the most ferocious ass whooping that I ever witnessed. I never disobeyed my grandmother until I was sure that I could survive a whipping like that.

Now as a young adult, I can clearly look back and realize that I didn't call the paramedics for myself, and that my mother had not left the door unlocked. As the years unfolded, I came to recognize that I had been chosen by GOD to survive and bring forth something great with the life he afforded me. It was clear why I had been placed in the care of a woman who was a saint, but at the same time could beat down a demon.

"Abraham, wake up. You're having a bad dream."

I had been tossing and turning and now Aaliyah was shaking me. "What? Huh?" I moaned out. I realized that I had been dreaming. I had dreamed of children sliding off of a giant cliff. I was trying to save them, but they were slipping one by one. It hurt to watch them fall. I was so busy trying to save them all that not a one had survived. What troubled me most is that in my dream, they had been following me.

"Are you okay?" she asked.

"Yeah... yeah, I'm cool."

"Why don't you take a shower? You were sweating."

I stood up. "Yeah, okay." We were in the apartment that Malik's family had lived in. I had cleaned it up and basically used it for a hotel. Most nights, I got a hotel as Malik had instructed me, but I had been working around the clock with Do or Die while Malik was in Baltimore.

I turned the shower on, but before I got in, I felt compelled to drop to my knees. *Father, I come to you on bended knees, asking for your forgiveness and continued mercy. I ask that you continue to watch over my family and friends. I want to thank you for allowing me to get my grandmother out of these projects. Though I am not sure that you approved my means, I ask that you take any negative done by my hands and turn it into a positive work under your force and direction. GOD, this is a dangerous place, these projects, in a dangerous world. I ask that you stay by my side and bear with me as I try to make it out of here as well. You know the desires of my heart before I even ask you. You know my nightmares, my fears, and my crimes.*

I will not ask you to protect me as I do crime, but where my heart is pure and my intentions worthy of your blessings... I ask you to put your hand in it. I know that you allowed Malik to enter my life for a reason. He fed me when my own mother left me hungry and has been my family every since. I know for sure that any plan he has is evil and involves treachery, but deep down inside, I know that he can be saved ... from himself. Please let him find you and be released from the demons that are causing him to change and grow into a dragon.

I ask that you let me form the greatest church that will serve as a protector of children and keep the blood of the innocent off of my hands. At this point, I acknowledge that you are GOD almighty and that I am nothing more than a speck of

*dust, and I ask for all these things in the name of your son,
Jesus Christ.*
Amen.

"Are you sure it's mine?" I asked Sondra. We sat on a
bench in Washington Square.

"I'm sure. And, Abraham, I wouldn't lie. I know this is
really awkward."

"It's a little more than awkward, this is foul. I mean look
at the whole thing. What am I supposed to do?" Her mouth
opened to speak and the she changed her mind. "I didn't mean
it like that...it's just crazy."

"Yeah, I know."

"Oh do you really? Do you know how humiliating it is to
be having a baby by a girl your best friend has been fucking for
months? Do you know how it feels to think you have met a
nice girl and she switches partners without you even
suggesting it?"

"Oh, so it would have been fine if you had commanded
me to be your slut, but since I have a mind of my own, you
can't take it. Well, for your information, I only did it because
Aaliyah told me that she really wanted you and that bitch has a
way of making a person miserable if she doesn't get what she
wants. She thought you were the one with all of the money, so
she wanted you."

I was stunned. "I didn't know. So you mean that you
were feeling me?"

"Abraham, I was digging you from the moment I saw you
in the store. You are just way more laid back than Malik. He
seems to take what he wants. Keeping it real, that nigga is
kind of scary."

I thought about it. "Yeah, but he wasn't always like that."

"Too bad that his change wasn't for the better. I want you to know that I already told him about this. He told me that he would pay for me to have an abortion and that I shouldn't even bother you about this."

"He said what?"

"He said there was no way that you would want to be bothered with this baby or me." She started crying. "I don't want to kill my baby, Abraham."

My heart began to sink into my stomach and I didn't know what to say. I reached over and put my arms around her. "Look, I just need some time to figure this out. But, I wouldn't ask you to do that, you know…kill the baby."

Sondra looked up at me, "Are you serious?" Then with tears in her eyes, she cried out, "Abraham, I wouldn't ask you to be with me because of a baby, but I promise you, I will be a good mother." She was rambling on about how she didn't care what her mother was going to say. "I just want you to be a part of the baby's life. I know Aaliyah is going to try to keep you from doing that but please…"

"Hey, hey, calm down. We don't have to figure everything out right here on this bench. I need some time to think about all this. This is a real bomb, ya' know?"

We got up and we started back to our cars. "Do me a favor," she said. "Don't tell Aaliyah yet. I want to be the one to tell her." I agreed but wasn't sure I would do that.

I told Sondra that I would speak with her in a day or two and urged her to relax. I didn't head straight back to Brooklyn. Instead, I drove around a little. I ended up parking my car over in the meat packing district and walking over to the pier. People were rollerblading, jogging and walking their dogs. I just found a seat and stared out at the Statue of Liberty. I remembered a time, long ago, when I had fewer questions about life. They were tough questions nonetheless, but still fewer. My life and the lives of kids growing up in the projects were different. Some of us had to wonder what we were going to eat or who would be kind enough to feed us. I remember every year around this time, Malik and I would walk thirty blocks to Dubarry Park where the white kids played freely. We wouldn't go there to play. We would go there because we knew that on a fall day like today, as soon as the temperature rose, a few of the white children would carelessly throw their coats on the ground. We depended on their complacency and carelessness to stay warm through the winter.

I thought about the baby that Sondra was carrying. If she was going to have it, I wanted to be a real father. I honestly didn't see how we could become an item, but I was willing to follow the guidance of my God. By the time I left the park at the piers, I was getting used to the notion of being a father.

"Hello," the voice answered at Aaliyah's aunt's house.

"Hey. Is A.J. there?" I had a Big Cookie in my mouth and was chewing into the phone.

"Yeah, she said she will be ready when you get here. She's in the shower. She said to tell you to come on."

I thought that was odd because I hadn't told her that I was coming for sure. "Alright, I'll be there in fifteen minutes."

"Okay, see you, Rico," her little cousin said.

Rico? Had she just called me Rico? It took only a second for everything to click and another one before I felt heat begin to wash over me. I was speeding across the Brooklyn Bridge. I was going to catch her in the act. Maybe her cousin had made a mistake. I tried to stay calm. I reached under my seat and felt to see if my Desert Eagle was there. It was. I headed up Flatbush Avenue at top speed. I zoomed past the Fulton Street Mall and didn't slow down until I turned left on Church Avenue. I came up on 37th Street and circled the block.

No sooner than I parked, did I see a white Range Rover come up the block, radio blasting. The driver never got out of the truck or hit the horn. He must have dialed in because in less than a minute, I saw Aaliyah come out the front door. She was looking damn good in clothes that I had paid for. She had on a tight jean skirt, a $300 pair of Prada boots, and a pink Baby Phat jacket that was my favorite. She had her hair in twists and her lips were shining clear across the street from her Mac lip-gloss. I started to leave, just pull off and never come back, but I had to know.

I jumped out of my car with my gun tucked at my waist. I walked up to her and caught her from behind before she climbed into the truck. I startled her when I grabbed her arm. "Where you headed?"

Her mouth said nothing but her eyes yelled, *Oh Shit!* "Abraham, what are you doing here?"

"What the hell you asking that for? What's up with this nigga, Aaliyah?" I looked into the truck and noticed the driver. He had a smirk on his face.

While I was waiting for a response from her, Rico said, "Yo kid, I'm gonna need you to back away from the truck. Aaliyah, who the hell is this chump?"

"Rico, he's just a friend, I swear," she said as if I didn't matter and her only concern was that she didn't upset him.

"He's obviously more than a friend. He's popping up over your auntie's." He climbed up out of the truck and walked around the front of his truck to join us. "What's the deal, kid? Are you more than a friend to my girl?"

"Your girl?" I had the smirk now. I looked at A.J. There wasn't the slightest look of remorse in her eyes. "A.J., you bitch."

"Fuck you, Abraham. You shouldn't have come over here without calling making trouble for me and my man." She then turned to Rico. "Baby, I swear I told him that it was over months ago. He just won't leave me alone. He's crazy."

"Is that so? Look, dude, you heard my girl. Beat it and don't come around here no more."

"Look here, Rico, I'm not tripping off this slut. I just don't appreciate being lied to. She came on to me…the night she fucked me and my best friend."

Aaliyah's mouth dropped wide open. Rico responded, "What? She did what? Oh, I know this nigga lyin'."

"Oh, I ain't lyin'. He fucked her first on the bathroom sink. I can call him now and he can tell you where both of her tattoos are as well as I can. Your name on that ass across that busted cherry and the butterfly on that thigh."

When he looked at her in disgust, she cried out, "I hate you, Abraham."

"Fuck you with a dirty dick, you skank." With that last insult, I noticed Rico pulling his pistol out. It was too late to try to grab mine as he had the jump on me, so I bobbed to the left and shoved Aaliyah into him. He fired a shot and missed before she collapsed into his arms trying to break her fall.

Instincts kicked in and instead of running, I lunged forward and threw a punch. I hit him directly on the temple and saw his gun fall to the ground as he stumbled back. I kept moving toward him throwing punches. I hit him with two left hooks and a right cross that landed on the bridge of his nose. His foot slid out from under him as if he was wearing skates. He went down on one knee but jumped back up quickly. I mistook him for soft and he hit me with a haymaker in my left eye. He followed with a jab and another haymaker that he missed because I ducked. He did catch the back of my head with his left hand and drove my head into his right uppercut. I felt my mouth fill with the salty taste of my own blood. I was dazed and he grabbed me from behind around the neck. I didn't know what he was trying to do but I changed his plans when I slipped out of his grip with an elbow to his cheek. He backed away and I saw him eying his gun that had slid under his truck.

We squared off with our guards up. We danced in circle for a moment and looked like Oscar and Sugar Shane. He was a good boxer and we traded blows, one after the other. What lasted sixty seconds seemed like and hour. His jabs felt like they were splitting my face open, but my right hooks to his head and body were wearing him out. I thought about the chance of him beating me in the fight and taking another shot at me and knew I couldn't allow it. Suddenly, I faked a right and when he flinched, I threw an overhand left that caught him directly on his chin and knocked him off balance. He fell back into a parked Honda Accord. Before he could regain himself, I threw my best right and hit him right in the mouth. I heard a crunch and a pop at the same time. His jaw was undoubtedly broken. He cried out and grabbed his jaw. I had no mercy where I would have normally. I swung my foot for his mid-section: the balls, the stomach and then straight to the knee, which cracked when I kicked it. There was a scream that could be heard up the block. He was on the ground rolling around probably in more pain than he ever thought possible.

I walked over to his truck and grabbed his pistol from under it. Aaliyah was standing there looking frantic. I faked as if I was going to smack the taste out of her mouth. She jumped back and I laughed. I looked back and saw Rico still on the ground. I wiped my mouth and walked away with his pistol.

"Abraham," I heard her call out. "I'm sorry."

I said nothing and just shook my head. I thought about it for a second and wanted to seize my opportunity to tear her down. "I only came over to tell you that Sondra is pregnant with my kid."

"What?"

"You heard me," I answered as I walked off."

I felt her running up on me. "What did you say mother..."

Before she could get the words out of her mouth I had spun around and grabbed her by the throat. He eyes were bulging out of her head and I stared into her face. I didn't have to say a word. My eyes said it all. I was feeling hatred for Aaliyah. What bothered me most was that I cared enough about her that I wanted to find a way to work the whole thing out. I wasn't in love and I knew that women played games. All of that didn't matter. Somewhere in the middle of the night, deep in our sins, I believed that we had connected and I wanted to pull her out of this street life along with me.

I realized that I was hurting her. "*Hatred stirs up contentions, but love covers over all transgressions,* Proverbs 10:12," I said aloud as I released her. She took a deep breath. "Never contact me again," I said.

In that second, I saw regret in her eyes. She knew then that she had made a mistake. I doubted that she had ever known love in her lustful relationships. Not romantic love, just human decency and kindness like I had shown her. "Abraham, I want you to know that..."

"Save it," I yelled back as I climbed into my car and screeched off.

I headed back towards the hood. I had to check on Do or Die. I also was eager to speak with Malik. I had to see where his head was. Some lines would have to be drawn—lines that would be uncrossable.

I put on Anthony Hamilton's CD and threw on track 6, *Comin' From Where I'm From,* and hit the repeat button. He was singing the blues and I was feeling like I could have written them.

While I headed toward the Towers, I said a quick prayer. I asked for forgiveness for the way I had cursed her, and for the physical beating that I had given Rico. I had allowed my anger to make me take his beating to a dangerous level. I then prayed for Aaliyah and hoped that she would have a good life. I forgave her and most importantly… I forgave myself.

SEVENTEEN

Anger not hate, is the greatest opponent of love.
Emotions such as frustration, jealousy, pride, disgust,
sadness, and anxiety can all form unexpectedly. Oftentimes
humans have trouble dealing with those emotions because
they have to be dealt with internally. The internal process
required for dealing with these emotions can be difficult,
confusing and sometimes too painful. For most it becomes
much easier to transform the feelings into anger. Anger then
easily lends itself to projection. The formula is as easy as
one, two, three. Get angry, blame someone, and attack.
Somehow, some way, the anger must be let loose, even if it is
on oneself.

"So you went and told him?"

"He had a right to know, Malik. I can't do this any more.
Even if he and I *aren't* going to be together. I can't disrespect
him like that if I want him to be a part of my child's life."

"Be together?" I knew that Abraham hadn't lost his mind.
"He started talking 'bout tryin' to be with you?"

Sondra shook her head. "Nah, nigga, you ain't got to trip.
He was just a gentleman about everything. He told me don't
worry about shit."

"So you're going to have the baby?"

"I told you it's too late for an abortion. I'm almost five months now, Malik."

"Sondra, this is New York. You can get an abortion the day before delivery somewhere in this city."

"Fuck you, Malik. I'm having my baby. You got a lot of nerve. I guess that's all you know about is killing. It don't matter if it's a baby or a man, huh?"

She stung me with that comment. "Bitch, fuck you. You don't know shit about me."

"Oh yeah, I know more than you think."

"Yeah, what's that supposed to mean?" She was saying all the wrong things.

"What? You don't know that everybody in Brooklyn is talking about you and Do or Die? Saying y'all niggas is the Black Mafia." I was silent. Sondra got up out the bed and started getting dressed. I stared at her belly. It was small for her to be so far gone. "Malik, this is the last time. I won't be seeing you again."

"Yeah, whatever." I stood up naked and walked to the bathroom to take a piss. When I walked back out she was fully dressed. She was by the door as if she was waiting on my permission to leave. "What?"

"I need some money."

"Don't you always?" I laughed. "So what you gonna do for cash if you ain't helping me out or fucking me?"

"I'll manage," she said looking at the floor. When I nudged her chin so that I could look into her face, I saw the shame in her eyes.

I walked over to my sweatpants and pulled some money out. "Here, take this." I handed her $1,000. She had provided many invaluable services for me in the past months. I hoped that if I really needed her, I would be able to call on her. "I understand," I said as she took the money from my hands, "But

I may need you one last time in a month or so. Can I call on you?"

She sniffed, but I saw no tears. "Sure," she answered and headed out the door.

Abraham and I did what friends and men are supposed to do. We talked. I wasn't a baseball fan, but my best friend loved the Yankees so I copped the tickets. ALCS tickets cost me $300 apiece, but Abraham was in heaven. The Yankees were playing the Boston Red Sox, but I wasn't really interested in the game. My whole focus was to find out where Abraham's head was in all this.

"So you know she's having the baby, right?"

"Yeah, I know," Abraham answered.

"So how do you feel 'bout that shit?"

"Man, at first I was a little bent out of shape. I didn't blame her though. It takes two, ya' feel me?" He went on to explain what had happened with him and Aaliyah.

"Yo, I never trusted that scandalous ho from the jump."

"Yeah, well I wish you woulda' hipped me. I almost crippled that nigga, Rico." We both laughed, though I knew deep down inside, the incident bothered him. That's just how he was. Abraham was a rumbler. I would pit him against most any nigga his size or fifty pounds heavier. He was just a natural puncher and had no problems breaking jaws... shoulda' been a boxer for real. If he was as nice with a pistol as he was with his hands he would have been the most feared nigga in the hood.

By the time we left the game, we had talked everything out—almost everything. "So, man, seriously, how do you feel about the fact that I've been hitting that for all this time?" I wasn't sure if it came out right, so I went on, "I mean, does it bother you?"

"Man, it is what it is. The real question is how do you feel about her? Do you care about her?"

I thought about it. "In a way, but not like a girlfriend. Angel, she's my jump-off."

Abraham laughed. "Well, man, I got to say that it might be a little awkward, my best friend dealing with my baby's mother." Then he paused. "Listen, man, you do what you think is best. No woman is going to come between us. She is carrying my kid though, and that has to weigh something with you. Don't stress her and if I do decide to give her a shot for the sake of the kid... stay out of it and we'll be cool."

I shook his hand and said, "Fair enough." He dropped me off at the Thirty Thirty Hotel where Angel was waiting and he headed back to the Towers. He had become the best Lieutenant I could have hoped for. He had respect as being my partner from the Do or Die Crew and Do or Die had respect from everyone else. In the last month, there hadn't been as much as one robbery attempted. The heads felt safe coming through there and the sales were through the roof. Cortez was my number one fan by this point. Even Doc and Wendell had softened to the idea of having to pay me every month. After seeing their profits go up week after week, they began to give me more and more respect. I still refused to trust any of them any further than I could throw 'em, but they were dropping that cash like it was hot every month so they had my protection.

I walked into the room and heard Angel yell out, "Wait!" She knew better than to startle me like that but she said, "Close your eyes. I have a surprise for you." When I heard that, a smile escaped my lips and I relaxed. I heard the spark of matches and then I heard her turn on the CD player. Beyonce's, *Me, Myself and I* came on.

I stood still as I felt Angel in front of my face. She tied a blindfold around my eyes. Then she began to undress me. "What you got planned girl?"

"You'll see," she said as she guided me to the bed. I was naked and laying flat on my back. "You trust me, don't you, love?"

"You know I do," I answered and felt her hands brush across my body. She rubbed my chest first then my stomach. Next I felt the wetness from her tongue. She stuck it in my navel as her soft hands gripped my penis. I moaned softly as her mouth reached me and took me inside. She had improved in the months that we had been dating. Her lips began sliding up and down on me coating me with her saliva.

"You like that, daddy?" she said with her mouth full.

"Oh yeah." She started working it like a pro and my back began to arch. My involuntary groaning let her know how much I was enjoying it. I felt her stop and I noticed how hard my heart was beating.

She then gripped my shaft with her left hand and told me to take the blindfold off. I leaned up and my eyes nearly popped out of my head. "Yeah, nigga!" Angel was holding a knife dangerously close to my dick.

"Girl... what the fuck?" I said angrily.

"Malik, who the fuck is Sondra? I went and got my hair done today and Dionne tells me you've been fucking this bitch the whole time you and I have been together."

I knew I couldn't stutter, but I needed that knife taken away from my dick. "Sweetie..."

"Don't give me that sweetie shit, Malik. I don't play that shit, Malik. If we are together, then we are together. You aren't going to cheat on me, there is too much shit going around."

I cut her off before she worked herself into a frenzy and did something that *I* might regret. "Now is this how you are always going to deal with shit that comes up in the street? You hear some bullshit about me in the hair salon and bring a threat to me instead of asking me about it. That's not right. I been takin' care of you from the day we decided that we was gonna try this." She still had her grip and the knife was an inch away. "Now you want to cut the dick off of the man who is going to father your kids."

"Malik, you gave that bitch a ring." Tears began to fall from her eyes. "Do you love that bitch, Malik? Tell me, do you love her?" she repeated.

"I don't know what you heard, but that shit isn't true. That is Abraham's girl. She is six months pregnant with his kid. He is thinking about getting married to her." I exhaled as an idea popped into my head. "I don't know what that bitch, Dionne, told you, but the only girl I ever bought a ring for is you, and now you messed up my surprise."

"Yeah right, Malik. Don't play with me. I swear I will slice this thing clean off and stuff it in your mouth." She was dead serious.

"Hand me my phone. It's right there." I pointed to the nightstand.

"I'm not letting go so you better slide your ass over there." I did as she told me and grabbed the phone. I smashed the button down on the Nextel and called Abraham. "Come in, Gilligan. It's the Skipper."

A second later, he came back with, "What up?"

"Nothin' much." I wiped the sweat off of my forehead. "Listen, I was thinking about what we talked about earlier. I think you are going to be a great father and that you should be excited."

"Straight up?" came through on the loudspeaker. I knew I had to guide the conversation so that I got only what I wanted through the phone.

"No doubt. Sondra told me that she cares about you and really respects you. Y'all are going to be great parents," I said.

"Whoa. She said that? That's big. I'm not mad that she's having it. No matter what the situation, children are a blessing from GOD."

"Yeah, I feel that." I moved right along. "Me and Angel might make one too, that is if she doesn't chop my dick off first." She was satisfied and let me go.

"What?" he asked, trying to make sure he heard me right.

"Never mind, I'll call you in the morning. Is everything straight out there?"

"Everything is copasetic."

"Alright then, peace."

"One."

A second later, Angel was in tears crying like a baby. She was apologizing hysterically. She seemed like she was about to hyperventilate. I didn't know whether to beat her down for threatening me with the knife or to call an ambulance. I begged her, "Stop. Calm down. It's alright, just relax." Holding her in my arms, I said, "I understand. I got a crazy temper myself." I even managed to laugh a little. "Don't make yourself sick up in here."

She held me tightly and I thought of how she had shown me her crazy side. I knew that she had to have one. Everyone did. Her being Phil Boogie's sister should have been warning enough that she had the rage of the devil inside of her for occasions just like this. "I love you, Malik."

"I love you too," I said. The words flowed easily off of my lips. I only had love for her, but I was still a young man. Though I would no longer be seeing Sondra, I knew that it would be hard to be a one-woman man. I had to reprimand her for her actions. There would be other times and other women eventually, and if she ever heard rumors, or worse caught me red-handed, she could not be allowed to think that she could haphazardly attack me.

She had calmed down completely and I got up to take a shower. When I finished and walked out, she was standing in front of the widow looking down at the cars passing by on the street below. With nothing on but a towel, I walked up behind her. She felt my body brush up against hers and responded by pushing her bottom into my pelvis.

In the next instant, I took the towel from around my waist and slung it around her neck. I clenched the ends of it so tightly, that it hurt *my* hands. She reached for the towel with both hands in a futile attempt to get some slack. I then pushed her face firmly against the window.

I kept my grip on the towel as she silently fought for air. She began to claw at my arms and I slung her from the window and pinned her even tighter against the wall. When I felt her body began to go limp, I dropped the towel and watched her fall to her knees. She then sucked in air as if it was gold as she collapsed onto the floor.

"Get your ass up," I commanded. When she didn't comply right away, I pulled her by the arms. She had the look of fear in her eyes. "I want you to listen and listen real good."

She stood there and her expression danced back and forth from fear to anger. I watched as her breathing returned to normal. Her body motion told me that I had her full attention.

"I don't care what you heard about me. I don't care what you hear in the future. If you want to live a long life you only have two options." I got real close up on her. "One, you can come home and ask me about it like a real bitch. Or, if you happen to believe what you hear and don't want to be around me…then you can leave…as long as you don't run to my enemy." I took my thumb and index finger and squeezed her cheeks. "But don't you ever try any shit like you did tonight. I don't believe in domestic violence. I got no time to go to jail for shit like that. So don't bring that craziness around me."

I made out a muffled, "Okay, I understand."

"You better because if I ever have to put my hands on you again, the police won't find your body." I let her go and laid across the bed. "…and give me that fucking knife."

I don't think either of us went soundly to sleep. Two hours later, we were in the bed and I felt her eyes open, even though she was turned away from me. "Angel," I said softly.

"Yes," came back in a whisper.

"I'm sorry that I had to do that."

She turned over toward me. "I'm sorry too." She sniffed and a tear crept out of her eyes. "I love you."

"I love you too." She reached for me and we kissed. Her lips tasted like a treasure that I had been waiting to discover all my life. As we grinded together, I appreciated the familiarity of her body, but appreciated it as if it was my first time touching her.

"Take that off," I said tugging at her shirt. She did and her breast bounced free. I didn't have to ask and she slid her cotton thongs off too. I was already naked and now I was hard. She began kissing me and I felt the temperature in the room rise. Her kisses spilled out of my mouth across my cheeks, neck, and onto my chest.

"You taste good, baby." She was licking and kissing me like there was no tomorrow.

"My turn," I said as I rolled her onto her back. I pinned her arms down over her head as I began to invade her mouth with my tongue. I slid down to her neck and then her breasts. They were so full and firm, yet soft like pillows at the same time. Her nipples sprang to attention as I cupped her breasts with my hands and gently pinched them with my fingers.

"MMmmmmmnnnn. That's my spot," she moaned as I began sucking on her pelvic bones. I danced there for a moment before I moved to her middle. When my chin slid across her clit she flinched. "Ohhhh, Leeeek."

"You like that."

"Hell yessss." I began licking her coochie. My lips suckled hers until I reached her middle. I sucked gently then flicked my tongue over her clit continuously. My face was soaked with her juices and it turned me on. There was her distinctive odor... it was a mixture of passion, sweat, lust, and purity all in one. I wanted to breathe her up and eat her up at the same time.

"Oh, I love it." I slipped out as I kept a slight sucking motion all the while applying steady but increasing pressure on her with my tongue. While I ate her, my fingers found her ass cheeks which were slippery from her wetness. She responded as I gave them a firm squeeze. I then slid my fingers up inside of her while I continued to eat her. I was gentle and I must have hit her spot because she screamed out.

"Maaaa.....uuuuhhhh..... leeeek." Five short breaths. "Unngghh." Ten quick breaths. "Umm... about to... to ... to....to... cuuuummmm!" Another scream and her ass came up off of the bed. She began to buck so wildly that I couldn't keep my tongue on her, but I tried. My mouth rode her pussy like a cowboy riding a bucking bronco at a rodeo. The more she squirmed the more I licked. "Got dammit, motherfucker. Oh no. I... I'm... still cumming."

Fifteen seconds later, she was still shaking and had curled up in a little ball. I reached for her legs to spread them apart.

"Give me a minute."

"Nah, fuck that." I reached for her legs. "You can handle this with your knife-wielding ass." I forcefully grabbed her legs and spread them. I crawled in between and slipped inside of her. She didn't open her eyes but instinctively began humping me.

We got into a rhythm like waves crashing against the shores after a storm. I slammed lovingly into her middle. She wrapped her arms around my neck and took all that I wanted to give her. We banged away all of our anger until there was nothing left but love. "Let me get on top," she commanded.

Once I was on my back, she glided up and down on me perfectly. I watched as she caressed her own breasts. With her hands, she reached back and separated her ass cheeks and kept riding me. She did it until I couldn't take the sensations anymore. When she knew I was ready, she grinded down hard, bumping her clit on my pubic area. She then reached down and began to rub herself into a frenzy. When my eyes rolled up into my head and I let out a groan, so did she. She was having another orgasm with me. "Oh, shit. I'm cumming, Angel."

"I know, baby. Give it to me."

"Oh, yes."

"Give me all that nut."

I let out a groan as I grabbed her hips and she arched her back one last time before she fell onto my chest. We struggled to catch our breath and by the time we had, we fell asleep with me still inside of her. There was no sex like make-up sex.

I left my pick-up point for the monthly payment from Cortez and company and did the usual. The usual meant doing something totally different from which I had done before. This was no different. I had asked for large bills from Cortez and he had done just that. The money fit into a backpack and I was able to look inconspicuous.

I watched over my shoulder and noticed that Cortez was moving toward his ride. As always, I assumed that he, Doc or Wendell would have someone attempt to follow me. I wondered if Cortez knew that I was having him followed. The private investigator had nearly every move that he had made for the last month written down, recorded, or photographed for me. If he wasn't watching Cortez, then he was keeping me clued in on Doc and Wendell. If Cortez was overconfident, then Wendell was careless. Doc however was simply sloppy. He kept picking up his drugs from College Avenue in the Bronx and drove them straight to his stash house in Bed-Stuy. He was bold or stupid enough to keep his drugs, money, and his woman under the same roof. I guess he thought the Bull Terriers and Rotties were going to deter the stick-up boys when they came.

I drove across the Manhattan Bridge and crossed over Canal Street. There was plenty of traffic, which made the trip a slow one. I kept a hand on my pistol of the day, the Wilson Combat 45s. I was prepared to be run up on by some killers, but hoped for the best.

Once I approached Pier Six at the East River, I jumped out of the car and moved quickly for the gate at Liberty Helicopter Tours. I had met with the pilot, Tim, the week before and when he greeted me, he already knew what was up. Within moments, we were up in the helicopter.

"Nice day for a ride," he laughed.

"No doubt," I said as we lifted off. Once we were in the air, we headed for the Statue of Liberty first, and then zoomed across the Hudson straight for New Jersey. When we made it to Fairleigh Dickenson's football field, I gave him $2,000 for his trouble and jumped out with the backpack firmly on my shoulder. I headed for the parking lot and into the car I had parked there earlier in the morning. Anyone following me that wasn't in a helicopter was short. I imagined Cortez's flunkies watching me take off wondering how they were going to explain losing me again.

I took the money out of the bag and counted it. I had just enough there to put the plan into effect. There was one problem. I was going to have to hold the paychecks of the entire Do or Die crew this month. I had a plan to appease them and hopefully they would comply willingly.

EIGHTEEN

Greed and unlawful acquisition are never far apart. Once the spirit of greed has taken over a man, he begins to plot on treasures that he has no rightful claim to. Eventually, he will break a law of man, nature, or GOD to get what he desires: money, power, fame and women. Most often he won't recognize his wrongdoing. He sees the wealthy, whom he admires, going in the same direction, so he too sets off on a path like a horse with blinders on, headed for a cliff with the devil as his passenger. The only way he survives is if he somehow turns back. If his greed is too overwhelming, more than likely he'll stumble along the way getting trampled by the stampede of lost souls following him. But every now and again, the greedy make it to the cliff going full speed. By the time they see the ground beneath their feet, the devil has ridden him clean over the cliff to certain disaster.

Each lieutenant sat on the rooftop staring blankly at Malik as he explained that there would be no pay for the month of November. I noticed a look on Wheeler's face that showed his disgust. He was the only one who was bold enough to show any disdain. "So what's up?" Malik asked looking directly into Wheeler's eyes. "Who got a problem with that?"

Wheeler shook his head as if he was making up his mind about speaking up. I didn't sense that he was afraid of Malik. He was a killer himself and had been in the streets long before Malik. He did understand though that Malik had a firm grip on his crew. If he went against Malik, he would have to do battle with each of the other members. Finally he stood up. "Look, man. It's like this. You could have given us some warning. Some of us plan on making moves with that dough."

"I feel you, Wheeler. That's why this is a discussion. If you need your dough, I'll break you off. I just asked that you all roll with me this month. I got a move that I need to make and it is going to take more cash on hand than I'm holding right now." Malik liked saying that. It gave the members of his crew the impression that he was grinding just like them. He didn't appear to be a rich nigga pimping their muscle. "I don't want you all to misunderstand me. I want your approval to do this. I'm not strong arming you for the money you earned. As a matter of fact, after this month, I plan to turn the whole operation over to one of you."

Wheeler nodded his head and seemed a little more relaxed. A hush came over everyone. "The whole operation? Why you gonna do something like that?" Terrell asked.

Malik smirked as if to say, "Don't question me". Then he went on, "Count your blessings, son. I got some moves to make that are going to keep me out of town for a while."

"Oh yeah? So who you planning on leaving in charge?" Wheeler asked.

"Depends on who looks like they're up to it. Might be a couple of y'all together. I ain't sure yet. No matter what though, the money is all yours after this month." There was dead silence and a few grins appeared. "So are you with me on this or what? The alternative is that I stay and you keep the same pay until I get what I need."

"I'm all in."

"Me too."

"I'm straight with it."

"It's whatever."

"Good. Then it's done." Malik stood and headed for the door to exit and we all followed.

Once everyone was back on post, Malik and I stood up against the fence of the playground. "So now what?" I asked.

"We got everything we need to do this. I'm gonna need you to get focused. We gonna meet next week with Double V's folks. You gotta come strong."

I realized that he meant I would need to come like a killer. I wasn't one and I thought about asking him if I could bow out, but I knew I needed to be there to watch his back. "Just keep my role to a minimum. All I'm focusing on ..." I was interrupted by the crack of a pistol and screams. I looked over and saw the police storming into the courtyard.

"Back to the building!" Malik yelled as he took off running.

I followed looking back. I saw two officers in ATF jackets running behind us. Malik reached the building and left the door swinging as I dashed in behind him. I wasn't sure which flight of steps he had taken until I heard his feet brushing the steps as he climbed them. Two seconds later, the door burst in behind me. I heard, "Freeze, police!" as I reached the top of the first flight. I didn't and a shot was fired. I was near the corner and when I turned it, Malik was crouched at the end of the hallway. He had his gun drawn and the laser was pointed directly at me as I ran towards him.

"Move the fuck out of the way," he yelled as I cleared him and headed for the next flight. He was still aiming for the end of the hall when the first agent appeared. He had gotten so caught up in the heat of the chase, he never suspected that

Malik and I could be armed. It proved fatal as the first burst of fire left Malik's pistol striking the agent in the eye. Malik continued firing and I heard his partner trying to return fire. I moved back down to where he was and pulled my pistol out. Malik ducked around the corner. "I need you to run up those steps loudly," he whispered to me.

"I got your back," I said squatting down beside him to show that I was armed.

"Nah, just do what I asked. Now run." I did and a few seconds later, I heard Malik yell, "Now you freeze, motherfucker!" Then Malik laughed. I walked back down to him and he was standing over the agent with his gun drawn. The agent had his hands up pleading for his partner. I was at Malik's side and the fed looked into my eyes and I could tell he was begging for mercy.

"Look, man. He needs attention," he said nervously to Malik.

Malik put his foot to the wounded man's head and nudged him. "He needs a coroner. He's dead." He stepped back.

"Listen, man, no need to make this any worse. If you surrender, you can fight this, but if you …"

"It can't get any worse, one body or two. Say your prayers." He aimed the pistol at his face. "He didn't think twice before he tried to shoot my boy in the back."

"No, Malik!" I yelled. "Just cuff his ass and let's jet."

I saw a grimace come across his face like I had never seen before. I didn't see it coming but I felt the butt of Malik's pistol strike me in the cheek. I stumbled back. "You just told this motherfucker my name." In the next instant, I saw the agent lunge for Malik, but he moved too slowly as Malik's body glided back out of his grasp. A foot to the skull and he was almost out. Then Malik fired two bullets into the back of his head.

He looked over at me. I stared back at him. It was the first time he had struck me in anger since we were kids fighting over a big wheel. I was holding my cheek and the sting that I felt ensured me that I was cut. I looked down at the two bodies in the hallway and felt sick. This was the death penalty.

"We gotta get outta here." He took off running. When we reached the front of the building and looked outside, it looked like there was a war going on outside. I didn't see any marked police cars, but there looked like at least fifteen officers and agents over in the courtyard. They were at least a hundred yards away. The officers were ducked behind the dumpsters and a couple of unmarked vehicles.

As we snuck out and headed in the opposite direction, I heard someone yell out. "There he is." Malik and I both thought they were talking about us and we looked back to see Terrell running from behind a building firing back over his head.

I froze in my tracks as I saw at least ten officers open fire, riddling his body with bullets. I was amazed that he was still running after being hit. He didn't fall until the shotgun blast hit him in the back of his neck almost taking his head off of his shoulders. I was paralyzed watching and probably would have sat there watching until they came over to lock me up until I felt Malik tap my shoulder and motion for me to take off behind him.

We ran for at least eight blocks. I was out of breath and my face was still hurting. When we stopped, Malik pulled his shirt off and put it back on inside out. He had a few spots with the officer's blood on it. We finally grabbed a cab. Malik didn't want to catch one in the vicinity of the Towers. Any cabdriver picking up young men from the area of the Towers during that time would be called in and questioned. If there had been an investigation, then our pictures had been taken sometime during the last few months. They probably would have our names as well so it was a necessary trek.

"It's over in the Towers," Malik said as we cruised. "We live in Jersey now."

I just looked at him. "Say what?"

"That's it. We ain't never going back over there again..." He looked at my cheek and went on, "... at least not to work. We got to send someone to make sure the apartments are all cleaned out, and I need to tie up some loose ends." He was thinking out loud, rambling on and on about the police raid. He seemed remarkably calm, but thoroughly disgusted that he would have to pull Do or Die out of the Towers before he had planned.

When the cab came to a stop in downtown Brooklyn, we got out. "You didn't see what happened to Terrell, did you?"

"Yeah, I saw. Fucked up."

I was feeling a little choked up. I thought about Terrell and how he had become a real soldier. "He was a good dude."

"Yeah, but he was born the wrong color in the wrong area code." He looked down and shook his head. "Charge that shit to the game."

"I feel you. You think we could send a little something to his folks to take care of expenses?"

"Of course, but I don't think we should show up at the funeral. Keep in mind, *we* just killed two federal agents."

I nodded in agreement. I was still amazed at how he was always thinking. Then I paused for a moment before I looked over at him. "You know I'm going to have to kick your ass for this later on," I said rubbing my cheek.

He smiled at me. "Yeah, I know, but we got shit to do right now."

I nodded, "Yeah, lucky you." I was dead serious and he knew it.

"I'll pick you up at Jimmy's Uptown around 9:00 tonight," he said. "Stay low until then." He gave me a pound and a handshake then he disappeared into the thick crowd of shoppers and workers buzzing around Fulton.

I showered and changed and decided to catch a movie while I was killing time. I wasn't sure why, but I had decided to call Sondra and invite her. She had been just as surprised to hear from me as I had been that I called her. We wound up meeting at Penn Station and checking out *Kill Bill*. After the movie, we went to get some ice cream and talked for a while about nothing much.

I was checking my watch to make sure I had time to get to Harlem by 9:00 when she asked, "So, Abraham, have you given anymore thought to our situation?"

"It's okay if you call *it* a baby." I smiled. "You're not going to freak me out."

She smiled back. "Okay, so have you?"

"I think about him all the time."

"Him?"

"But of course." I laughed. I couldn't believe that amidst all the chaos I was encountering that I was able to find enough inside to find humor.

"So look at you, the proud Papa already. Wow." She told me that she had always wanted to be married to whomever she had a kid with, but since that didn't seem possible, she was glad that I was the father.

"That reminds me," I said and pulled out a receipt to use for paper. "You have a pen?"

"Yeah, hold up." She dug in her purse. "Here."

I scribbled down an address and no name. "Listen, after you have the baby, if anything happens where you don't hear from me or Malik for over two weeks, I want you to hop on a train or bus and go to this address. When you get there, just tell them that I sent you and about the instructions that I gave you."

"I don't understand."

"I've done some things to make sure that you and the baby will be okay. Just promise me you'll do it." I was holding her hand.

She looked back into my eyes. "Okay, I promise."

"Alright, I got to run." I stood up and we exited the restaurant. We headed back to the subway entrance where we hugged before we parted ways.

"That's him," was all I heard as I stood outside of Jimmy's Uptown. My heart quickly fell into my stomach as I turned around to see if it was me who had been made. "Hey, man." It was Bing, the kid that I had saved from getting jumped in the summertime. "Abraham, right?" he said as he walked up on me.

I was relieved it was him instead of the police. While I tried to relax and slow my heartbeat down, I answered, "Hey man. What's good?"

"Everything. What's good with you?" I noticed that he was dressed very nicely. He was wearing slacks, Kenneth Cole boots, and a designer sweater.

"I'm just holding it down." One day, I wanted to be able to say that I was holding it down for my Lord and Savior, but for now, I was nowhere.

"I hear that. Hey look, I wanted to introduce you to my sister, remember, I told you about her." He stepped to the side and when his sister stepped forward, I had to do a double take. I still didn't think it was who I thought she resembled. I extended my hand.

"Hey, I'm Abraham," I said. "Nice to meet you."

"Tasha Robb. Nice to meet you." She ignored my extended hand and embraced me. "Mmmm you smell nice. What you wearin'?"

"Nervousness and mayhem," I laughed out. She joined in.

"Hey, my brother told me what you did for him last summer. That was real decent. Why don't you come in with us and have a bite to eat? It's on my record label anyway," she said matter of factly.

She confirmed what I was wondering. Tasha Robb was the hottest new rapper out. She had just dropped her single and they were playing it on Hot 97 every hour of the day. I had to catch myself before I walked in and left Malik. "I got a partner meeting me up here…"

"What's his name? We'll leave his name at the door."

"Hold on he's calling me right now?" I answered the phone and listened to Malik tell me that he was tied up. I assured him that I was fine for the night and would catch up to him in the morning. He seemed overly excited and rushed me off the phone. "Peace," I said hanging up. I had to admit that I was glad that he wasn't going to show up. I was hanging out with Tasha Robb. She was celebrating her new single and was showing me a lot of love.

"You ready?" she asked.

"No doubt," I said as I walked into Jimmy's as part of her entourage.

NINETEEN

Crime pays in many ways. Done well and on a large scale, it pays major dividends. Done perfectly, and the criminal winds up living a life that most dream of. The only problem is that a crime never registers as perfect until the life of the criminal is over. Up until the day he dies, the only thing a criminal can do is hope and imagine that he has gotten away with the crime. Time eases his apprehensions, and years erase evidence, but the mind and conscience always haunt the average criminal. Sometimes though, crime pays an immediate and exact revenge on the committer. This is the offender who goes out in a blaze of fire, or is locked under the jail. This is the criminal who finds out that he is the small fish in a pool of sharks. The spoils are never enjoyed or wind up bringing about a worse state of being than existed in the life of the criminal before he even decided to take part in the act in the first place. This is the crime that is never worth committing.

When Ferris called and told me what was going on at his aunt's house out in Bushwick, I sped over there. He'd told me that his aunt's boyfriend had come to her job and beaten her earlier. She had no sooner made it home from the hospital with fourteen stitches and her left eye swollen completely shut before he was at her door trying to force his way into her house. Her daughter had called Ferris and he in turn rang me.

I would have come to help him out no matter what, but what I heard when I got there made the whole ordeal almost too good to be true. When we pulled up, he had just left. Ferris' cousin let us in. She was frantic and crying, saying that he was going to come back and kill them like he had killed the old woman.

"What the hell are you talking about?" Ferris asked. My ears had been pricked and I was listening attentively.

"Shut up, girl." Ferris' aunt yelled out.

"He's crazy. That nigga been robbing people left and right. He's the one that killed that old lady up on Marcy last month. He didn't get nothing but $60 from the lady."

"How you know that?" Ferris asked.

"You sure about that?" I chimed in.

"Damn right, I'm sure." She was pacing back and forth. "He had the nerve to brag about that shit."

Ferris' aunt sat in the corner by the stairs, rocking. A closer look at her revealed that her face was worn well beyond her forty years. I could tell that she was once beautiful. There were signs of drug use and it all came together. She and her man both shared a habit. He just so happened to be one of the worst types of criminals on the street. He was a junkie, a violent one without a conscience.

Ferris' aunt began arguing with her daughter about running her mouth. At this point, my blood was boiling. I began thinking about getting a hold of her boyfriend. The phone rang and startled each of us. His aunt answered it and was trying to calm him down and talk some sense into him, "Cardo please…"

I instinctively snatched the phone from her, "Yeah, faggot, you like putting your hands on women, huh?"

"What?" the voice yelled back. "Who is this?"

"It's the nigga that's gonna rip your head off of your shoulders and piss down your neck," I barked into the phone.

Cardo began yelling back into the phone, making a wide range of threats. He ended with, "I'm on the way back around my woman's house right now and I'm killing everything."

"This is my woman now. Come later, we busy right now."

"What?" he yelled.

"You heard me."

"Do you know who I am? Nigga, I keeps it gully. You ain't ready for this death I'm bringing," he was yelling at the top of his lungs.

"Whatever, sucka. I'm right here," I shot back and then I hung the phone up.

"Why?" Ferris' aunt was in tears. "Why would you do that? He is crazy. He hasn't been home for more than a year and believe me, he ain't afraid to go back."

Ferris, who had been observing my manner with a sense of pride chimed in. "Aunt Cee Cee, we ain't scared of that nigga. If he come around here, he's gonna get dealt with." Ferris pulled up his shirt revealing a snub nose .38 in his waistband.

"Ferris, what are you doing with that?"

"Oh you know what I'm doing with this. Y'all called *me* remember, not your brother. I don't have time for bullshittin'."

I started thinking and planning for what might go down. I thought back to the anger I felt when I heard about the murder of the old woman. I realized that this was a golden opportunity to exact some real street justice, and it had fallen in my lap.

I had been looking forward to hanging with Abraham and taking him out to the apartment in Jersey. Knowing him, I was sure he was grieving over what had happened to Terrell, and I wanted to be there for him.   Somehow though, I felt a connection to this mission. It was spiritual.

The first bang came to the door and I watched Ferris jump. I stayed in the kitchen getting prepared. I had sent Cee Cee and her daughter, Fran, upstairs. She had actually pleaded with us not to hurt him. I laughed when I thought about her ignorance. He was getting what he deserved.

"Tell him to back away from the door and you'll let him in Ferris," I commanded. "Then run your ass back here into the kitchen."

Ferris did as I told him. He yelled from the window next to the door and Cardo saw that Ferris was a youngster. It didn't stop him from stepping to the bay window where Ferris stood and hurling an oversized rock straight through the window at him.

"Now!" I yelled. Ferris quickly unlocked the door and headed back toward the kitchen. Cardo burst through the door like the Hulk and saw Ferris headed for the kitchen where he followed right behind him.

"Come here, you little faggot. I got something for your ass." As soon as he cleared the entrance to the kitchen, I gave him the surprise of his natural life. There was a grimace that turned into a high-pitched scream when the pan of scorching hot fish grease hit Cardo in the face. I had fried all the grease in the old Crisco cans sitting on Cee Cee's stove and put it to use.

"How you like that shit?" I laughed out loud. He was on his knees covering his eyes, more than likely blinded for life. "I can't hear you, Al Green."

"Aaaghhh, I can't see. Muthafucka, I'm gon' get cha'." He was fumbling around on the floor, trying to locate the ice pick that he had in his hand.

"Nigga, you ain't in the joint no more. This is Brooklyn, homey." I lifted my knee almost to my chest before stomping him on the back of his head with my Timberlands. I repeated the same stomping motion until I lost count. By this point, there was a puddle of blood mixed with the grease on the floor. "Come here, Ferris!" I yelled. "This nigga was gonna stick you with this." I showed him the pick. "I think you need to hit him in the ass a few times to let him know that shit is un...motherfuckin'...acceptable."

Ferris reached over and took the pick. He looked into my eyes and if he had any reservations about punishing Cardo, he hid them well. I didn't see any fear. Ferris stepped over Cardo's body, which was face down. I winced a little when I saw him slam the ice pick directly into his ass crack. I was thinking cheek, but Ferris kept it gutter and hit him three times in his shit hole. Each time, Cardo's body gave an involuntary jerk.

His body looked almost lifeless, as he was in a state halfway between consciousness and shock. I gave Ferris instructions to get a few items out of my car while I rolled Cardo over. Once I had him on his back, I took notice that his face was a mess. His skin had already formed blisters from the obvious third-degree burns. His nose looked like a swollen lump of flesh and his mouth had been busted wide open. I called Cee Cee down to the kitchen and when she walked in she began to cry, "Oh, no."

Ferris hadn't come back in yet and I grabbed her by the shoulders. "Listen, you got to calm the fuck down."

"Why did you..."

I cut her off, "Are you fucking crazy?" I shook my head in disgust. "Do you realize he was coming to kill you? He said that while you were upstairs."

"Nooo."

"Yes. He was going to gut you like a pig. He said you knew too much." She began to cry in a light whimper. "I want you to listen and listen good. I am only going to say this to you once." She nodded her head trying to keep from crying. "Are you with me?"

"Yes."

"He is not dead yet," I looked down at him, "however, make no mistake about it, I am going to kill him tonight." Her face showed fear. It was obvious she had some form of love for the man. "Don't grieve for this man. He didn't have any mercy on that old lady he beat to death. Did he?"

She didn't answer so I moved up into her face and screamed the question. "Did he give a damn about her family, about her life, who she left behind?"

She shook her head no.

"What if it was your mother he had killed? What would you want me to do to him?" She was silent. "He ain't worth a damn. Tonight I am going to make an example of this man. Tell me what he stole from the old lady."

She was still whimpering. Ferris walked back into the kitchen with the duct tape, some bolt cutters and rope. "Just some money."

"Did he give you anything? A VCR, jewelry, anything?" I stared into her eyes. "You better not tell me any lies, Cee Cee."

Nervously, she ran out of the kitchen and up to her room. When she came back, she had Citizen watch. "This is it. There were some pearl earrings, but he took those to the pawn shop."

"Okay, cool. Wipe your prints off of it and put it in a plastic bag." I looked down at his body. "Ferris, tape his arms behind his back, then tape his ankles together… extra tight." I then instructed Cee Cee to get some damp cloths. "I want you to nurse this nigga back to health. Get some ice for his burns. Crush five Tylenols and dissolve them in some water." She was moving real slow so I stopped her. "Are you following me, Cee Cee? I *am* going to kill this nigga and if you know what's good for you and your family, you are going to do everything I tell you to do and you will never speak on me or this nigga again." I put my left hand on her shoulder and my right hand was on my Wilson combat pistol. "You understand?"

She looked down. "Yes...yeah. I mean okay."

"Good, now hurry up."

Two hours later and Cardo had fully regained consciousness. He was mumbling. His mouth had been duct taped so we couldn't make out what he was saying. I had sent Cee Cee upstairs because she was having trouble watching the things I was doing to Cardo. I had been asking him 'yes' or 'no' questions about what he had done to the old lady. Each time he he gave me an answer that I didn't like, I would put a lit cigarette out on his chest.

It wasn't long before he was struggling to free himself. Each attempt to undo his hands was greeted with a kick to the ribs. I had Ferris handle the stomping because I didn't want to do it too hard, putting him out of his misery before I had a chance to do what I needed.

It was midnight when Cardo finally broke down. Tears were pouring out of his eyes. I had Ferris take the tape off his mouth just enough to make it possible for me to understand him. "Please," he begged. "It hurts so bad."

I was smiling. "What hurts?"

He was crying his words out, "My ass, my face is burning. Please..." He was begging. "...please let me go to the hospital."

"Okay, I'll take you to the hospital. I swear my life on it, but you have to do one thing."

"Anything," he said and I watched as Ferris' eyes perked open.

"Tell me about what happened and why you killed the old lady."

He closed his eyes tight, stopping the tears and he began, "Man, I was high. I just wanted some money. I knew she had some because she had just left the store and I saw her put change into her purse. I followed her home." He paused. "I almost didn't do it. But when I knocked on her door, she opened it. I forced my way in there and when I demanded the money, she wouldn't give it to me."

"Why didn't you just take her purse and leave?"

"She had taken the money out of her purse. Then she wouldn't tell me where it was. The next thing I remember...I was in a rage. She fell to the floor and..." He began to ramble, "Little bro, you know the game out there. C'mon. I respect you man. I respect your gangsta. I respect you."

"Okay, I heard enough." I hid my disgust. I was in the presence of a man who truly had no real right to walk the Earth. I finally felt compelled to do GOD's work. "Help him up, Ferris. Tape his mouth back shut."

"But you said..." he forced the words out before Ferris had him taped up, "...you said you would take me to get some help."

"I am. I just don't want you yelling outside, trying to call attention to us. You are going to hop your ass to the car. I need your address and your momma's address. If I hear about this from the police, everyone you know dies. Ya' feel me?"

He nodded like he had just won the New York Lotto.

Within seconds, he was on his feet hopping to the car. Ferris cut his hands free and he wrote the addresses down.

Ferris held his gun on Cardo while I used the cuffs in my glove compartment to secure his hands behind his back. "We takin' your car," I said and nodded in the direction of the beat-up Chevy Lumina.

"Okay," he mumbled.

"Wait right here. Ferris, go get everything you took in the house." He returned with everything and I packed it up. Cardo stood patiently waiting for his ride to the hospital. When Ferris returned, I whispered instructions into his ear. He started Cardo's car and walked around to the back where we were. Ferris had popped the trunk and Cardo looked to see what we were putting in it. Ferris then ran to my car and returned with a can of gasoline that he put in the Lumina's trunk.

Cardo's eyes showed puzzlement and then he looked in my direction just in time to see my fist coming straight for his jaw. I hit him and he stumble back. I hit him twice more and he dropped to his knees. I then kicked him in the back causing him to fall forward. He was as defenseless as an old woman, I thought to myself as I began wrapping the rope around his ankles. I tied his ankles so securely that I could have dangled him over the Brooklyn Bridge in 100 miles per hour wind, and he would have dangled for hours. I then tied the other end to the iron beams inside of his trunk.

Ferris then taped the trunk down as far as it would go over the rope. "Okay follow me. Stay close, but not too close," I said with a smile pointing to Cardo who was on the ground squirming.

I put the car in gear and pulled off flooring the pedal. I dragged him mostly up and down the residential streets in Bushwich. I ended up on Myrtle headed west. As fate would have it, I was catching every light. Ferris was right behind me. He was only fourteen but could drive his ass off. I imagined the pain that Cardo was feeling as he was dragged at forty miles an hour. I hung right on Bushwick Avenue and then left on Flushing. Once I reached The Woodhull Medical and Mental Center I stopped. I moved lightening fast. Within moments, Ferris and I had dragged Cardo's body into the passenger seat of his car. His clothing and the first three layers of his flesh had been left on the pavement. The only sign of life was the involuntary twitching that he was doing. I was sure it was nothing more than the exposed nerves, but if he was alive I wanted him to feel even more pain. I emptied the container of gas inside the car, lit it, and got into my car and drove off. I had sworn on my life to take him to the hospital and I had delivered good on it.

Twenty minutes later, Ferris and I were eating cheese steaks at Ernie's Pizza in Little Italy. After we ate, I called the police station and told them whose body they would be trying to identify. I had left the watch in a bag next to a tree ten feet away and quickly explained the reason for Cardo's murder. I took Ferris home and headed back to Jersey.

I seldom slept past 9:00 in the morning, but my body and my mind had finally become exhausted. I didn't plan on climbing out of the bed until noon. It was 3:00 a.m. already. I couldn't wait to reach the safety and comfort of the place I would call home for the next day or two. We never stayed in any hotel for more than two nights. I didn't want our faces to become familiar to the front desk workers or maids.

Angel had become an excellent sidekick and I had begun to give her my blind trust. I would call her at night and she would give me the name and address of the hotel that we were staying in.

When I reached the Embassy Suites on I-17, I found her and Diamond, Phil Boogie's daughter, curled up in one of the beds together.

I looked on the counter and saw that there was a shopping bag filled with new underwear, socks and T-shirts. There was another with a fresh pair of Levi's, crisp white shirts, and a new pair of wheat-colored Timberlands. On the ironing board were the *New York Post, The Times*, and the *Herald*. I was anxious to read any coverage of what had happened in the Towers yesterday.

On the front page of the local news, it was there. *Three Officers Slain in Raid in Brooklyn*. The small print under the caption read, *Four gunmen killed and two taken into custody as ATF operation turns deadly*. I read the articles. I had killed Joshua Cavetti, 29, and Chris Jonesboro, 35. It didn't say anything in there about them firing first as we fled. The Towers were going to be on lockdown while the investigation continued.

I looked at the names of the gunmen, and there was Terrell. The other three I didn't recognize the names of. I shook my head and wondered which soldiers had fallen and which were headed up the road.

The shower felt good and I let the water beat down on me for almost a half an hour. While I washed with the foaming black soap, I reflected on my life and what I had become. I had money buried and enough in the safe at my apartment to handle the plan that Double V had devised. I even had $73,000 in a cereal box that belonged to Abraham. He had no idea how much money I had put away for him. He never asked about money, be it getting more or how much I held for him. It wasn't important to him. Besides, he trusted me and knew I'd always have his back.

Every so often, the water would get extremely hot and the burst would burn me. I flinched but didn't move away. I figured it was either GOD or Satan sending me a message… punishment for my deeds or a preview of the heat I was headed for. I climbed out of the shower and crawled into the bed and slept like a baby.

Angel crawled into the bed with me at dawn and we made love quietly as possible while Diamond slept. After we finished, I rolled off of her and fell back into my spot still breathing heavily. Without my having to ask, she began to rub and stroke my back until I fell back to sleep. She had come to know me so well. She was my lover, my homey, and the way she nurtured me, she was more of a mother than I had ever had. She was damned close to perfect.

"Why Planet Hollywood?" Cortez asked when he walked up on me in the lobby. "I thought the ESPN Zone was your spot."

I smiled. "I never get attached to any one spot. You never know where you gonna find me or which way I'm comin' or goin' for that matter."

"Yeah, I'll bet," Cortez replied. "So what's up?"

"That's what I was hoping you could let me know. I'm assuming things are tight in Greenberg?" I asked as the hostess led us to our seat.

Cortez gave a slight chuckle. "That's an understatement."

"So what's up now? Where do you think we need to take it from here?"

"I take it slow. Real slow," he said calmly. The waiter came and brought us menus. We both ordered wings and water.

"So you shuttin' down?" I was taken aback.

"I don't see where I have a choice." He leaned over toward me. "Look, Malik, you looking at one of the few niggas to beat a charge that would have placed me under the RICO Act. I have tiptoed around conspiracy charges, witness intimidation, numerous weapons offenses, obstruction of justice…you fucking name it, I have beat it. But what happened up in the Towers is too much for me to tangle with. The heat is up in that spot right now. Pataki is all over the news for visiting the families of the slain officers. Bloomberg was up in the Courtyard telling residents that a task force is going to clean up the block. Any nigga out there hustling right now is committin' suicide. All it would take is one of my workers to get popped and flip on me and I'm through." He shook his head no. "I don't need it. I'm moving my operation into another gear."

"Oh yeah, and what does that entail?"

He gave me a smirk letting me know he wasn't talking. "Listen, I've put enough dough away to walk away from it all. I'd be a fool to stick around until it's too late for me to move on."

"So what about Doc and Wendell?"

"What about them?" he said in a tone indicating that he held some contempt for the pair of kingpins that he had shared the Greenberg projects with. Our wings came and we both dove in. "They'll move a few blocks over and try to take over some new territory. To each his own, but if I were you, now that the Towers is a done deal, I would stay away from those two. They never really liked you much. And now, you are as they say… expendable."

I nodded and I had to admit I appreciated that he shared that info, but I wasn't the least bit worried about either of them. "So I guess this is it for us?"

"Just about," he answered and smiled at me. "I won't be needing your services for our operation, but I do have a surprise for you. It's sort of a token of my appreciation for your hard work and what you did that night in the Courtyard when the animals tried to take me out of the game. Though I already squared up with you for the other thing you did, or should I say *overdid,* I am indebted to you for that as well."

"Oh that's great but you owe me nothing. You compensated me well. I have no complaints."

Cortez pointed at me like a wise man schooling a fool. "You don't even know what I am going to give you. Slow your roll, youngster." He pulled a sheet of notebook paper out of his jacket pocket. "Do not lose this. As a matter of fact, it would be best if you can memorize it."

He slid the paper over to me and I opened it. I looked and saw six addresses. I looked at him with a puzzled look, then shook my head and laughed. I slid the paper back to him.

"Those are the addresses for Doc and Wendell, their stash houses, and where their girls live," he said thinking I would be impressed.

I sipped my water and stood up. "What makes you think I didn't already have that information?" There was a look of utter surprise on his face as I extended my hand to shake his. "Stay up," I said as I headed off.

I headed for the bathroom before I left to exit the restaurant. On the way into the restroom I made eye contact with a waitress who looked familiar. She was beautiful but innocent looking. She had that "college-girl" look to her and was sporting a customary smile for the customers that was just inviting enough to secure a nice tip, but distant enough to show that she wasn't interested in making friends.

I walked into the bathroom and handled my business. I readjusted my Sig Sauer because the holster had been pressing down on my thigh. I washed my hands and looked into the mirror. I poured over myself for a second wondering if I would have the good fortune to complete everything that I was planning to do.

I walked out of the rest room and was about to leave the restaurant when I felt an arm tap my shoulder. "Malik?" she asked.

Looking at her up close, it came to me and a smile formed on my face. "No," I said, "I know this ain't..." I hadn't seen her since she moved away.

"Malik." She extended her arms to hug me. The waitress that I had seen was Marcella, my childhood sweetheart.

"Girl, it's so good to see you. How the hell you been?" I was shaking my head back and forth. "What happened to you? Where you been?" I had a million questions to ask her.

She stood back. She pulled a strand of hair from her face. "I been just chilling you know, growing up." She laughed a familiar giggle. "Trying to put some dollars together. I'm saving up for school next fall."

"Oh yeah. Where you going?"

"Haven't decided yet. I have the grades for Columbia, but the money for City College." She giggled again. "But it's no thing. I'll do what I gotta." I nodded, "But what about you?" she asked. "I see you still a cutie."

"Stop that for real." I didn't want to feel so crazy, but it was like I was a kid all over again about to ask her to check yes or no in a box. *Would you be my girl?* -style. "I'm just holding shit down. Trying to raise capital to start a business."

I wanted to ask her how much she needed for college, but I didn't want to come off like I was stuntin'.

"Look, I gotta get back to work, but it was nice to see you." She paused, "You have a number?" she asked.

"No doubt." I gave her my cell and two way and was about to walk away.

"Excuse me," she said. I looked at her and she had her hands on her hips. "No Good-bye hug? You too hard or grown for that now?"

"Of course not." I showed her my teeth again.

"Bettah not be frontin', son," she gave me the New Yorka accent. "You know I remember you when you was drawing Dragon Ball Z tattoos on your arm and trying to rap like Lil' Bow Wow."

I held my head down. "Yeah okay." We embraced tightly.

I could smell the scent of her perfume behind her ears. Her lips brushed against my ear as she whispered, "I never forgot about you."

We pulled away and she reached inside her shirt and pulled out a necklace. The necklace was new but the charm I recognized. It was the gold cross that my grandmother had given me one Christmas when I was ten or eleven. I had given it to Marcella on her birthday.

"For protection," she mouthed. That was what I had said to her when I had given it to her.

"For protection," I said back and walked out of the restaurant.

I walked out of the doors wanting to turn back inside to catch another glimpse of Marcella. I made it halfway down the block trying to fill my mind with thoughts of Angel, but it didn't stop me. Moments later, I was back inside. I told the hostess that I had left my eyeglasses. I stood off to the side watching Marcella. Her complexion reminded me of the chocolate river in Willie Wonka's Chocolate Factory. She had jet black silky hair like an Indian. She looked good even in her waitress clothes. She hadn't grown an inch since her thirteenth birthday, but it was fine. She had filled out in all the right places and was on her way to becoming a perfect ten.

There was way more to her though than her physical appearance. I could feel something from her clear across the room. I couldn't put my finger on it but her presence was moving me in ways that I had never experienced. I took in all of her that I could before I left for the second time.

TWENTY

Fantasies are closer to reality than most people ever dare dream. There is an imaginary line created by society that separates most people from their dreams. The line is called normalcy. What is normal for children growing up in the ghetto is unacceptable for those who grow up in an upper class world. The world teaches people to be average, but only applauds those who excel. It's simple logic. Without the normal, the extraordinary don't shine. Choosing to make one's fantasy a reality is no more difficult or scary than choosing and subjecting oneself to live a life of normalcy. It's up to each individual to choose what constitutes an incredible life for them. Everybody doesn't need a bunch of fame and fortune. However, everyone should strive to live out his or her ultimate purpose. For the best part of the fantasy isn't the destination... it's the journey.

Tasha was doing a good job of keeping my mind off of everything that I had been thinking about. We had a great time in Jimmy's and had spent most of the night talking to each other in the booths by the bar. People were staring, trying to figure out who she was and why she was being catered to.

We ended up hanging out two days later to do some shopping and then went out on what felt like a date the following Friday. Things were slow since the Towers had been shut down. Malik had instructed me to stay at the Marriot over in Englewood, New Jersey for the week. Since I had nothing but time on my hands, Tasha's calls for company came as a welcome diversion.

The morning after we had gone out, she called me and asked me to meet her at her new apartment out in Queens. She said that she needed someone to talk to and when I arrived, she was acting a little frantic. She'd greeted me at the door in a NYFD T-shirt and a pair of cut-off jean shorts. I noticed how short they were as the bottoms of her cheeks jiggled as she made her way into the kitchen. "Take a seat at the breakfast bar, Abraham," she commanded.

Moments later, I had a plate full of home fries, eggs, and French toast. "Wow, it's like that?"

"Yeah, I love to cook, especially when I'm nervous. I get to cookin' and eatin' every damned thing I can find." She patted her belly, "Luckily, I never gain a pound."

"Oh yeah, that's a good thing with you being a celeb and all." I paused and blessed my food before I dug in. "Good, real good," I said as I took in another fork full of the French toast.

"Good, I'm glad you like it." She wasn't eating but came out of the kitchen and took a seat next to me. "So listen, let me tell you why I asked you over."

She then began to explain why she was feeling so uptight. She was having problems with her manager who happened to be a pretty popular producer. "This nigga been threatening me. Telling me that if I don't sign certain papers, that he is gonna make life real miserable for me." She gave a detailed account of the affair that made it obvious that the guy was seeing dollar signs. He hadn't been as interested in her until she had been offered a high six-figure deal. Now he wanted a piece.

"So what is he threatening to do?"

"You name it. One day violence, the next day some other shit."

I was curious so I didn't hesitate to ask, "Like what?"

She stood up and walked over to the couch and plopped down. "I messed around and fucked this nigga a few months back. He videotaped it and now he talking 'bout the internet and a bunch of other shit."

"How do you know he has the tape?"

"He sent me a copy, and believe me it's real clear."

"So he wants money, right?"

She put her foot up on her glass coffee table. "You could say that. If I sign with him, he'll get a third of everything I make for the next three years."

"Alright, so you said you have a copy of the tape, right?" She nodded. "Why don't you release the tape yourself? It's going to happen anyway. He will never destroy the tape. He'll just come back and hold it over your head again in three more years." She was silent. "You sell it to the bootleggers for a chunk of change. You come out with a press conference telling the young girls not to make the same mistakes. You look like a martyr and you defame him at the same time."

"I would be so embarrassed."

"Well you *did* what you did. The only way to overcome it is to face it head on. Don't let your fear of him or public shame, rule you. Fear nothing but GOD."

"You're right, ya' know?"

"For sure. I mean you could seriously flip this to your advantage and go on the Wendy Show and generate more publicity before your CD drops."

Light bulbs must have been going off in her mind. Her eyes brightened and she added, "Look at Paris Hilton."

"Who?"

"The little rich bitch with the TV show. Someone has a fuck tape of her and all that shit did was generate mad press." She kept on, "There was a time when her show would have been pulled before it even hit the air, but now all it did was probably raise her visibility."

"Word. It's all about the spin and the perspective. If it comes from your mouth, it's not like you're the victim."

There was silence and she stared directly into my eyes. "You know something, Abraham? You're right." I smiled as I got up to clean my plate, but she jumped up and said, "No, I got it." She cleaned it and set it to dry in her stainless steel dish drainer. When she finished, she walked over to me and gave me a big hug. "Thank you so much."

Her hair was curly and flowed down past her shoulders. It was a combination of sandy brown with blond highlights. It matched her pecan- colored skin. I hadn't yet made out her ethnicity. She could have been black, Cuban, Dominican, or Puerto Rican. She was finer than a model though and fit the role of a rap chick. The diamonds in her ears screamed, *Pay me.* Even in her round-the-house clothes, she was conveniently sexy. During the hug, I felt myself harden and when she noticed, she backed away and bit her bottom lip.

"Come with me up into the loft," she said seductively. She took my hand long enough to get me to the stairs. As she moved up the steps, I watched the bottoms of her cheeks as they peeked out from under the frayed edges of her shorts.

I couldn't believe that it was happening. Why she was choosing me, I didn't know. She was Tasha Robb, the hottest thing out right now. She had been all over the Kay Slay mix tapes and was soon to be the talk of Wendy Williams once the home video hit the streets. There was no doubt that she was lusted after by the masses already. I had to admit that I had dreamed and even masturbated thinking of her since the first night I had met her. Now here I was following her to her bed.

I had rushed over when she called and hadn't taken a shower this morning, so when I made it upstairs, I asked if I could take a quick shower. She ran the water for me and said, "Hurry," as she placed a thick yellow towel and facecloth on the toilet seat.

The steam was hypnotic and I painted the picture of what I was going to do with her once I got out of the shower. Every time I thought of her, I got nervous and had to let the warm water beat on my back and on top of my fro to relax me. I stepped out of the shower and put my wet feet on her rug.

I quickly wiped off the excess water and headed out of the bathroom. Her room was darkened. The curtains must have been thick because it looked as if the sun had set and the only thing that kept the room illuminated were the ten-inch candles burning on the nightstands.

I crept slowly into the room and noticed Tasha's movements on the bed. As I moved closer to her, I saw that her head was hanging off the edge of the bed. She was squeezing her breasts with one hand, massaging her pussy with the other. I could hear her breaths increase as I moved toward her. When I reached the edge of the bed, I could see that her hair was hanging to the floor and she opened her mouth as she reached for me with her hand. She guided me into her mouth and began sucking me like she owned my manhood.

My knees buckled slightly because the tongue action was just that nice. The way that she was positioned, her tongue was stroking the top side of my penis, tickling the head. Instinctively, I leaned forward and found my mouth at her entrance. She tasted sweet and I licked with my best effort.

"Oh yeah, baby," she said. She tried to continue sucking me, but it was obvious that I was messing up her concentration.

"I can't take it," she breathed out and removed me from her mouth.

"Spin around. Put your head on those pillows." She complied and scooted back onto the bed. I crept up on her like a lion onto fallen prey, pinning her legs up into the air. My hands were on the bends of her legs, spreading them apart as I moved my face back into her neatly trimmed bush.

"Shit. Oh no. Ohhh Shit!" she screamed as my tongue began to dance inside her. I painted a picture running my lips across hers only stopping on her clit. "You need to write a book, boy." Two short breaths. "Nobody has ever licked me so perfect." I kept at it but let her legs down.

Eating her felt so good, it was as if I was the one being pleasured. It was a dream come true. I thought about all the men who had probably dreamed of doing to Tasha exactly what I was doing. When she began to hump my face, I knew that I had found a rhythm that would take her over the top. I French-kissed her clit, pulled her lips apart with my tongue and guided the tip of it across, around and over her clit until I felt her drench my mouth and face with her juices. Her stomach muscles tightened and she let out a grunt. "Oh, oh, I'm about to... oohhh. Yeah baby, yeah baby...I'm there. Eeeeehhh, yeah...I'm cumming...I'm cum...I can't stop cumming... I...can't...I'm...still....stop...what...you...tryin'...oh yeah! I love it... baby, don't stop." She was bucking uncontrollably, grabbing my head and humping my face. Her whole body shook, tensed and then collapsed onto the mattress.

"Give me a second," she asked. I did not comply. I began rubbing the tip of my dick against her pussy. I asked for a rubber. She didn't move. I tried to think sensibly but was too wound up and pushed my dick inside of her. More moaning. I was stroking her long and hard. Her eyes were glassy. "You can have this. I belong to you, Abraham," she was talking seductively, making promises that I'd heard before. "You feel so good." I was drifting inside her ocean. I could make out the flames in the background. I could see her head thrashing back and forth, and I could feel her fingers on the small of my back, pulling me deeper with each stroke. What I couldn't feel was the passage of time. It seemed like hours since I had left the rest of the world behind as I entered hers. I was halfway dreaming, halfway feeling when she interrupted me.

"Let me ride you," she offered. I rolled off of her and flat onto my back. She climbed on top of me with her back facing me. I watched her hair as she leaned forward and back, grinding her crotch against me. She grabbed my ankles and placed her feet flat on the bed as she began to bounce. "Oh yeah, I can cum like this, baby," she screamed and she did. She collapsed this time and fell back onto my chest. I rolled her over onto her stomach and entered her as she lay flat on the bed. I pushed one knee up so that I could slide easily into her. She opened up and began to breathe heavily. I felt my orgasm building up and couldn't hold it any longer. I had every intention of pulling it out, but I got lost in the mix as I began squirting into her. "Oh cum for me, baby. Feel good, baby. Shoot it all."

I let out a terrific sigh as I fell off of her and rolled to her side.

Moments later, we were staring at each other. I was wondering how often she had unprotected sex and why she had allowed me to. I figured she had to be thinking the same thing.

"Abraham, I've never had unprotected sex in my life," she said as she ran a finger across my lips. "I know that you probably have, but I just didn't want you to think that... you know, I've told you about the tape. I just didn't want you to think I was some slut."

"I didn't think that at all. As a matter of fact, this is only the third time in my life I've slipped up and done something like that."

"That's good 'cause I got a lot to live for."

"No doubt."

"I meant what I said," she shot at me.

"Oh yeah. What part?"

"It's yours if you want it. Whenever you want it."

"What makes you think you want me? You could have anyone you want, a baller...shit, you could get a nigga like Baby from the Cash Money Millionaires. You did a song with him right?"

"Yeah, but I just want something real."

"What makes you so sure I'm real?"

"Like Common said, *It don't take all day to recognize sunshine*. You the real thing and it shows. You got a good vibe. Spirituality. I can feel it. I'm drawn to it." She sat up and said, "You know what's kind of strange?"

"What's that?"

"From the moment Bing came home and told me about what you did for him, I wanted to meet you. He described you and I felt like I had to know you in some form. I was so turned on by you and didn't even know you. The only thing I knew was that when I saw you last week at Jimmy's... I wasn't letting you get away." I smiled and closed my eyes. I felt valued and wondered what role we would play in one another's lives.

I was drifting off to sleep when I said to her, "Yo, T."

"Yeah, baby."

"You're beautiful and everything is gonna be alright."

"Thank you. I needed that."

"You know what else?"

"No, tell me."

"You are my fantasy come true."

"That's so sweet, but guess what?"

"Now I'm your reality."

I let it marinate as I drifted off into the deepest sleep I had enjoyed in months.

"Why are you having so much trouble answering the call, Abraham?"

"Who is that?"

"Oh, my son, you know who this is. Now answer me. With all this wickedness, where are you headed?"

I didn't have an answer. I couldn't make an excuse and I felt shame wash over me.

"Surely you don't think you are doing my work. Do you think I brought you this far for you to become a star on the other team?"

"No, I know better than that."

"Well then. Haste makes waste, my child. There is much work to be done starting with you."

"What do you mean?"

"There are many mysteries and much knowledge unattainable to man. But, Abraham, my son, I know that you are aware. Simply take a look, a long look at yourself. You will soon need to make the tough decisions and move forward. Move toward what you know is right. I'll be waiting."

"How will I know when the time is right? How can I be sure?"

"You have all the answers you need already. Just remember to share what you know and feel. It will enable you

to bring someone with you. Someone who you don't think will come willingly is going to surprise you. Just ask them to join you in your quest to find favor in my house."

"What if I make the wrong choices?"

"Then you will have the blood of the innocent on your hand. The children will be lost on your watch."

When I heard that, a chill shook through my body, then another. I was so cold and fighting to get warm. The next moment, I awoke when I felt the cold air blowing across my legs. I sat up and saw that the window was open. I looked over and noticed that Tasha wasn't in the bed with me anymore. I stood up and closed the window. I headed down the steps and saw no sign of her in the living room then I heard her in the kitchen. I walked into the kitchen ass naked and jumped back when an older Hispanic woman was in the kitchen cooking.

She smiled at me. "You were expecting Miss Tasha, no?"

"Yes I was," I said covering myself.

"Well, she had business in the city. I am her cooking and cleaning." She used her hands to speak. "No minda me."

"I'm sorry. I didn't know you were here." I headed back upstairs. I heard her giggling as I moved quickly.

"She say to tell you she be back in two, three hours. You can stay. Have some bean salad. I make it so delicious. Miss Tasha ask for it all the time," she shouted up the steps.

"Okay," I yelled back. "I may run out for a while too." I was so embarrassed there was no way I could wait there after the senorita had seen my goods.

"Suit yourself," she said.

Three minutes later, I was out the door and on the Long Island Expressway headed nowhere doing fifteen over the speed limit.

TWENTY-ONE

Planning is necessary in order to launch any attack or movement that hopes to have measurable success. Great planners are those who plan from experience. Gifted planners are those who are able to effectively plan from the experiences of others. Wise are those that can combine the two. While textbooks, training and simulation are all great means of preparation, nothing compares to battle-tested nerves and experience. Naturally, it pays to be good at what you do in the heat of battle, but warriors use their instincts as well as their intellect. Both the elements of fear and surprise are vital in overcoming opponents. However, when it comes down to it, a wise man once said, "It's just as important to be lucky as it is to be good."

I pulled up in front of the address on St. Nick, hit the horn and circled once just like he told me to. On the second time around, I saw a light flash in an apartment and took a space across the street. "You ready, man?" I asked Abraham.

He nodded his head but I wasn't convinced. I was beginning to really doubt if his heart was in it. "Listen, man," I said. "If you ain't down, just say so. You can cash out now. I got close to seventy-five gees for you in the safe at my spot. You can bounce with that and I won't love you any less."

Abraham's head was down and I realized he was praying. "Man, what the fuck you praying for, nigga? We ain't going to church. We up in Harlem and you know what they say."

I had interrupted him and he was irritated. "Nah Malik, what do they say?"

"They say there's Hell up in Harlem." He laughed. "C'mon, my nigga. You strapped right?"

We got out of the car. I looked at Abraham as he moved around the car. We both had on black cargo pants, black Eddie Bauer ski jackets, so he at least looked like he was ready to put in work.

As we crossed the street and headed toward the building, I noticed a few guys out in front of the building. "Keep your hands visible, Abraham. We don't want to spook anybody, ya' feel me?"

"No doubt."

The way we were dressed, I didn't want to look like the stick-up boys.

"What's good, son?" one of the guys said. I ignored him and walked right past him. "It's like that?"

I kept it moving, giving no expression. Abraham followed suit. The hallway was dimly lit so I pulled out the toaster and walked cautiously up against the wall. I hit the second floor and Abraham was right behind me. I was glad to see that he had his pistol out without me having to tell him.

I cleared the banister and walked back toward the apartment where the light had flashed. I was two steps away from the door's entrance when it swung open. I paused for second and heard, "Boy, get your ass in here." My Uncle Kelly was standing in the door.

I smiled and walked inside. "Hey Uncle, this is my partner." He extended his hand to Abraham and shook it firmly.

"Nice to finally meet you, son. My nephew has spoken of you often."

"It's good to meet you too."

As instructed, I used no names and none were used on me. I had gone over that with Abraham ten times before we arrived. He had learned his lesson and I had warned him that a slip-up around criminals of this caliber could bring his life to an end.

Once inside the apartment, I realized that I was the last to arrive. The front room of the apartment was empty and it was obvious it had just been painted. There was plastic all over the floor in the living room and rollers in the corner. There was commotion in the next room and we followed my uncle there.

Immediately, my eyes met with my grandfather's and a rush of emotions rolled through me that I contained. I had never seen him as a free man and I was overjoyed, but none of the men in the room were to know that we were related. He was seated at the end of an oversized glass dining room table. He was looking like he had never left the streets. He was wearing a black Hugo Boss sweatshirt, black and grey fatigues and a pair of Nike ACG hiking boots. He had on a doo-rag, covering his tapered haircut. The only way you would know that you were in the presence of one of the most notorious criminals in the history of New York City was the way he commanded and received respect from everyone in the room.

Double V nodded at me and winked an eye. "You gentlemen can have a seat. We're only waiting on one more person, I believe."

Abraham and I took a seat at the far end of the table. I took a look around at the six men seated. They all looked to be older than thirty-five. A couple of them looked older than my grandfather. I noticed one of the men staring at me like he knew me. I was getting annoyed and was about to ask him if he had a fucking problem but knew that my outburst wouldn't be appreciated by my elders, so I just chilled and shot him an ice grill right back.

I felt a little out of place with all the old heads until I thought about the fact that I was the one funding this whole operation. I could smell that someone passed gas and immediately my attention was stuck on the fat guy across from me. He looked too jolly to be into crime with his stinkin' ass, but if he was gangsta enough to be in my grandfather's presence, then he must have been down. My eyes flashed back to the front room when I noticed my Uncle Kelly flash the light on and off. I assume he was signaling the last person coming.

"Anyone hungry or thirsty? Grab it now because once I start, there won't be anything going on but listening." Double V got up and headed into the kitchen and grabbed a bottle of tomato juice. He took it straight to his head and opened a second. Two more of the men walked into the kitchen to grab beverages and by the time they were seated, my uncle had let the last man in.

Just then, Abraham leaned over to me and carefully whispered, "Yo Malik, you recognize that big dude right there?"

I turned and took another look at who he was talking about. It was the guy with the staring problem. "Nah, you?"

"Remember in the summer when we came up here to eat and the girls went to that book fair? That's the same guy we almost got into it with in front of the soul food spot." I took another glance and it came back to me. He looked roughly the same, but with the skull cap and the thick hoodie on, it was difficult to make him out. But, I instantly remembered the teardrop tattoos under his eye.

"Oh hell yeah, I remember his ass."

He must have heard me, because he turned and looked at me and a smile appeared on his face. "What's up, little nigga?" he said and extended his fist to me.

He held it there. I decided to give him the respect of a pound back. "What's good?"

"Holdin' shit down, 'bout to make this power move." He gave a half-hearted laugh. "I told you we'd get to dance another day. Let's be glad that it's on these terms, fair enough?"

I nodded my head. "Yeah, let's be glad."

Just then, the door opened and a white dude walked in. Double V walked out of the kitchen and commanded everyone to sit. "I will assume that everyone knows why they're here. I also assume, sir, that you will respect my time from now on and take whatever means necessary so that you are precise with your times of arrival." The last comment was directed to the white dude.

"My apologies. I don't get up this end much. I got a little turned around."

Double V nodded his acceptance. "No need to apologize. Just understand that whatever adjustments you need to make to be prompt are mandatory. I guess you could say it's always a life or death kind of thing, ya' dig?"

The man nodded his head.

"Okay, gentlemen, here we go." Double V stood up. "My name is Vincent Vaughn. I'm also known as Double V in the streets and the ladies call me Double Deep between the sheets, but that's whole nutha' story. The bottom line is this. My name is the only name that any of you need to know in this room. I am also the only one who knows each of your names. It is no secret that I know where your parents live, where your kids go to school, where your fucking dogs get groomed." He began walking around the table and stopped when he was positioned behind me. "I don't beat around the bush or sugarcoat anything, so here is the law. If any of you ever speak my name to anyone, friend or foe, and I find out about it, and make no mistake, I will find out, I will annihilate you and every living thing that you care about. I don't say this to scare you. I say this to keep things, as the youngsters say, *real*. It won't get any realer than me having the fingers chopped off of your six-year-old or having your momma's tongue cut out her mouth. If you really piss me off, I will fuck around and cut the tail off your dog and pull his ass inside out, ya' dig?" The room was so quiet, you could hear a mouse shit on cotton. "The bottom line is this. We are about to get paid. If everything goes according to plan, none of us in this room will ever have to think about lifting a finger for the rest of our lives. But..." He cleared his throat. "...There's always a but. With every move, there is always the chance that shit could go wrong and any one of us could be left holding the bag. Of course that would bring a shit-load of time. So if you are ready to do the crime, be ready to face the time."

"On my honor," one of the men said.

"I'm all in."

"I know you are all in," Double V said. "You all know too much anyway by now. Bottom line is this, we got this thing sewed up tight as it can be. The odds are in our favor."

"We are about to pull off the heist of the century and disappear into thin air. Each of you has indicated to me where you would like to relocate. Once we meet up after the job, I will, in exchange for a slice of your portion, provide you each with two identities and properties in your chosen locales. Now, since I am trusting you, you have no choice but to trust me. I have always operated in a code of honor and integrity. Greed has never ruled me and I advise you to be sure that it doesn't get the best of you."

Double V outlined the plan. It took him two hours to go over each detail. We were robbing a super-armored car that would be leaving Atlantic City heading to Philadelphia after the Bernard Hopkins and William Joppy fight in two weeks. Double V's contacts had told him that the truck would be carrying the cash receipts from six major casinos. This could mean anywhere from thirty to forty million dollars.

The men asked him all sorts of questions, starting from how we were going to transport the money once we had stolen it. I was the only one who he didn't give a job to. He even assigned Abraham a position as a driver. Once he finished with the questions, he stood and said, "Alright gentlemen, I will be in touch with you and give you all the directions you need regarding when and where we will meet next. I would also like to commend you all on your choice of attire tonight. I told you to come dressed in your work clothes and I am satisfied with your appearance tonight. Remember, silence is golden. I am leaving now and my assistant will dismiss you one at a time. He will give you specific directions on which way to drive when you leave here. Failure to follow his directions will be taken as gross disrespect and could prove to be very hazardous, gentlemen. Thank you for your time." He was up and out the door. My Uncle Kelly dismissed the white man first, then me and Abraham. I made eye contact with the teardrop as I left the room. He gave me a bad feeling.

I followed the instructions Uncle Kelly gave me and Double V was on the corner of 118th Street waiting for me. Abraham jumped into the back seat and my grandfather jumped in.

"Son, it's so good to see you."

"I know. I can't believe you're home." I smiled. "What does it feel like?"

"Shit, it feels like work. That's all these streets ever meant to me. I work these blocks, cities, states and governments like the whores that they are. No time for nostalgia. Always business... almost always."

He gave me a series of directions and as I drove, he gave me the lowdown on each of the men that we were working with. He told me the names to match the faces then we drove to the spot where each one lived and frequented. He told me that in case something happened to him within the next two weeks, I needed to be able to handle the entire operation. Abraham sat quietly in the back.

"You okay back there, son?" Double V asked.

"Yes, sir."

"Well alright then. I don't like no quiet motherfuckers behind me. Sing or make some fucking noise, boy," Double V barked.

Abraham was still quiet as if he was wondering what he should do. After a few seconds of nervous quiet, he spoke up, "What you want me to sing?"

Double V looked at Abraham and then to me. The next thing I knew he burst into laughter. "Boy, you alright." He laughed loud. "Malik says you family. Lighten the fuck up. I'm just foolin' with ya', son."

Abraham breathed a sigh of relief as my grandfather continued on with his conversation. He started back up about the scheme.

I was surprised when he disclosed the jobs that some of the men seated at the table held. One of the men, named Lawson, had done fifteen years for armed robbery and had gotten a whole new ID, work history and a CDL all from Double V the day he had come home from the pen. Now he drove a tractor-trailer dragging BMW's up and down I-95.

Jeremiah worked in Richmond, doing demolition for a construction company. He had rigged a few explosive devices for the right prices over the years. The white guy, Dennis, was a pilot. He flew the personal jet of one of the members of the Walton family. When they weren't using the jet, they sometimes rented it out for $100,000 per weekend. He was paid well by them, but not well enough to keep him from wanting to steal a couple million dollars. Bobby was the fat guy. He owned a warehouse that was located off of the Black Horse Pike fifteen miles outside of Atlantic City. He was also a New Jersey State Trooper. Caldwell was the big guy with the teardrop tattoos. I wasn't surprised to find out that his talent was muscle. The sixth man, Navan, was a driver for Bricks Armored. He was responsible for sharing the entire layout and routine for the company. There was no surprise that he had taken the job two years earlier with the purpose of setting up the robbery.

My Uncle Kelly, was a mastermind at finding information that people wanted to keep private. Double V explained that he limited Kelly's involvement in his plots because he had learned long ago that his brother didn't have the heart to put in the hardcore work. He also knew that Kelly was of better use to him by remaining fairly legit and on the streets. In the event that the police ever questioned my uncle, he would have nothing to tell. Early on the two of them had agreed never to discuss anything other than what was absolutely necessary regarding Double V's activities. He explained that he could pay Kelly for info without disclosing why he needed it. Other than the occasional visit, they had also kept their contact to a minimum, and never spoke of one another to anyone.

We drove around for another forty minutes until he directed me to pull into an empty parking space on Audubon. "C'mon, you two. Your car will be fine right here."

It was almost 2:30 in the morning and I was hoping he was ready to call it a night, but he walked two cars up and opened the doors to a black Crown Victoria. He went to the trunk and pulled out a paper sack and jumped into the driver's seat. "Damn, it's getting cold out here," I said as I locked the doors to the car.

"You ain't lying. Hey, where you think he's taking us? I was supposed to meet Tasha about two hours ago."

"Just come on. Whatever you do, don't ask him shit. You'll see her whenever we finish with him."

The engine started and my grandfather yelled out of the window. "Step lively, youngsters. I ain't got all night. I got some pussy waiting on me in the Bronx when we finish."

Abraham and I just looked at each other and laughed as we got in. He turned the volume up as he pulled off. He had some old school music blasting. "Who's dat?"

"The late, great, Minnie Ripperton. You like that?"

"It's alright."

"Alright my ass. That's music right there. I used to date her. She was something else."

He began telling us stories about his great romance as we headed up to the GW Bridge and cruised into Jersey. Double V stopped at a 24-hour mart and grabbed some donuts and coffee and came right back out to the car. Fifteen minutes later, we were in Secaucus rolling down a residential street. "It shouldn't be long now," he laughed out loud.

"So what are we doing out here?"

Double V sipped his coffee and at the same time began to fumble with the sack that was next to him. "This house belongs to a secretary down at the District Court of New York.

She also happens to be the mistress of Judge Simon Roby. That Cadillac in the driveway is his."

Minnie was crooning about going back down memory lane and hitting the highest of high notes. Double V's eyes closed as if he could see her singing them.

He went on. "He usually heads home between 3 and 4:00 in the morning to his wife. Tonight he won't make it home."

"Why do you want to kill a judge?" Abraham asked.

Double V's eyes were closed even as he spoke. His words flowed almost lyrically. "First off, I'm not going to kill him. You two are. Second, he wasn't a judge twenty-five years ago. He was an assistant district attorney. He's the reason why I did so much time. Originally he worked out a deal with my lawyer where I would do three to five, max. Then, at the last minute, he pulled it off the table because the state indicted me on additional charges. He was so connected downtown that my lawyers were unable to get my trial delayed. Later it came out that he never intended to accept my plea and only presented it to keep my lawyer, Harold Troy from preparing properly."

"But wasn't that your lawyer's fault too?" I asked.

"Damned right it was." He paused and bit into his donut. "That sonofabitch has been dead for twenty-three years." He then pulled out a black Browning nine-millimeter pistol that had a silencer on it. "When the lights come on I want you to go over behind that tree, son." He was talking to Abraham. "When he is getting into the car, kill him and take his wallet and the car. Then, follow me closely. We'll dump the car and make it look like a car-jacking and robbery."

Abraham was silent. "But don't you want him to know why he is dying? What's the point in killing for revenge if you don't make the victim stare into your eyes and beg for mercy?" Now my grandfather was silent. "I'll do it for the hell of it, but

I think you owe it to yourself to walk up on that fucker and make him remember your name."

"You might be right, son," he answered. It was strange, but suddenly I felt a lack of respect for my grandfather. I was a little displeased that he had asked Abraham to kill for him. He didn't know Abraham well enough to assume he would handle a job right or if he was in fact a killer at all.

Moments later, the lights came on upstairs followed by the porch light five minutes later. The front door opened and I was surprised to see a black man come out of the front door. He kissed the woman on the lips and headed down the steps toward the driveway. Double V reached to unlock the car door and began to open it. "Wait," Abraham yelled out.

"What?"

"She's still at the door," Abraham said. "She's watching him to his car."

"Damn," Double V said as he watched Simon climb into his car and start it. His fingers were tapping on the steering wheel as he watched his Cadillac back out of the drive way and head up the street. "Put your seatbelt on," he said as he took the last hit of his coffee. He pulled out and smashed on the gas. Simon made a right at the first stop sign and we turned right behind him. At the next corner, the light turned red and when Simon's car stopped we barreled right into his rear. Double V wanted to make sure that the Crown Vic was still rolling, so he backed it up a little. "You two duck down in the seats and don't come up." Then he pulled up to the side of the judge's car. Simon looked a little disoriented. Double V jumped out and asked, "Hey, you alright?"

Simon opened up his car door holding his neck. "What are you, drunk or something?" He walked around to the back of his car and screamed, "Jeezzus. Look what you've done.

This is a brand new car. Let me see your registration, license and insurance infor…"

"I know it's a new car, Simon," Double V said pulling the pistol out of his coat pocket.

"Hey," he yelled out. "Don't shoot. It's okay. It's only a car. I'll fix it myself, you go ahead."

Double V laughed. "Simon, now you and I both know that a square shooting pit-bull like yourself would never let anyone slide. You'd write my tag number down and have every cop in Jersey and New York looking for me."

"How do you know my name?" he asked nervously.

"Look at my face. Or have you sent too many of us to jail to remember faces. How about a name?" Simon had a worried but blank stare on his face. "Does the name Vincent Vaughn ring a bell?"

There was a pause before, "I think it does."

Simon was shaking now. I was looking and couldn't take my eyes off of the drama. Abraham was still ducked in his seat. "That was so long ago."

"You damned right, it was almost half a lifetime ago for me. I see you have moved right up the ranks. I've been following your career closely. From crooked D.A. to crooked judge, I presume."

"Hey, man, I was just doing my job."

"Bullshit!" my grandfather yelled. He then went on to explain the details of his case. "You have any idea what it's like to be locked up for five times longer than you should have been? Of course you don't. But here tonight, I am going to send you to your permanent cell, you piece of shit."

"But… but…"

"But what?" Double V moved closer to him.

"But… you were guilty of all those crimes." The man was crying. "They told me that I had to get a major conviction and slow the crime down. Harlem was going downhill. You were feeding off of your own people."

"The same way you fed off of me. I launched your career. You made a decision, but you didn't weigh the cost."

"I don't know what you're talking about."

"I'm sure when you were busy fucking me into a twenty-five-to-life sentence, you weren't counting on me holding a grudge all this time. Now my time is served and yours is up."

"Noooo. I have children...I..." The silencer made the shots unnoticeable other than the fire that erupted from the barrel. I watched as Double V hit the judge twice to the chest and once to the head.

He climbed back into the car and we pulled off. "So how you feel?" I asked.

"Like a million bucks," he said. I looked back at Abraham and the look on his face told me that he simply didn't understand.

Abraham told me that he was headed out of town with his new girl for Thanksgiving. He had been acting real strange since meeting this girl. I wasn't sure if he was in love or going through some changes about Sondra's pregnancy. All I knew about his new love was that her name was Tasha. Usually, he told me every detail, blow by blow, when he starting getting a new piece, but he had kept unusually silent about this girl. I didn't care, it was his right to keep silent. Knowing him, I figured that either he wasn't tapping the ass or he was on some respect type hype with her.

I had started creeping around a bit myself seeing Marcella. Things had changed in the time that we had been apart. Angel was my heart, but I couldn't stop thinking bout Marcella. It was like unfinished business with her. Angel never got suspicious or asked questions because I had run the streets the entire time we were dating. As far as Marcella, I had been spending a lot of my down time at her apartment. She had gotten real comfortable, walking around in wife beaters with her ass jiggling in her thongs. The first night that I had tried to push up on it, she had told me she wasn't ready. She said that she was feeling me, but she wasn't into casual sex, so I took my time. I had taken her on a weekend trip down to D.C. to do some shopping. We had gone to see R. Kelly at the MCI Center and shopped up at the Mazza Gallery. I let her go crazy in Filene's Basement and Saks. The way to a woman's heart is through the mall.

We stayed in D.C. at the Four Seasons Hotel for three days and I didn't even try her the first night. On the second night, she climbed all over me in the elevator, kissing my neck, pulling my shirt up. I pulled the emergency stop and we got busy for the first time right there between the seventh and eight floors.

It was strange sharing passion with someone whom I had been so connected to yet given up on so long ago. I entertained feelings of hurt and excitement all at the same time. She had vanished from my life without a trace. Though I knew it was beyond her control, I still harbored some resentment. When she moved away without so much as a good-bye, she reinforced for me the belief that women were undependable. My mother had introduced it. That night in the elevator glaring into each other's eyes, she showed me with her passion that perhaps she never had given up on me and that maybe young love never died.

TWENTY-TWO

Love is by far the most powerful emotion. At the same time it is the most mysterious and difficult to control. Most people long for it yet never invite it into their lives. Some love junkies get a taste of it and crave more than they can afford. This often proves disastrous because, contrary to what most say, love does cost. Love is the emotion that demands all the attention and spotlight. Not answering love's call causes it to wither and die, or worse shatter into pieces of rage, jealousy, hurt, anger, resentment and sometimes vengeance. Nurtured though, love is a many splendid thing. It can make an old man feel young and a young man feel like dancing. Real good love is like a favorite song that never stops playing.

"**What** you mean you don't feel like dancing?" Tasha was pulling on my arms and I knew I had no choice but to hit the floor with her.

The rest of the club was packed but we were behind the VIP rope. I had been sipping champagne on a couch with Tasha Robb draped all over me. I had been catching stares from men and women alike wondering who I was and why she was all over me.

We made our way onto the dance floor and people were screaming at Tasha, "Great show!"

"Thanks," she had yelled back. "CD drops December 16."

We hit the floor surrounded by security. We danced for an hour straight until we were both sweating. The club had been packed for Tasha's performance and was getting hotter by the miute. It was a promotional event arranged by the record company but paid for by a local promoter. He had made a killing because when we arrived, the line at Liquid was wrapped around the building. It was the night before Thanksgiving and people had come out ready to party. We were in South Beach and people partied every night of the week regardless.

In the morning, we were driving up to Fort Lauderdale to have Thanksgiving dinner with my grandmother, but tonight we were enjoying ourselves. Since I had met Tasha, my whole life had revolved around spending time with her. I know that I enjoyed being in her presence, but she seemed like she was becoming a bit overbearing. If I wasn't with her, she was on the phone asking me when I was coming to her side.

She treated everywhere we went and had even sprung for the tickets to Miami and the H2 that we had rented. At first, I questioned why she seemed so attached. It just didn't fit the image of the rap star or jibe with the lyrics in her songs. But the day she was on Wendy Williams, she spelled it out. Without saying my name, she talked about feeling safe for the first time in her life with a partner. She admitted that she had been hurt by men all her life, even touched by an uncle as a child. She said that she wanted to empower women with her music and not just sexually. She said that her goal was to encourage sistahs to follow their dreams, to be real to themselves and the people in their lives, to live within their means, to open a bank account for their children instead of buying them Jordan's every other month, and by all means to read a damned book every now and then.

Before the show had gone off, she had looked me in the eye as she talked about the sex tape that would more than likely surface. She had even added that she wasn't ashamed, but would be suing the gentlemen for every penny he owned for threatening her and releasing it. Wendy had slapped her five and gave her mad props for being a down-ass bitch.

We left the club and headed back to our hotel. We were staying at the Royal Palm Crown Plaza. It is the only minority-owned hotel in South Beach and the accommodations were excellent. We walked out onto the grounds and contemplated getting into the Jacuzzi, but the temperature had dropped to about sixty degrees and I wasn't trying to catch pneumonia.

We did walk out onto the beach holding hands. The tide was roaring and I was in awe of the sound of the ocean. I was ashamed to admit that it was my first time at any beach other than Jones Beach, so I said nothing as I stared out into the darkness.

"What are you thinking, Abraham?"

"I don't know. A little of this, a little of that, I guess."

"C'mon you can do better than that," she replied. She wrapped her arms around my waist. "Tell me."

I continued staring out at the ocean. "I guess I was just thinking about how my life has changed in the last year and how I want it to wind up."

"I know what you mean."

"Do you?" I looked down into her eyes.

"Yeah, of course. Like last year this time, I was working at H&M during the day and waiting tables in the Shark Bar at night. I was just about to sign my deal, but everyday it was like something new was coming up threatening it." She shook her head. "I remember being afraid that success was so close, but that somehow I would lose it before my dreams became my reality."

"But look at you now, balling out of control." I took her chin by my fingers and said, "What GOD has in store for you, no one or nothing can take from you."

She smiled. "I guess."

"No need for guessing."

"Yeah well we all can't be as grounded as you, Abraham. But hey, how about you? What was your life like?"

I smiled and answered, "I definitely didn't have the hottest new female rapper in my arms." I went on, "Seriously though, I have been on a journey during the last year. This is undoubtedly the year that will define me."

"Why do you say that?"

"When you talk with your creator, he fills you in on things. I am definitely aware of how the things that I have done and will do in the near future will shape my mission in life. This will be my season of remembrance."

"What do you mean?"

"Everyone has a time in their life that they can look back on as their turning point. It doesn't matter if you're six, sixteen or sixty. There is a time that you look back on with fond remembrance or regret, sometimes both. I feel that season for me is coming to an end and when it is all said and done, my future will be determined."

She just looked up at me as if she was wondering where it was coming from. "Abraham, you really make me wonder about you sometimes. When you talk like that, it's kind of scary."

"The future can be scary." I paused for a moment and looked out at a light flashing in the ocean. "Listen, Tasha, when we get back home, I might need to disappear for a couple of weeks."

"Two weeks! There is no way..."

I cut her off. "I really care about you and believe me I don't want to lose what we have, but it has to be that way. I have some things I need to help a friend take care of and I don't want you affected in any way.

"You mean, Malik?" I had filled Tasha in on the history of me and Malik's friendship. I hadn't, however, given her the complete details of the murder and mayhem that I had participated in at his direction. "Abraham, I don't have a good feeling about your involvement with him. I know he's your best friend and all, but if he's the man he thinks he is, then he can stand on his own."

"You don't understand. He has been a big help to me and my grandmother." I thought about the thousands of dollars that I had made because of him and most importantly, how I was able to get my grandmother out of the projects. This last scheme held the promise to all the dreams my future could hold. I knew it was wrong to base one's dreams on monetary goals, but I wanted my own church and youth center one day. Malik estimated that we could walk away with two or three million dollars each.

I had played out the scenarios of how I would hide my portion of the money for five or even ten years before starting my church. I was in no rush and was too smart to be one of those fools who runs out and buys a Porsche the day after robbing a bank.

Tasha interrupted my thoughts. "What if I can't wait two weeks?"

"Then I guess what we have isn't that strong, and I'll have to wish you the best."

She broke away from me. "Oh, it's that easy? You could just walk away." She began to walk away.

I grabbed her arm. "Listen, T., I love being with you, but my plans are bigger than both you and I combined. Just like you want to reach people with your music, I want to do the same with my vision. I want to save lives, help children. I also want to make sure that I have my own money..."

I hadn't realized it, but there were tears in her eyes. "Money!" she yelled out. "Is that what it's all about? I don't care about how much money you have. By this time next year, I'll have more than enough to last us a lifetime."

"Us?" I was taken back by her comment.

"That is if you want there to be an us." Her face went down and she wiped her tears away.

"Tasha, how can you be so sure *you* want there to be an us? I mean here you are just starting your career. Before long, the whole world will be at your feet."

"Hmmph," she breathed out. "I can't believe you of all people don't understand." She took me by my hand. "Listen, Abraham, all my life I have been forced to be a protector of my brother and a partner to my mother. I started working nearly forty hours a week cleaning office buildings at the age of thirteen. My mother spent all her money taking care of my grandfather's medical bills because he was a Vietnam vet who got screwed by the government. We needed every penny I made to keep a roof over our heads and the freaking lights on. I spent all my teenage years providing food for me and Bing. My mother worked two jobs and I don't ever remember her being there to tuck me and my brother in at night." I just listened quietly as she continued, "We didn't live in the safest neighborhood. There was crime on every corner. I grew up terrified that one of the older men who said all kinds of nasty shit to me everyday would come and get me after my mother left for work."

"Damn."

"That ain't the worst of it. The first boyfriend I ever had was shot and killed by his best friend, Dwight. I know because I was on the phone with him when he did it. For two years, I feared for my life until Dwight was found dead in an alley in the Bronx. You see, I haven't ever felt safe or looked after. Nobody ever made me feel like they wanted to do something for me without getting anything in return, not even Bing..." She looked into my eyes and said, "...that is until you came into my life."

I was touched and I kissed her on the lips. "I'm not going anywhere."

"I just want you to understand that all the money I make will mean nothing to me, unless I have you in my life. You make me feel safe, Abraham. Our connection is spiritual and I don't want you to do anything to jeopardize it."

"I won't," I said. It was the first lie I had told in a long time.

She responded by taking me by the hand and leading me towards a stack of reclining chairs that were chained together. She had a leather skirt on and once she was able to lean up against the chairs, she lifted it above her waist and turned her back to me. "Make love to me. I want your baby. If it's a girl we'll name her Miami." I laughed as I walked up to her. I unfastened my pants and let them drop to my ankles. The sight of her muscular ass and calf muscles excited me. I eased up to her and began to pull her thongs to the side. "No, rip them off."

I responded by doing just that. In seconds, I was pushing myself into her to the rhythm of the Atlantic. Her breathing was heavy and she reached back over her shoulder and put her hand behind my head. She arched her back and poked her butt into my mid-section. We were grinding in a perfect rhythm with the breeze at our backs. With each stroke, she made promises to always be mine. She begged me to stay with her forever.

She grew wetter by the second as her cream was all over my manhood. I told her I would in fact always be hers. The passion was perfect this time and the connection was electric. I felt us bonding in ways that we never had before. It was more than ordinary sex or lust this time. It felt like she was giving me a piece of her soul to keep and I responded by giving her a piece of mine.

"Ohhhh, it feels sooooo good," she sang out.

I felt a tingling and in the darkness I saw bright colors. My knees grew weak and I felt myself letting go of every fear that I had about our relationship. My orgasm was strong and I flooded her insides. She began to shake and I tried to keep humping her through her climax. Tasha bucked wildly and before I knew it, I had lost my balance and fell onto my back into the sand.

She was still panting from her orgasm and began to laugh at the same time as she turned to see me on the ground trying to keep the sand out of my butt. She extended her hand to help me up, still laughing at me. I had to admit it was funny. Once I got myself together, we headed up to our room and hit the shower.

She got in first and I climbed in with her. She sang Ginuwine's, *My Whole Life Has Changed* to me while she washed my back. She got out before me and when I climbed out, I noticed that she had turned all the lights out. There were candles lit and she told me to take a seat on the bed. I noticed that her hands were behind her back. "Now close your eyes."

"What is it?" I said smiling.

"Just close your eyes."

I obeyed, "Okay."

"Are you peeping?"

"No."

"Lean your head toward me."

"What are you up to?"

"Just do it."

I leaned forward and felt her hands brush the sides of my hair and something hit my chest. "Okay, look," she said all giddy-like.

I opened my eyes to see a chain on my neck with a diamond encrusted cross charm on it. "Oh my GOD!" I couldn't believe it.

"Now you bling blinging for the Lawd," she giggled out. "Six carats on white gold."

"I don't believe this."

"Why?" She reached over and kissed me softly on the lips. "Anything for the man I love."

I was speechless. It had been a month and she was telling me that she loved me. I knew that I was somewhere between infatuation and love with her. "If we could freeze a moment in time... I would stay in this one with you."

"I would do the same." She stood up. "But we can't and it's okay, because you have work to do that's bigger than us."

"You okay with that?" I asked.

"Yeah, baby." She nodded. "As long as I'm by your side."

In that moment, I had a feeling that I had found my first lady. We climbed into the bed and held each other. I ran my fingers over the cross on my chest again and again. I began to think about the whole robbery thing that I was going to do with Malik and felt a fear come over me. I didn't want anything to come between what I had with Tasha.

With her, I had a sense of peace and I felt like I would get my church even if I didn't commit the crime. I lay holding her, staring at the ceiling until I heard her heavy breathing signaling that she had fallen asleep. "Here's to Miami," I said as I kissed her on the back of her neck.

She surprised me because I thought she was sleeping. "Only if it's a girl," she whispered back. "If it's a boy, we'll call him Abraham." Then she whispered, "Abraham, don't go back to New York. I love you and I need you more than Malik."

I was speechless.

Then she added, "Whatever you need, I got it. There's no reason for you to go back into the fire."

She pierced my whole being with her words and I began to wonder if the words coming to me were from her or *through* her.

TWENTY-THREE

Intuition is the vision mastered with the third eye. Unfortunately, most people are too busy taking in sights with the two physical eyes to ever develop the third and most important. The physical eyes report every physical thing they take in and leave the brain to sort the information out and create the message. The third eye takes in messages from that which is unseen, including energy, good fortune and especially danger. A highly developed sense of intuition is the reason why certain people appear to be lucky to be alive or undeservingly prosperous. The simple phrase, "I can feel it," is not a mere saying. It is the mantra of those who are watching with the third eye. "Don't go out tonight," "Turn left instead of right." You hear the voice and heed the message. The next moment or day you say, "Damn, if I had gone out that could have been me". There's no such thing as coincidence just happenstance created by those who see with the third eye and those who choose to listen to or ignore its messages.

"**Man**, fuck it!" Casper yelled out. "We going back in the Towers. "I don't give a damn if Mayor Bloomberg sets his office up in the courtyard."

Wheeler joined in, "For real, he can get it too." They all started laughing. It had been weeks since I had seen my crew from Do or Die, and they were as crazy as I had left them.

We were sitting in the World's Greatest Carry Out on Atlantic and Grand. I missed the hotcakes from that spot. Every since the Towers had been shut down by the huge police presence, I had no reason to come around the way. My cousin, Carlos, had cleaned out both me and Abraham's apartments and in exchange, I let him keep the guns that I left had behind.

I was still getting word that the feds and local police were snooping around asking questions, harassing folks and making promises of rewards. They were wasting their time around there. People around Greenberg would grow wings and fly before they would snitch on the killers that dwelled there.

"Listen, my niggas," I said. "That right there would be suicide. The po po's got that spot locked down. You've seen the news. They still got candles, flowers, stuffed animals and shit sitting in front of the building where those agents got killed."

Wheeler commented, "You say it like you ain't the one that did it." He took a Newport out from behind his ear. "You the one that heated up the spot. Now we can't get no fuckin' money in our own hood, and don't think we forgot that we didn't get paid that last month." He looked around as he lit the cigarette. "I mean, Terrell ain't gonna use his pay where he is, but I got shit to do." His comment about Terrell was disrespectful.

The tone at the table changed. "You talking real slick about a fallen soldier, Wheeler. Terrell was a good dude."

"Yeah, whatever. So what you got going on? You plannin' to take over another block? 'Cause if you are, make sure it ain't Garvey Ave. 'cause we playin' for keeps up there." He looked at me and I could see he wasn't with me at all. My feelings weren't hurt. The moment I stopped being his source of income, it was just a matter of time before he looked at me as his enemy. *"Never put your trust in a hired gun,"* Double V had told me when I first described the members of my crew.

I looked across the table at Ferris who had fear in his eyes. He was the one who had called me to come talk to the crew. On the phone, he told me that they wanted to find out how to reach Cortez in order to get a supply of heroin. Now he was sensing the growing tension at the table. "Oh yeah, I got big plans, Wheeler," I said as I ate the last of my breakfast. "But I won't be making anymore moves in Brooklyn."

"Why's that?" Casper asked.

"It's getting too crazy in these trenches. I need some peace, you know?"

Wheeler laughed. "Sounds like you getting soft on us." He was trying to agitate me.

"Wheeler, my man, I don't know what's getting into you homey, but if you disrespect me one more time, we gonna have to take it out front," I said staring right into his eyes. Then I looked at Casper.

Wheeler stood up, "Anytime you ready, nigga."

Casper yelled out, "Dog, sit down and stop tripping man." He took Wheeler by the arm. "This Malik, man. He came up here to help us out and you gonna start tripping like this."

I was trying to make Casper out to see if he was with Wheeler on the bullshit he was trying. I had already made out two niggas parked outside in an Explorer. They had been parked out there the whole time that we were in the carryout. If they weren't with Wheeler, then he would have surely noticed them and commented on them by now. "Yeah, I came out here to help you out. As a matter of fact, I came down here to bring you all some dough so you could make some moves, but with all this attitude you giving up, you kind of forcing me to reconsider."

"Now see," Casper said then he tapped Wheeler's arm. "I told you Malik was gonna look out."

"Yeah, you did," Wheeler said. "Malik, my bad, dog. I just been a little frustrated. I was doing so good with you and now it's like a nigga gots to start over."

"I understand, man. I brought you fifteen each." I then looked at Ferris. "Little man, you kind of quiet. You a'ight?"

"Yeah," he muttered out staring down at the food he had barely touched. "I'm alright."

My cell rang and I pulled it off my hip. "Yeah, what's up, baby?"

"You alright?" Angel asked on the other line.

My heart started beating fast when I heard hear say that. "Yeah, why you ask that?"

"I just was thinking about you and I was wondering if everything was cool."

"Yeah, yeah." I told her to hold on. I turned to the fellas, "I'm gonna run to the car to grab that cake and be right back."

Wheeler nodded his head and I saw Casper smile. I walked out the door of the carry out, hung up on Angel, and reached into my waistband. My car was parked up the block about thirty yards off. I noticed that the Explorer had moved from its spot and I suspected that it was in the alley I was about to walk across. My hand was on the FNP nine millimeter. I sped up as I reached the alley and it was empty. I breathed a short sigh of relief until I heard Ferris yell out my name. I turned in time to see Wheeler running at me with his gun drawn. Casper was trailing him with a sawed off shotgun.

My eyes grew wide and I fired first. Wheeler ducked toward a parked car and my heart moved to full throttle as I watched Casper turn towards Ferris and blast him with the sawed off. Ferris' young body was lifted off his feet as the buck shots ripped through him. "Y'all muthafuckas!" I yelled at the top of my lungs as I fired shots in Wheeler's direction first and then at Casper.

Wheeler returned fire but revealed that he was either a lousy shot or he was scared because he shot the windows out of two cars that were parked up the street from me. Casper, meanwhile, looked as though his pistol grip was misfiring. When he realized he was in the open with a gun that wasn't working, he tried to run for cover. I took advantage of his situation and fired six shots at him. I saw two hit him in the back, and rejoiced quietly when I saw his head snap forward letting me know that I had spilled his brain matter on the streets. He fell flat on his face and the gun slid under a parked car.

I had four shots left in my gun, but I was trying to see which end of the car Wheeler was hiding behind. "I got your man, son. You next!" I yelled.

"Let's do it, nigga," he shouted back.

I took the extra clip out of my jacket and put a fresh one in the gun. Just as I stood up, I heard the revving of an engine as the Explorer came up the street. I took aim at Wheeler and fired twice as he looked at the Explorer. I missed him, but the passenger of the Explorer didn't. I didn't hear a shot but watched in disbelief as I saw an arrow go through Wheeler's forehead. He dropped like a deer in the wilderness. I heard sirens approaching and the Explorer stopped.

"Get in, baby boy." I looked in the truck and saw none other than Wild Steve, in the passenger seat.

"Hell fuckin' no!"

"Suit yourself," he said. Just then, I saw two more niggas in masks running down the block towards me. One of them had an AK and raised it to spray when the back door of the explorer opened. I was surprised to see Cortez seated in the back seat.

"Come on, Malik!"

Something told me to jump in, so I did. Just as I did, I felt the impact of shots hitting me in the back. The truck pulled through the alley and Cortez reached over to pull my door shut.

My back was stinging as I had been hit twice. I was bucking back and forth as Steve leaned over the back seat with a knife in his hand. "Nooo!" I yelled as his hand gripped my neck. With the other hand he dragged the back of the blade across my coat.

"Stay calm, man, you gonna live." I realized that he was cutting my coat off me to assess my wounds. My back was stinging so bad that I had forgotten how prepared I was for the ambush.

"Yo, this nigga got on a vest!" Cortez half yelled, half laughed out.

Wild Steve, realizing that he had ripped my coat for no reason said, "My bad, shorty. That was a nice coat too."

I calmed down as the pain subsided. "Malik, you are one lucky SOB."

I thought about Ferris back there laying on the ground. "I want y'all to take me back. I need to go check my little shorty, Ferris. I need to get him to the hospital."

"Man, don't be silly. A grown man wouldn't have survived that hit. He was a mess."

When he said that, tears fell from my eyes. I pulled my gun from my waist and put it to Cortez's head. "If ya'll wasn't in on this then how do you know about this whole set-up? Somebody bigger than Wheeler's ass set me up. He couldn't organize his way out of a damn paper bag."

"Hold up, Malik!" Cortez shouted. "Take that tool down." Just then, I felt the tip of Steve's blade at my neck. "Malik, if you shoot, Steve will jam that blade into your throat so smooth, you'll drown in your own blood before your gun cools off. "Now act like you got some sense, boy. If we were trying to hurt you, you'd be dead already."

Steve smiled and nodded at me. "You know he's telling the truth." He was. Steve put his knife away.

I pulled the gun down and Cortez shook his head in disgust as he said, "You have a horrible attitude, son."

"So what's going on? Something ain't right."

"Yeah, it's a hit out on your ass. Fifty gees dead, a hundred alive."

"Every gun in Brooklyn is pointed at you," Wild Steve laughed out. "Doc and Wendell don't like you very much."

"Those faggots, huh? So is that why you want me alive?"

"Malik, you have to use your head. Would we tell you about a contract on your head and let you ride with a loaded gun if we were trying to kidnap or kill you?" Cortez asked. "Malik, with me, it's all about honor and integrity. Not only did you help me get money, you saved my life. Now I've saved yours. I've paid Wild Steve here $125,000 *not* to kill you." Steve turned around and showed me all of his teeth. He was a maniac on another level. It was then that I noticed he had on a camouflage outfit as if he was hunting in the wilderness. "Now he works for me. I have a new operation that I'm setting up if you're interested in coming aboard. A man can never have too much muscle or be too safe. The money is flowing and the weather is nice."

"I'll keep it in mind. But now I need to deal with these clowns."

"Well, unfortunately, I have some bad news for you."

"Oh yeah, what's that?"

"It's not only Doc and Wendell you got beef with." He paused. "You deal with a chick named Angel, right?"

I sat up quickly and the question echoed in my head. *You deal with a chick named Angel, right?* "What?" I didn't believe that he had just spoken her name in connection with the drama.

"Yeah, that's Phil Boogie's little sister," he continued. "Apparently, the word is out that you had something to do with his untimely demise. As a matter of fact, your name is surfacing in a number of homicides all over Brooklyn." He chuckled. "They calling you the new Murder Inc."

Wild Steve joined in. "Your young ass is hotter than a firecracker. You don't need to worry about adding any more bodies to your count. You need to be concentrating on your escape from New York before you wind up in Sing Sing or upstate at Eastern."

"Where did you get this shit from... about Angel?"

"Oh don't go getting sentimental now, Malik. You seem to have forgotten that the streets are always watching. It just so happens that now they talking."

I didn't want to believe that Angel had set me up. But I thought back to the words my grandfather had shared with me. *Some bitch is always plotting.* "She would've said something to me. She's too emotional to keep something like that in for this long."

"When was the last time you saw her?" Cortez asked.

"A couple of days ago," I said not realizing until that moment that I had been spending more time with Marcella lately.

"Well we just got the word today that she tipped Doc off as to your whereabouts. As for your crew, those idiots were working alone. It was only a coincidence that Doc and Wendell's guns were coming down the street when we pulled up. Apparently, you told her where you were going to be this morning. Doc and Wendell put a couple guns on it and then they called Steve here as an insurance policy. If the two monkeys didn't get you, Steve surely would have. Lucky for you, he was working for me and let me know that the hit was gonna go down."

I took a deep breath. I could still feel the pain pulsating in my back from the shots, but I was glad to be dealing with some pain as opposed to holes. My thoughts were racing. "I'm indebted to you for everything, Cortez and you too, Steve." I asked them for reassurance on how Angel could have gotten the word on me.

Cortez broke it down for me. "Apparently, after you killed Phil, you took some drugs and a gun off him. It just so happened that you showed the gun to some kid named Black Sid over on Marcy and you gave him some product to sell. His big brother, Levi, took one look at the red-tops and knew that they sold those in the Towers. Sid mentioned the pearl-handled gun that you had on you and eventually Levi ran into Doc. Of course they talked. Everyone knew that Phil loved that gun and the rest is history.

We were cruising up Flatbush Avenue when I yelled out, "Drop me off at the Fulton Mall."

"You sure? I was going to have my man, Horace, take you into the city. You'll be safer out of Brooklyn," Cortez advised.

"I got this."

"Suit yourself." We drove and they did as instructed. When we came to a stop he said, "I don't suppose you're going to walk around the mall with that bulletproof vest on like you 50 Cent or something," Wild Steve said.

I took the vest off and folded it. I now had on nothing but a t-shirt. It was nice out for November, but I looked a little out of place. "Thanks for everything," I commented.

"Hey, Malik," Cortez said. "Think about what I said. I'll be heading down south at the end of the week. You all alone out here and every thug in the BK is looking to collect off of your head. Don't get caught slipping."

"I won't," I said and started to walk away.

"Malik!" I heard Wild Steve yell. I turned and he motioned for me to come back to the window. "Here, take this jacket and put your vest back on." I walked back over and he handed me the camouflage jacket that he was wearing.

I took the jacket and thanked him. He winked and said, "It's no thing. Make sure you check the pockets. Stay up." And they pulled off.

I put the jacket on first then headed for the store on the corner so I could put my vest back on. I reached into the pockets and found a professional hunting knife and some fishing wire in one, a ski mask and a pair of handcuffs in the other. I ran over to the next street and hopped in a taxi. I dropped him a twenty and gave him specific instructions.

When we reached the spot where the shooting had just taken place, there were cops crawling all over so I couldn't get my car. I gave the cabbie another twenty and had him head out to Queens. I called my cousin, Carlos, and told him to meet me at the 24-hour Laundromat on Myrtle Avenue. When he tried to tell me he was in the middle of something, I went off cursing into the phone causing the driver to look into his mirror.

"Just fucking drive the cab!" I yelled. Getting back to Carlos, I said, "If you ain't at that spot when I get there in fifteen minutes, you're finished."

I gathered all the guns that I felt I would need and left Carlos' apartment. I didn't want to bring him with me because I wasn't sure if I was on a suicide mission. While I drove back to Bed-Stuy, I phoned my Uncle Kelly and filled him in on my drama and asked him to relay the message. I told him that I didn't want to dial Double V directly. He had instructed me to make minimal contact with him until the day we were leaving for the heist. That meant none.

I then tried to call Abraham, but his cell was turned off. I had no idea where he was. I hadn't heard from him in almost a week. Knowing him, he was off romancing his new lady while contemplating GOD's plan. I wasn't mad at him even though I needed him. I was actually glad he wasn't here for this. While I didn't fear dying, I didn't want to take him with me. I was hoping that he wasn't in Brooklyn because a hit on me meant he was a target as well.

As I cruised down the BQE, my phone rang. "Yo."

"Son-son." My grandfather was on the phone.

"Hey." Before I had a chance to say another word, he went on.

"Listen up. Head up to Harlem before you make a move. I'm rolling with you. Meet me at 106 and Third. Dial this number when you hit the block." Click.

I wondered what he was doing up in Spanish Harlem. I seldom went up there, but I knew there had to be some attraction. I dialed Marcella and she answered on the first ring.

"Hey, Malik. I was just thinking about you." Her voice was smooth and silky.

"So what were you thinking?"

"I was just thinking that I want to see you." I could hear her heels click-clacking against the sidewalk. "I'm on the way to work. I get off at midnight, you picking me up?"

"I'll tell you what. If I'm there by midnight, it's me and you. Don't wait for me though."

"That sounds real shady, bro," she laughed into the phone. Her laughter was soothing like a calm in the middle of a storm. "But if that's the best you can do, I'll take it because I really want to see you."

"Marcella."

"Yeah, baby?"

"I"m really glad to have you back in my life."

"I feel the same way about you. As a matter of fact…"

I cut her off. "No, listen here. If I see you tonight, this is your last night working there."

"What?" I must have sounded strange to her.

"If I make it there, I'm gonna take care of you. You won't have anything to worry about other than school. You can turn in your name tag. I got you. I know it sounds crazy, but I just want you to trust me."

"I do, baby. I trust you one hundred and fifty percent. If you say quit 'cause you got me… then I'll quit. Simple as that."

She was the first person in my entire life to ever say anything like that to me. The only other person who's trust I owned like that was Abraham. "Thanks," I said. "That means a lot to me." I told her that I had some drama in the streets to take care of and that I wanted her to say a prayer for me.

"I will. Be careful," she said. "I'll see you a little before midnight."

"That's a bet," I replied and hung up. *I hope*, I thought to myself.

I reached Third Avenue and dialed the number that Double V had called from and got no answer. I approached the corner of 106th Street and saw my grandfather on the corner talking to a Hispanic man dressed like a chef. To his right, was the man he called Caldwell with the teardrop tats under his eye. Every time I saw him, I felt uneasy. Whenever he was around, I felt the presence of death. I wondered if I gave niggas that same feeling.

I came to a stop and Double V walked up on me. "Listen, Caldwell and Raul are going to ride with you. I told them your name is Son-son so answer to that. I got some business to handle, so I can't take the ride with you. I want you to take care of the bitch first. Then do what you got to do in Brooklyn, but if the block is too hot out there, Caldwell will let you know. Listen to him, he knows what he's doing." Before I could respond they climbed into the van.

I was a little nervous and drove straight through a red light. "Whoa, take it easy, Lil' Nigga." Caldwell said. He kept calling me Lil' Nigga as if I had requested he do that.

"Don't get us pulled over, Son-son," Raul said in a thick New Yorican accent. "We got guns and shit in here." Raul held up a small case. "I ain't never going back to the pen, so be careful unless you want to act out a scene from the movie *Heat*. I'll be like DeNiro, airing shit out." He laughed.

We stopped and I got gas before I jumped on the West Side Highway and Caldwell explained the plan. I was blasting Cam'ron's *Come Home With Me* CD to get me in the mood for what I had to. We made it to Angel's block and parked.

"That's the house right there." I pointed to her door.

"Do your thing Raul," Caldwell said as he handed him a cell phone.

"Nombre, Son-son," he said. "I need the phone number to the house."

"Oh okay. Uh, 718-555-1905. Angel's her name. Her last name is Knox."

"It's ringing," he said. "Hello. This is Hector Dominguez from WHIT 95.9 and I'm calling because Angel Knox has won $950 from our station. We are calling to verify that she is at least eighteen years of age…"

"Excuse me. What radio station? How much did she win?" she said to Raul.

He repeated himself and then asked, "Is she home now? She has to verify that she entered the contest herself."

"Well this is her mother and she should be in the house in about fifteen minutes. She and her boyfriend only went to return some videos. Try right back, okay?" Raul had repeated her word for word. When he said she went with her boyfriend, I felt a twinge of jealousy. Angel obviously moved as quickly as I did.

We sat and waited in the van. Caldwell and Raul carried on a conversation while I thought about the whole situation. I cared for Angel. I even thought that she could have been the one. I imagined how hurt she must have been when she heard that I had killed her brother. As if he was reading my mind, Caldwell interrupted my thoughts. "Lil' Nigga, don't be back there getting all sentimental. She had a hit put on you and she knows too much. If the streets don't get you soon enough for her satisfaction, then pretty soon, she gives your name to the cops. I been through it all and did sixty-six months behind a bitch. But hey, if your heart ain't in it, then we can roll."

I didn't appreciate him questioning my fortitude, but he was right. "Nah, I'm fine. I was just thinking some shit over in my mind."

"Getting your game face together, huh, Son-son?" Raul added.

"Exactly," I lied. I was having second thoughts about killing Angel.

"You ever killed a woman before?" Caldwell asked. He was picking my brain like a shrink. "'Cause it's a little different than killing a man."

I decided to man up and regain my composure. "Killing is killing. I'll snap her fucking neck and go eat a sandwich. As a matter of fact, I don't even need you for this. After we finish, I'll see what you got when we get down with the niggas on the block." Doc and Wendell had a new block where they were moving their product and I was ready to pay them a visit.

Ten minutes passed and I saw a cab drive past my window. Angel was in the back seat and when the cab came to a stop, she climbed out accompanied by a kid with baseball cap hanging off of his head. He had what looked like a bottle of liquor and she had two grocery bags.

I gripped the steering wheel waiting for the right moment when Caldwell screamed out, "Lil' Nigga, what the hell you waiting for? Drop that bitch." I was frozen. I was angry, but for some reason, I couldn't get out the car. Caldwell jumped out the van and headed for Angel. He crossed over to the sidewalk in front of them and drew his gun.

Somehow my feet hit the ground and I felt myself moving toward Angel. I pulled the ski mask from my pocket and pulled it down over my face. I didn't have my gun drawn as I walked towards her. She was on her steps fumbling for her keys when she looked over and saw me coming towards her. As I got closer, she must have recognized my walk and her mouth dropped open and she screamed, "Oh my God, Kirk, that's Malik!"

Her counterpart turned and looked in my direction. He caught a glance of Caldwell walking towards him with his gun drawn. Then with the grace of a cheetah, he pushed Angel to the ground and ducked behind the steps of her mother's brownstone. Caldwell fired at them both and sounds of the shots echoed up the block. He fired again and the bullet ricocheted off of the bricks and struck a car window. The sound of glass shattering was followed by car alarms going off. Caldwell continued to walk up on his impending victim when all of a sudden the guy reached around the steps and returned fire. He missed Caldwell with the first shot but scared the hell out him.

For a big man, Caldwell moved quickly. "You already dead, boy, so you might as well come out from behind the steps."

"Fuck you!" he yelled back.

I continued to creep up the street. When I circled up the block, I could see Angel crouched into a ball in the corner and her new man was protecting her. He was glancing up the block in my direction, but didn't see me until it was too late. I jumped out from between a Cherokee Jeep and a Mazda MPV and opened fire. I hit him six times in the back and legs. Angel screamed as blood poured out of him.

"Nooo, Kirk!" She yelled out and tried to shake him back to consciousness. I recognized the name as the boyfriend she had who was locked down. "You killed him. He just came home last week, you bastard. I hate you!" she yelled out at me. "You killed my brother too and pretended to be his friend." She was crying hysterically. I shook my head no, but it was no use. "You killed Phil too, I know you did." She stood up and tried to charge me. Caldwell yanked her from behind by the neck and threw her down to the ground.

"Hold up, wait," I said to him. I tucked my gun and snatched her up off of the pavement. "Listen to me." She was shaking and screaming. "Listen!" I yelled as I smacked her. "Your brother was raping my sister. That's why I killed him."

"You liar!" she yelled repeatedly.

In that instant, I jerked back when I felt the warmth of Angel's blood splatter across my face. There was a hole in her forehead and her brains were on the sidewalk. I looked at Caldwell as I dropped her body to the ground. "We gotta move, Lil' Nigga." He turned to walk quickly back to the van when her mother's door swung open. I looked to see Angel's mother running down the steps, screaming frantically, with a butcher knife in her hand.

"You killed myyyyyy baaaaaby." She lunged at Caldwell. He leaned to the side and grabbed her head as her momentum carried her his way. He palmed the back of her head as he grabbed the arm with the knife in it. I watched in amazement as he slammed her face into a parked car. In the next instant, I heard a crack as he yanked her arm up behind her back. There was a clank as the knife hit the ground. A half second later, Caldwell jammed the end of his .357 into her mouth, pulled the trigger, and pushed her lifeless body to the ground with no more care than if she was a sack of potatoes. He was an animal. I thought briefly about what he would have done to me that day in Harlem if I hadn't got the jump on him. As I stepped over her body to move toward the van, I noticed Phil Boogie's daughter standing there in the doorway.

I moved in slow motion and thought for a second about shooting her. Not because I feared her identifying me, but because I had destroyed her future and she was still a baby. Then I remembered something that Abraham always said: *God looks out for children and fools.* I mouthed the words *I'm sorry* to her and rushed off to the van.

I was ready to run and head back to Jersey to my hide out. For the first time, the killing was feeling like it was too much.

I wanted to get away from these cats that my grandfather had put me with, but I knew my day wasn't done. If I took them back without dealing with Doc and Wendell, I might never have a chance to.

"Lil' Nigga," Caldwell said. "I feel you trippin', but everything's cool. You did what you had to do. Double V told me that she was responsible for you gettin' a price tag put on your head. There's only one way to respond to that." He cracked his knuckles as he made a snorting sound with his nose. "You didn't have a choice, ya' know. Unless you want a tag on your fuckin' toe. I'm not bullshittin', now it's either them or you."

"That's right, Son-son. Let a muthafucka put a hit on me. He better be damned sure he has the guns and the know-how to take care of the job."

I started thinking about their words. They were right. I knew from that time at the ESPN Zone that it would come to this one day. I had made a lot of money with them and helped them. But instead of them respecting the code, they decided to go gutter on me. Inside, my feelings of regret for what had just happened with Angel began to turn into hatred for Doc and Wendell, but especially Doc.

"This is it," I said as we rolled down Marcus Garvey Boulevard. There were at least ten men on the corner and another five posted in front of the building. I recognized one of Doc's workers as we cruised up the block. I drove fast, trying not to be recognized, and went an extra two blocks past before I made a turn to circle back.

"So did you see them?" Raul asked.

"No I saw one of their workers though."

"Keep driving," Caldwell said and I did.

"Oh shit!" I yelled out.

"What?" They both asked at the same time.

I looked over and saw Wendell cruising down the block. He was in a maroon Mercedes ML. I smashed on the gas and rushed back around the corner. When we circled back, he was parallel parking just up the block from the building where everyone was standing. When he did, a female got out of a Honda behind him and walked up to his car. She had on a short pink coat, showing ass for days.

I explained that he was only half of my problem, so Raul stated, "You will need to get them both at the same time."

"Don't worry," Caldwell said. "The other one will be around shortly."

"How you figure that?" I asked.

"You said that they just started operating down here, right?"

"Yeah."

"Well any hustler worth his paper will keep a close eye on his new grind. How will he know if he's being cheated if he doesn't know what his normal take should be?" He pointed, "You see, there's some steady traffic coming through here. But he needs to know which hours are busiest, how often the police roll through, and if the stick-up boys are preying on him."

"Yeah, you're right," I replied slightly impressed with his knowledge. "I guess you an O.G., huh?"

"For sure, Lil' Nigga. I was setting up strips and shutting 'em down by the time you stopped shitting in your diapers."

I had gained respect for this dude. He had some knowledge and was a stone-cold killer. "So we should just sit here and wait?" I asked.

"You got something more important to do?" he asked and then laughed.

I guess I didn't. So we sat and watched. Wendell walked into the building with the girl in the pink coat and came back out an hour later. His car never moved and shortly after the sun went down, a black Nissan 350z rolled down the block and parked behind Wendell's Benz. When I saw Doc climb out, my heart raced. "That's him, right there in the leather coat. He's the one." I was excited but remembered, "I mean, we need them both, but he's the ..."

"...the one you want," Caldwell said, finishing my sentence.

"Yeah," I answered.

"Okay look. You wait for my move. I'm going to head up the block and cause some confusion," Raul said. "When I move for your men, light this block up and get straight back to the van. You understand? Damn, that's a nice ride he has." He looked at Caldwell and smiled. "You think I could get the papers on that."

"I don't see why not."

"Okay, you two, try not to shoot that car."

"Are you serious?" I asked.

"I'm most sincere," he said and laughed. "If you see me pull off in that, don't worry about me. I'll make it home."

I looked at Caldwell and he stared back and said, "He's serious."

"I'm on a mission," Raul said and climbed out of the van. He walked up the street with his hand in his jacket pockets. To the dealers, he looked like a potential sale so a couple of them approached him on the way up the block.

"Okay, it's your show Lil' Nigga. When he diverts their attention you run up on them and handle your business."

"What you gonna do?"

"I'm gonna wait here and watch you. When I see you have the mission accomplished, I'll pull up and you can hop in."

I stepped out of the van. For the first time in a while, I felt nervous about what I was about to do. With all the guns that were surely out here, I had no room for error. I moved for the corner and watched as Raul headed back down the street on the same side of the block that Doc and Wendell were on. They were standing out front talking to one of their workers. I could hear Doc's car stereo thumping G-Unit's CD as I posted up against the building. Doc looked like he was cursing his worker out and when he finished, he sent him back off to work. He was riding high, profiling, when I heard Raul yelling at the top of his voice. "These muthafuckas sold me some soap. Where is my money?" he yelled.

I saw Wendell looking up the block to see what the commotion was all about. "Hey, man, chill." he said trying to calm Raul down.

"Calm down? Calm down? Look at this bullshit." He was now a couple feet away from Wendell. I was wondering what he had in his hand. When he reached him, he showed him what he had purchased from one of his workers. "Man, are you crazy? That ain't no damned soap. That is grade A rock, man. Get the fuck out of here." He started backing away and then added, "We don't do that around here. If that shit don't get you high, you come looking for me tomorrow and I'll make sure you get high."

"Tomorrow?" Raul laughed. "You won't be out here tomorrow."

"Yeah, I'll be here. Come see me."

"That won't be necessary." Wendell was puzzled at his sudden calmness. When he saw the sick look in Raul's eyes it was too late. Raul lunged at Wendell and took a box cutter to his throat. When Wendell reached for his throat Raul swung his foot in a roundhouse kick that landed on Wendell's temple knocking him out cold.

"You muthafucka!" Doc yelled as he ran towards Raul.

"Doc!" I yelled out. He turned and looked at me and yelled out.

"Steve?" He recognized the jacket but was surprised to be staring down the barrel of my gun.

"Nah," I said. I pulled the mask up, revealing my face.

"Well I'll be damned," he said and began trying to save his life. "Hey, man, the whole hit was Wendell's idea. I told him that it was going to bring too much drama."

"Well I can't ask him now can I?" I glanced over to see Raul going through his pockets. When he finished searching him, he pulled a nine-inch knife from the side of his boots. Doc grimaced when Raul plunged the blade into Wendell's chest.

"I think he's dead," Raul said laughing aloud. Then he stood up to look around and keep watch.

"Now it's your turn, you little bitch. You know you really shoulda thought long and hard before you put a hit out on me." I raised my gun and said, "Say hello to Phil when you get to Hell."

"You gonna kill me like this in cold blood, my nigga? We could squash this whole thing. On the real, I got plenty of money." He was rambling, "I'm talking so much cash that you wouldn't ever have to hit the block again."

"Nah, that's alright."

"C'mon, Malik, I don't even have a pistol on me."

"That's too bad," I said as I began squeezing the trigger. BOOM, BOOM, BOOM! I hit him in the legs on purpose. The shots were like a cannon going off and people began to scatter. I knew that some of them were running to grab their guns and would be coming back so I moved quickly. I walked up to Doc's body and he was on his back grimacing. I looked over at Wendell and noticed that his eyes were open, but his body was still. "Doc, you know I killed Phil Boogie and I have to admit that I wanted to kill you the first time I spoke to you."

"Go on then, you little faggot. But you gonna get yours," he said. BOOM! With the last shot, I sealed his fate. I got down and reached into his pockets and yanked his money and keys out.

"Hey, give me those keys," Raul said.

I was about to toss them when the rattle of an Uzi went off. Shots went right over my head. I looked over at Raul and just that quick he had been hit in the chest. He fell forward onto his face and I knew he was dead. The same shots rang out again and I saw that they were coming from behind me, the same direction that I needed to go in. I was about to take off when I saw shots coming from the van.

Caldwell was trying to cover me but it was a bad mistake, because the young hustlers opened up fire on the van and turned it into Swiss cheese. I knew that there was no way that I was getting out of this spot alive when I remembered that I was holding the keys to Doc's Z. I jumped in it and pulled off. I sped towards the corner and saw two gunmen running out of the darkness from in between the buildings. I heard a loud series of pings as they hit the sides of the car.

I sped to the corner and hung a right. I circled the block just to make sure that Caldwell was in the van. I crept slowly and when I reached the van, the other shooters had run up to see Doc's and Wendell's bodies lying there lifeless. At the same instant, I looked over and saw Caldwell slumped over the steering wheel with his left arm hanging out of the window still holding his .357.

I put the car into reverse and sped back up the street. I was thinking quickly and went to the nearest gas station. On the way back to the van, I heard sirens and knew it was grace. The block was empty when I made it back because everybody knew the po po's was on the way. I doused the van with gas and lit the can. As I pulled away from the van, I thought about how Caldwell's death came in connection with me. He had saved my life when I feared he would take it.

We had finally had our chance to dance together and like he said, it was lucky for me that it was under those circumstances.

TWENTY-FOUR

Order is the way in which the Master operates. For everything that must happen, happens divinely. What good is it to question why something happens? There is no answer for such a question. To be a true servant of the Master is to not only accept the lessons of life, but to embrace them with one's whole heart. It would be foolish to consider life's harshest teachings enjoyable by any stretch. They are often painful and disheartening at the very least. The joy comes in the knowledge that order will bring positive from negative because it has to. Having the knowledge of the fact that through living in acceptance of God's order, means understanding that the unbearable has meaning, that all the pain has a purpose. Personal growth will allow it to be understood that wrongdoing must exist so that good can reveal itself as the Order of the Creator.

Malik picked me and Tasha up from the airport. He had left twenty messages on my phone in a three-hour span. Though I hadn't checked them in two days for some reason, I had randomly listened to the messages while I watched the Knicks play the Heat on TNT. His words had been frantic and he sounded as if he was panicked. When I returned his call, he begged me to cut my trip short and get home.

Me, on the other hand, I had been living a life of pure bliss. Tasha and I had spent Thanksgiving Day with my grandmother and great-aunt and then checked back into the Royal Palm. We had spent the days by the pool, sipping daquiris and bathing in the sun. We both had gotten two shades darker.

When we walked through the doors to exit the airport, Malik zoomed up and scooped us like a hawk. We barely had time to get into his Mercedes before he was pulling off. Tasha was wearing her hair pulled back in a ponytail and she was wearing a Bebe baseball cap pulled down to her shades. Malik didn't recognize her and I was fine with it.

I introduced her simply as Tasha. She smiled and winked at me from the back seat as they exchanged greetings. "So where do you want me to drop her off?" Malik asked.

Before I could answer, Tasha interrupted, "Oh no. I'm going with Abraham. Where he goes, I go."

"Is that a fact?" Malik asked sharply.

"That's for real, my nigga."

"Oh okay, I see." Then he turned to me, "So Abraham, I see you done hooked up with a little shot caller, huh?"

I laughed, "It's all good, baby." I turned back toward her, "Malik and I need to talk alone for a bit. He can drop you off in Brooklyn or better yet..." I turned back to Malik, "Where you sleeping tonight?"

"That's why I called you home. Tonight, there won't be much sleeping so we might as well take her to the nearest hotel so we can drop your things off and you can get changed."

I wasn't sure if it was what he said, the tone of it, or the fact that Tasha was around. Either way, I was irritated. "So what we got going on, Malik?"

He nodded his head toward the back seat and said, "You'll see."

I looked back at Tasha and saw her scowling at me. Fifteen minutes later, we had a room at the Crown Plaza across from the airport. Malik handed me a bag of clothes that he had grabbed from Dr. Jay's and told me to change and meet him downstairs at the car.

Once we put the bags down, Tasha started in, "Abraham, I don't feel good about this. Five hours ago, we were sitting in Miami, chilling, now here we are back in New York and you're about to head out to do who knows what with your boy, Hannibal Lecter, out there."

"Listen, everything is gonna be cool and I'll make it up to you when I get back, I promise." It was shortly after midnight and I knew that Tasha would be sleep when I got back.

Then she asked a question that I wondered about myself, "So why does he have you dressing in all black. Look at you." I looked down at myself. I had on a pair of black cargo pants, a black pullover medium-weight Northface jacket and some all black Timberlands.

I said, "It's cool, don't worry. I'll see you when I get back."

"Abraham, I may not be here when you get back."

It stung a little, but I knew she was just being spoiled, so I replied, "Then, baby, you gonna miss a good thing." I planted a kiss on her forehead and headed out the door. Malik was waiting in the car out front.

Malik started right up about all that I had missed, "You wouldn't believe the day that I've had." Then he proceeded to tell me about everything that he had been through since the morning. My mouth dropped and my heart sank when he told me the tales of death and destruction. I couldn't believe it. Angel, Casper, Wheeler, Ferris, Doc, Wendell, the tear drop-tattooed big guy, Caldwell, and a few more people that I didn't know, were all dead.

My head was spinning as he went on describing the details of the day. It sounded like something out of a movie, but I knew he was dead serious. I didn't mention it to him, but I wondered if he had some great purpose in life that had yet to be revealed. I couldn't imagine him escaping so much death and be able to tell me about it. Finally, I looked over at him. "So how do you feel?" I asked him.

"What the hell are you talking about?" he shot back.

"After seeing all of that death, tell me for real, how do feel?" I kept checking the rearview mirror as we sped up the Grand Central Parkway.

Malik was silent for a few moments, and then he answered, "I don't." We exited the parkway. "I don't feel shit. You see, Abraham, all these fools wanted to take me out the game. I never sought out to kill anyone. I did elect to get into the game and I know that plenty of shit comes along with it, but I never planned to kill anyone who didn't deserve it.

I nodded my head. He thought that it was in agreement, but I did so because I realized that he had gone over the deep end. He actually thought that he was justified in what he was doing. "So where are we headed?" I asked.

He was blasting Nas' *God Son* CD as we pulled up on a residential street and parked. "Malik, where we headed," I asked again.

"Here," he answered. Malik turned the engine off and the radio down. Then he reached into the console and pulled out two sets of keys. "This is Wendell's stash spot. I need you to just come and watch my back while I grab that loot. It's just a matter of time before the police or his family comes looking for it, so we might as well get it first."

I nodded my head in disgust. I hadn't had the chance to tell him that I was ready to turn over a new leaf. I wasn't feeling this craziness. I was ready to take the seventy grand or so that he had stashed for me and call it quits. While it had been nice to have the money to improve my lifestyle, it wasn't worth the price of my soul. I wanted no more of it. "I don't know about this, Malik."

"What?" he yelled out. "You gots to be kidding me! There is free money up in there. He can't use it where he is now." He shook his head to show his disapproval. "Abe, man, you done gone crazy, kid. You've let that bitch get in your head."

When he said those words, my vision got blurry and my head felt instantly warm. I didn't feel myself reacting, but in the next second, my hands were around his throat and his head was pinned back against his headrest. "Watch your mouth. Don't ever disrespect her or me like that!" I squeezed down purposely just to let him know that if I wanted to, I could crush his windpipe with almost no effort. His eyes were big, but he said nothing. His cell phone rang and he muffled out an, "Okay, okay, man. Calm the fuck down."

I let him go and he reached to answer his phone. "Got damn, Abe." He rubbed his neck and stretched it as he hit the button to put the speaker phone on. "Yeah," he answered.

"Malik, what the fuck is going on out there? I just saw Caldwell's name on the fucking news—all shot up and found in a burning vehicle?" Double V shouted into the phone. "Get your ass up here to the same spot I saw you at earlier. I need to speak with you!"

"Yo, I'll be there, but I can't come right now. I can't really explain, but I'm in the middle of something. I'll call Kelly when I finish." Malik shot back.

"What?" Double V was cursing and then said, "Thirty fucking minutes. I'll be there and I suggest you don't have me fucking waiting, Son-son."

"Pops, don't wait for me. I said I'll call. And another thing, you ain't my fucking father, so don't bark on me like that."

"Oh, you a bad mufucka now. You disrespecting me? I taught you the fucking game you playing, but you know it all now, huh?"

"I know a lot. I know I'm in the middle of something and besides, what's the big damn deal?" Malik replied. "People die every day. Honestly, that big muthafucka gave me the creeps anyway."

The phone was silent. I was shocked at how Malik had spoken to his grandfather. Then Double V said something that shut Malik up. "Well... I don't know how to tell you this, but honestly, that big muthafucka... he *was* your father, you little piece of shit." The line went silent.

I broke his glare. Malik had been staring out the window for five minutes. "You alright?"

He snapped out of it. "Yeah, I'm okay." He then turned the engine off.

"Did you hear what Double V said?" I asked. I was in shock and didn't know how he couldn't be.

"Yeah, I heard him." He paused and took a deep breath. His voice cracked a little as he said, "I don't believe that shit. I didn't look anything like that nigga."

"Well man, you look exactly like Lindsey."

"Abe, let that shit go. I don't have time for that right now." He was trying to act unfazed but I thought I could see water in his eyes. Then he clapped his hands together and cracked his knuckles. "Alright, let's make it fast," he said and pulled out two pairs of latex gloves.

While we were putting them on, we noticed five men pull up in a Volvo Station wagon and stop in front of the house we were watching. They were all wearing masks as they quickly piled out of the car and headed for the front door. "Hold on," I said to Malik as I pointed.

"Oh shit," he said as he watched the front door lifted off of its hinges. He was quiet for a second then he said, "Abraham, you might want to run back up Bushwick Avenue and catch a cab."

"Why you say that?"

"Because when these niggas come out the house with the money…"

I didn't need to hear the rest. "Okay. I'm out." As soon as I reached over to open the door, unmarked cars came speeding up the block and a van that was parked across the street from the house opened up and agents began climbing out. Within seconds, the entire house was surrounded. We watched in amazement, realizing that he and I could have been inside that house. Malik waited two minutes and backed into a driveway to turn around. We could hear the helicopters on the way as we drove down the street in silence.

I broke the silence, "So where to now?"

"I'm going to drop you back at the hotel. Then I'm going to head uptown. I need to speak with my grandfather."

Malik told me how he planned to go and rob Doc's stash house as well, but figured that they must have been under investigation and that he was just going to chill. "It's a good thing we didn't go in that house, huh Abe?"

"Yeah, it's a good thing."

"I guess God was on our side tonight."

"Don't you believe that for one second. Our demise just wasn't in his plan. Not yet anyhow."

We made it back to the hotel and Malik pulled up in front of the door. "So listen, Abraham, I'm sorry for disrespecting your girl, calling her out her name. I had no right..."
"Man, it's all good. I'm not even thinking about it."
"Yeah, and I guess you owed me one for me hitting you with that pistol."
I laughed. "Oh, I still owe you for that one. That choking was strictly for the disrespect. I'm still going to bring that whooping to you at a time so ordered."
"I'm looking forward to it, my nigga." he said back, almost sounding serious.
"So you goin' to go see your grandfather?"
"Yeah, if I can find him."
"Promise me you won't go near Doc's crib."
He promised and I could hear that he was lying in his voice. I didn't say anything and I turned to head toward the hotel. "Hey, Abe," he called out.
"Yeah."
"Tomorrow, I'm going to meet you with the money I have for you. After that, I won't be around until it's time to do the big thing. I'm taking Marcella and going to set up camp somewhere. If you still down, let me know. I know that you might not think that you need this dough, but you can do a lot of GOD's work with a couple million dollars. Just think about it. You have a few days to make your mind up. We might need to replace you."
"I understand." I did. I looked into his eyes and said, "Malik, be careful, man. You my brother and I love you."
He didn't say anything. He pulled off and headed for his destiny. I headed upstairs to pray for him.

When I reached the room, Tasha was sleeping. I didn't want to wake her so I went into the bathroom and began to pray.

Father,
I come to you on bended knee, thankful that you have spared my life and Malik's life for yet another day. Father, I ask that you watch over him. I know that he is up to no good. Even as we speak, I anticipate he is headed to commit more crimes against the laws of man. Right now though, I ask for forgiveness for all of the transgressions that we have both committed against your laws. I know that you are merciful and that you are forgiving. Malik so desperately needs your mercy. Father, his life is a complete mess. He is under the control of the spirits of greed and violence. He will not survive much longer, so I beg you to bring him out of this bondage. I ask you to please turn his negative life and use it for positive. I ask that you forgive me for the hypocrisy that I have practiced. I have stolen, fornicated, and proven a false witness to your glory. My faith has been found in want and I beg of you to forgive me and move me to a place where I can find your favor. Lastly, I say to you, Father, if I cannot save Malik, then please remove him from my life in whichever manner you see fit.
I acknowledge that you alone are GOD Almighty and that I am nothing but a speck of dust. I acknowledge that you can reap punishment on me and exterminate my life like a vapor in the wind. I ask you to use me and move me to a position where my life can serve as a testament to your power.
I ask these things in the name of the Son.
Amen.

I woke up and turned on New York One. There was up to the minute coverage of the night of violence.

Joan Harris, from channel 8, was live in a neighborhood just off of Marcy Avenue. She was standing in the front yard of Wendell's stash house. "At about 1:00 a.m., a combination of ATF and New York City officers raided this home and foiled what appeared to be a robbery attempt. It appears that the police were waiting for a warrant to arrive when five armed gunmen pulled up and stormed the house. The officers, who were staking out the house, called for nearby back-up and they were able to arrest four of the five gunmen. One of the gunmen was able to escape. We have officer Chad Cunningham on the scene to tell us more about what happened."

Sue asked him to elaborate and placed the microphone to his mouth. "Yes, Sue as I announced earlier we were able to arrest four of the five suspects. The fifth man apparently climbed out of a window on a top floor and made his way onto the roof. He then climbed across the wires connecting the two houses together. We saw him briefly and sent the K-9s after him."

Sue interrupted. "You said that he was able to elude the dogs."

Cunningham then sounded a little choked up. "No, he was not able to elude the dogs. He killed the dogs, one of them with an arrow and the other with a hunting knife."

"Excuse me, officer. Did you say an arrow?"

"Yes. It was not shot but he used the arrow to puncture the lungs of Rex 3. He cut the throat of the second dog, Ojay."

He was really choked up. "Two damned fine animals. We will catch the culprit."

"Do you have any leads?"

"I can't discuss that at this point. But if anyone out there has any tips on who may be using arrows to commit crimes, please call us at 718-555-9990. We will say that we believe that this is related to a series of homicides committed earlier in the day. Thank you."

"You heard it," Sue said as she recapped the information. I flipped the television off and covered my head with the pillow remembering that Malik had told me that Wild Steve had killed Wheeler with a crossbow earlier in the day. *Poor dogs*, I thought to myself. I was drifting back to sleep when I felt Tasha's hands rubbing my thighs and butt.

"I know you aren't sleep," she said in a groggy voice. "I heard the news. You were looking to see if Malik's face or name showed up, huh?"

She knew me already. She leaned over and rolled on top of me. I was silent. "Make love to me," she said. "I want you inside me."

I rolled over onto my back and she stayed on top of me. "Tasha, I need to tell you something."

"What is it?" She was staring into my face.

"We can't keep doing this. I can't keep fornicating with you like this. It's killing my spirit." Her stare showed me her disillusionment. "I'm sorry."

"So what does that mean?" She folded her arms. "No premarital sex for you, big boy?"

"Actually yeah. That is what it means." I was expecting her to say okay, but to plan her exit. Instead, she leaned over and kissed my forehead.

"Then I guess we got to get married then." She smiled and went down on me.

I began to drift off to ecstasy as her tonsils massaged the tip of my penis. With my eyes closed, I mouthed the word, "Exactly."

TWENTY-FIVE

Misdirection is the teaching style of the devil and here's the curriculum: Spend a billion to send a camera to Mars but tell the school children in Oakland, Houston, D.C, Harlem, Philly, Detroit, Cleveland and those in any other inner-city, sub-par public school system to wait on books and that there is no money for them to have breakfast in schools. Captivate fifty million viewers worldwide with reality TV each night, but never show families destroyed by drugs, AIDS and improper imprisonment. Paint a picture that makes everyone stop and stare—a picture of the ultra-rich, ultra-beautiful and super powerful. Make everyone concentrate on that picture and wonder how they can become a part of it. Blind them with the glare of an easy life filled with sunshine, sex and self-indulgence. Wait until they forget everything else that matters— family, friends, children and GOD. If they start to snap out of the hypnotic state, sedate them with music, movies, and books filled with non-knowledge. As they pour out the desires of their hearts, entice them with all things that they fancy. Treat every vice with an addiction. Numb the minds with small crimes against humanity, until atrocities are viewed as everyday occurrences. Let all things that are detestable to the Master, become the things that are bragged about until good becomes bad and bad feels good.

Let the occasional explosion of news serve as a divider of public opinion and the explosion of religion serve as a divider of men. Let the destruction of families never reveal itself to be anything more than a symptom of the true ills of a misdirected society. Tell the man of color that all the evil in the world is the white man's doing and tell the white man that it is everyone else. At this point, any who haven't been fooled by the teachings of the devil, stumble them with the promise of access to information, just like the Devil did to Eve in the Garden. Once they are caught up in their own ability to gain knowledge and prosper, sell them the final dream from which they never wake from. The dream is that they have nothing but time. Tell them to live life to the fullest today and they can wait to change tomorrow, next month or next year. The only rule in this school is not to reveal to men the price of their education until after they buy it. When it comes to the selling of souls: no refunds, no exchange. All sales are final.

A light rain coated the highway as I headed up I-95. I had abandoned New York City for the past ten days. I had created so much heat and had lived through so much drama, that I had to get away. I had been holed up in three different hotels down in Maryland, trying to stay inconspicuous. I had taken Marcella with me and hadn't done anything other than eat sleep and fuck the entire time. One night, she had begged me to take her out so we hit a club called the VIP in DC. I had taken her to Saks Fifth Avenue where she had picked up a black Vera Wang dress and a pair of Jimmy Choo pumps. She was so thrilled to be treated, she nearly cried. I promised her that as long as she was with me, her life would always be that way. I was a millionaire almost twice over.

The night I dropped Abraham off, I had gone straight to pick up my cousin Carlos. I paid him $5,000 to simply break down the door and leave the scene. Once I saw that he had made it out of the house and up the street without the police coming, I went in and found Doc's money in a suitcase and a cooler. It was so easy, I almost shit my pants laughing as I drove off. I remembered the time Carlos sent me to do his dirty work for a cut of the money. I never thought once about sharing more of the money with him. I had killed a lot of people to get that money and there was no way he was going to reap the rewards that almost cost me my life. Carlos was lazy and stupid, and it appeared that life had brought our relationship full circle. If the police had nabbed him at the door that night, I would have driven off like Val Kilmer did in *Heat*. Instead, I left New York, paid in full.

I was afraid to leave the money in my apartment unattended so I purchased some ugly ass furniture the next morning before I left and had it delivered to a storage unit in New Jersey. I had hidden the money inside the couch and mattress and left it there while I contemplated where I would keep the money. I had plenty of time to come up with a plan and I did.

As I neared Dover, I thought about the dreams that I had been having since Caldwell, who I still couldn't believe was my father, had killed Angel. I kept dreaming of her and the times that we had shared. I kept hearing her yelling at me and cursing me for destroying everyone that she cared about. I kept seeing Phil Boogie's daughter and I wondered how her life would turn out. It was torture that I felt I deserved, so it was therefore bearable.

It was 1:00 in the morning and Marcella was sleep with the passenger seat reclined. Looking at her brought me comfort. She was the type of girl a man needed if he was making moves. She hadn't questioned me about my business one time nor had she appeared to be spoiled. She was definitely a rider. It tickled me a bit when she told me that she was going to be there for me even while I got over Angel. Of course she didn't know that Angel was dead. All she knew was that I had just gotten out of a troubled relationship.

It meant a lot to her that I wanted her with me while I went through my time of trials and she showed her appreciation in a lot of ways. We pulled over at a rest stop so that I could take piss and when I came back out, she was naked from the waist down. "Hurry up and close that door, it's cold out there," she said.

"What the hell are you doing?" I said, sliding into the seat.

"You just told me that you are going to be gone for a couple of days, right? Well I want you to take care of me, right here right now. You can't get a sistah hooked and then leave her hanging all weekend."

"You serious?"

"Just pull it out and climb over here," she said seductively.

"You ain't got to ask me twice," I said as I slipped off my boots and slid my jeans down. I remembered that this was how the D.C. sniper got caught, fucking around at a rest stop, but it didn't stop me.

I was on top of Marcella and began kissing her on her neck and behind her ears. She began to breathe heavily and pushed me up enough to pull her sweater and bra up over her breast. I looked at her nipples and they were standing off of her chest. The moonlight was coming in through the roof and I could make out the beautiful designs of her body. I began sucking her breasts as my dick grew harder by the second. I could feel her hands rubbing my chest and massaging my nipples as I brushed against the opening to her vagina. Her dampness coated the tip and I was ready to plunge in. "No, not yet," she said. The seat was reclined and she turned her back to me and slid up the seat until her belly button was resting against the headrest. "I want you to lick it."

"Then turn around."

"No, lick it from the back," she said. I hadn't seen her freaky side yet, but I was enjoying the way she was taking charge and asking for what she wanted. "C'mon, Malik, lick it like a lollipop."

I looked around the parking lot and didn't see anyone near us or coming and before I knew it, I was tongue deep inside of her pussy. Her clit was hanging down and swollen and made it easy for me to get it into my mouth. I gripped it between my lips and began to savor the feeling that her juices provided my lips. My mouth was alive at the thought of giving her pleasure.

"Uh huh, uh huh. Oh shit, yeah," Marcella cried out. "That's right. Lick it, suck it."

I did as she asked and began to put pressure on her clit with the tip of my tongue. I still held her lips between my lips and fought her pelvic movements to keep them in my control. My hands were on her ass pulling her cheeks apart and I found my nose right against her asshole. The only scent was of the Victoria's Secret Body lotion and wash that I had purchased for her. My face was dripping with her juices as I continued sucking and licking.

"Okay! Okay! Okay!" she screamed louder each time. Finally, I felt her thighs begin to tremble. "Oh baby! Please don't make... don't make me... cum like ... thiiiiis."

I made several slurping sounds and put three fingers inside of her. In the next instant, she jumped and bucked hard against my face. "Is that how you like it?" I mumbled into her pussy.

"Oh, fuck yessss! Malik, right... there... yes... unnnnh..... ruuh...iiiite... there," she grunted out and her whole body shook for about fifteen seconds.

She slid down onto the seat and I plunged straight into her from the back. The *R in R&B* CD was playing softly and *Your Body's Calling* was playing. If I didn't know better, I would have sworn that she was backing into me to the rhythm and beat of the song. I was enjoying the ride as I watched my dick disappear inside and back out again as her lips milked me. I was glistening with sweat and the cream from her glazed my manhood.

"I love the way you feel. I didn't know it would be so damned good."

She was getting off on me talking to her. "Keep talking to me."

"What you want me to say?"

"Whatever, daddy, just say anything. I just like to hear your voice while you pound this pussy from the back."

"Mmmmmph," I grunted because her dirty talk was turning me on. "Bring this pussy to me!" I shouted.

"It's yours, daddy. I feel you deep in there."

"I'm makin' you sweat. I'm watchin' this phat ass bounce up and down and it looks so good."

"Good enough to eat."

"Oh yeah, I already did and it tasted so good." I smacked her across the ass.

"Oh yeah, I like that," she said. "Keep doing it."

"Oh you like to be spanked?"

"Only by you, Malik." Good-ass answer.

I spanked her more while I kept plowing into her. "You like it nasty, don't you, girl," I said as I began to grip her hair in my hand.

"Oh yeah, I'll be nasty for you," she breathed out as my pace quickened. "I'll be your slut."

"Oh shit!" I screamed out. I began to yank her by her hair and pulled her head back as I slammed hard into her.

"Owwww," she moaned out as I pounded her like a man possessed.

"Take that dick. You said you wanted to be my slut, now take it." I kept pulling her hair and she began to erupt with moans and cries of her second orgasm. She was so wet that my thighs were coated with her juices. As she came, I leaned into her and felt the rush of my own climax. "Oh baby... I'm cumming. Oh, it feels so gooood." My dick started to tingle and I thrust into her until I had emptied myself into her. I collapsed onto her and rested there for what felt like five minutes.

She slept for the rest of the ride and when she woke up, we were outside of my apartment. I helped her in and we climbed into bed. I didn't wake until the phone rang. Marcella had gotten out of the bed already and I could hear her watching the television in the living room. It was noon on Saturday, the day of the Hopkins and Joppy fight, and my Uncle Kelly was calling with my instructions. "Hello."

He spoke back and went on, "I need you and your partner to meet me at 9:00 tonight at Fishhead's, it's a soulfood spot in Atlantic City." He gave me the address. I scribbled it down and asked for directions from the AC expressway. "Whatever you do, don't be late. You know Vincent is still a little pissed with you about the way you handled the whole thing with your father."

"Hey Uncle, he wasn't my father. He wasn't shit to me, okay?" I shot back.

"Yeah, okay, son. You just be there at 9:00, you and your partner." I hung up and thought about the fact that I hadn't heard from Abraham in ten days. I had dropped him off the $75,000 and told him that I didn't expect him to be around. He accepted the money and told me to be safe and that he would be in touch with me. The writing was on the wall—he was out of the game.

I wondered what I was going to do for a partner and decided to call Abraham. He didn't answer, so I left a message. I laid staring at the ceiling, thinking about where I was headed. I had over two million dollars to my name. Once I found a way to hide the money, I would be free and clear. I began trying to come up with reasons as to why I was going through with this robbery.

The only thing that I came up with was that I didn't have anything else to do. I wanted to be rich forever like most every other person in the world. If I stopped now, not only was I already rich, I was in a position to live off of the money that I had stashed now for a few years, and eventually start my own business.

Then I thought about the kind of money that rappers like Jay-Z and P. Diddy had and I thought about living like them. A couple mill wasn't going to cut it. There was no promising that I would be able to make a score like this again. Plus my grandfather was going to help me hide it and move to a better place.

I sat up in the bed and dialed Cortez. He answered on the first ring. "Hey, compadre. I see you still kicking. You are one elusive, lucky son of a bitch."

"Yeah whatever, I need to get in touch with Wild Steve," I said.

"I believe I can help you with that. I'm sure he's going to want to speak with you. I'll call him and tell him that you want to speak with him."

"Okay."

"Oh… Malik, wait up."

"Yeah."

"Word has it that you used some info that a certain brother passed on to you. If that is true, then congratulations are in order."

"I don't know what you're talking about."

"Sure you don't," he laughed.

I paused for a second. I don't know how he knew but he did. I guess he was a lot smarter than I gave him credit for, yet I still stuck to my story. "I really don't."

"By the way, can I give you one bit of advice?" he asked.

"Sure."

"Malik, remember, never become wise in your own eyes."

I had heard that somewhere before but couldn't remember what it meant. "What exactly do you mean by that?"

"I mean that you shouldn't be walking around here thinking that you are untouchable or that your time won't come. You're trying to build your life off of catching other people sleeping. You need to be mindful that every shut eye ain't sleep."

I paused and took in what he said. "I'll remember that."

"Yeah, do that. Also, know that Cortez didn't get where he is today just by being lucky," he laughed again. "You weren't the first person to follow me where you thought I lived. I will say this for you though. You would make a good detective if you weren't so adept at killing them. You did good though, I was never able to follow you home either. But did you honestly think I would fly my money out of the country without me accompanying it? Get real." Then he laughed once more. "Malik, take care of yourself and don't spend it all in one place. I'll have Steve call you." Click.

I couldn't believe what I had heard. That Cortez was a slick mufucka. I reclined back into the bed and my cell rang five minutes later. "What's good, my nigga," I heard Wild Steve say.

"Yo, I got a move for you to make with me. I need a partner and I don't have one. If you down to roll with me, you could see something major."

"Major?"

"I'm talking ten times what was on my head."

"Word?" he answered. "What I got to do for that, shoot a plane out the sky or knock off an armored truck?"

"It won't be anything outside of your normal bounds."

"Well count me in."

"Cool, then meet me at One Fish, Two Fish, on the corner of 97ᵗʰ and Madison."

"What time?"

"Four."

"Do I need my vest and equipment?" he asked.

"You could bring the vest, but leave the arrows, poison darts and all that other Crocodile Dundee shit behind please, bro."

He laughed. "Man, you crazy. Alright, I'll see you then."

"And, Steve." I said.

"Yeah."

"Please don't try to kill me, we got too much money to make tonight."

"You have my word. One."

Before I left, I felt compelled to tell Marcella what was going on to some extent. I wanted her to know that there was a chance that I could get into some real trouble. She began to cry hysterically and it took me a full hour to calm her down. I promised her that tonight would be my last night of crime. Once I pulled this off, we could disappear and be together forever and live everywhere and nowhere.

I gave her the key to my storage bin and told her the security code to get into the gate. I wrote Abraham's number down and told her if something happened, to call him. I also told her that the bill for the storage would come to the apartment in about two weeks. Only then would she know which storage company I used and the bin number. I explained that she would find enough money to start a nice life.

I gave her all the instructions she needed in order to tidy up my life in the event that I was taken out by the police. I didn't mention the money buried at my mother's. That money was for my legal fees in the event that I was ever taken alive. Once I was sure that she had an understanding of everything necessary to carry on, I made love to her one more time. I showered, got dressed and with a sick feeling in my stomach, I left her in my apartment.

Wild Steve and I ate a quick lunch while I told him more in depth what we were about to do. He agreed with a mouth full of stuffed catfish as we finished our food. We paid the bill and we headed out of the city bumping to the Black Album.

"Yo, you think this nigga, Hov, is really gonna stay retired."

"I doubt it. Would you?" I asked.

"And walk away from all that money?"

"Well, he got enough money. That can't be his inspiration."

"Ain't no such thing as enough money, Malik. Ask Bill Gates if he has enough money. When you ever see a rich mufucka stop making money while he was breathing?"

I nodded. "I see your point."

Then he surprised me when he said, "But you know, money ain't everything. You proved to be a soldier and a man of your word and that holds a lot of weight with me."

I nodded again. "I feel you."

"For real. That's why I didn't kill you. I saw that you had honor and it spoke to me. You lived up to the deal you cut with Cortez, Doc and Wendell. The Towers was never as safe as when you were protecting that spot. You had every stick-up crew in Brooklyn too damn shook to move on you. Doc and Wendell, them niggas simply wasn't feelin' you because you scared them, but you didn't break on 'em until they broke on you. You was good to your word. Now they ain't here and you are. You got a lot you can do in this life once you get past this crime shit." He paused. "That is if you live long enough."

"You think so?"

"Hell yeah. Man, I'm not planning on doing this shit too much longer. I'm trying to open up a discount hunting supply store down in Virginia."

"That's big. What you gonna' call it?"

"Wild Steve's Hunting Supplies."

"I like that."

He nodded. "So what would you want to do other than rob, kill and extort mufuckas?" He laughed.

"I don't know."

"C'mon now, everybody got something they interested in. Stamp collecting, some shit. Titty bar? You probably want to be a cop deep down inside."

"Hell no."

"Well I know it's something. You like to shoot ball, right?"

"Yeah, but not like that. Honestly... I like to rap."

"Word? Let me hear your flow. What you got? I'll bet you flow like Fifty or something."

"Nah, I got my own style."

He reached over and skipped the track on Nas' God's Son CD to *Made You Look* and said, "Go ahead. Rock it for me one time."

I was a little put on the spot. I used to spit rhymes in the car all the time, but never aloud for anyone else to hear. This was my first time, but for some reason, I just came off the top of my head. "Alright." I started bobbing my head to the beat and waited for a break and then I just started,

"Can you handle a look through my eyes,
Are you going to judge me or even worse despise?
If you don't like or can't understand what I represent,
Will you damn your own fate by passing judgment?

If my God ain't like yours and I don't believe what you do,
Will you doubt my spirituality or worse try to seduce,
others to believe, that I am a plague on mankind with no
purpose or use?

Though I feel your resistance I am simply too strong,
You should know that it's not war that I want, just a stage to
perform.
We all got a story to tell and I got a right to tell mine,
I may learn from you, and you might feel me in time.

All this and still no credibility, you think it's a mirage,
It's the mirror of life, the art is in charge.
Do I have to describe fear to prove I've been scared?
You wanna see my world, like the Staple Singers I'll take you
there.

If you hearing my story then you baptized by fire,
Though I never seen GOD I know there's a being that's higher,
Until I feel that power, I get rougher by the hour, so if
you cant handle the rage then don't turn the page."

"Oh my gawd, my nigga. Nigga, you nice. I'don't believe that shit." Wild Steve was tripping in disbelief. He had me really thinking that he was impressed."

"You bullshittin' me?"

"I'll show you if I'm bullshitting." He pulled out his cell and dialed a number. "Hey, what's good, my nigga…yeah ain't shit popping…but yo, Kon, you ain't gonna believe this young cat I'm with. He got crazy flow, man. You need to get this nigga in the studio. You in the city? Yeah, well I'm gonna bring him over there tomorrow for you to check him out… huh… okay." He handed me the phone and said, "Yo, Malik, hit that same joint you just did for me. He wants to hear some."

"Who is this?"

"That's Kanye, the hottest producer out there." Wild Steve replayed the song and I did my thing once more. When I finished, Kanye told me that he'd see me tomorrow night. I couldn't believe it. My mind started racing with all types of thoughts. Could I become a rapper and then I wondered if I would I even make it to tomorrow?

"Thanks, man," I said to Wild Steve. "That was real decent."

"It ain't no thing," he said but it was to me. Wild Steve was a decent dude.

We talked the whole way down to Atlantic City and when we got there, it wasn't quite 7:00, so we decided to go and hit the casino. We walked around The Taj Mahal, taking in the sights. Everyone was in furs, looking their flyest. The honeys had come out dressed to impress. Meanwhile, we had on black pants, sweaters and boots. We didn't give a fuck, we were on a business trip.

We headed to the meeting spot and got there a little after 8:30. I was a little hungry and decided to order a fish sandwich. Wild Steve asked me to grab him one too while he waited in the car. When I came out ten minutes later with the sandwiches in my hand, I noticed that Wild Steve wasn't in the car. I opened up my door and put my sandwich on the dashboard and looked around the parking lot. I walked back inside and checked the bathrooms, but there was still no sign of him. I looked on his side of the car and noticed his cell phone was on the ground. "What the fuck?" I said aloud. Then I heard a sound coming from the side by the dumpster. I headed around the corner and as soon as I cleared the side of the building I was punched. The first punched dazed me and I stumbled to the ground. Then I heard his voice.

"I hate to have to do this to you, but it's God's work." It was Abraham.

"Man, what the fuck is wrong with you and what are you doing here?" I had no idea what was going on, but before I could gather myself, he threw another punch to my midsection dropping me once again.

"Wild Steve is over there handcuffed in my backseat. I looked across the street and saw Abraham's car parked. Sure enough, Wild Steve was in the back seat. He looked like he was sleeping. I'm saving your life, Malik. Your luck has run out. I can't let you go through with this thing with your grandfather. The time has come for you to take what you have and just quit. We can move away and you don't ever have to worry about any more of this bullshit. We've already won. Matter of fact, I'll give you all of the money you gave me back and I'll sell my grandmother's house if it's money you need, but I can't let you do this. I have a feeling that tonight something terrible is going to happen and I'm not sure what, but I can't let you go through with this madness. If I have to put you in the hospital tonight I will."

I was a little delirious from being hit twice, but I knew that Abraham had lost his mind so I climbed to my feet. "Abraham, listen," I said breathing heavily. "You got your two good licks in. If you hit me again…"

"You gonna shoot me?" he cut me off. "I doubt it. You don't have a gun on you. Double V told everyone to leave their weapons behind because he would supply them. I know you listened because I searched your car while you were inside and you don't have one in your belt."

He was right. I knew that if I didn't get Wild Steve and be ready when Double V pulled up, there would be hell to pay. With that in mind, I lunged forward and punched Abraham in is jaw. His head rolled with the punch, but his body hardly moved. He took a step back and I threw a left and connected with that too. Still, he bounced into a fighter's stance and his hands went up to protect his face.

"C'mon, give me your best," he said. I was about to throw a jab but he beat me to it. His hands were lightening quick. The second jab caused me to see a flash of light and the right hook that followed sent me flying into a stack of bread crates that were propped up against the building. I bounced up quickly as possible and lunged at Abraham's mid section. As I grabbed his waist, attempting to tackle him, his knee came up and caught me in the face. The pain was immeasurable and my mouth filled with the warm, salty taste of blood. I collapsed on all fours.

"Abraham, I'm gonna..." I was filled with rage as I got up and threw haymaker after haymaker at his head. I missed three times but he lost his footing, trying to dodge my blows and slipped forward into the last punch. My fist caught him on the cheek, right under his left eye and I heard the crunch of my hand on his cheekbone. He hit the ground with a thud and my hand felt like the bones had shattered. He rolled on the ground like a punch-drunk fighter and I fell to my knees in agony holding my hand. I grimaced and stood, starting to head toward his car. When I got to his car, I realized that Steve was handcuffed to the headrest and that I would need the keys from Abraham. I tapped on the window and saw Steve coming to. His eye was swollen shut, indicating that Abraham had knocked him out cold. I laughed and then saw Steve's eyes widen. I knew what it meant but by the time I turned around, the punch landed on my temple and the lights went out.

I never saw or heard the sirens, but when I came to, I was in the back of an Atlantic City squad car. I had been arrested for assault and public disturbance. Abraham was in a car right next to me. The police had taken the cuffs off of Wild Steve and questioned him. He had claimed that he got caught in the middle of a lovers' quarrel. He told them that he didn't want any further involvement due to the fact that he had a woman at home. He was released and I was able to give him the keys to my car to drive back to New York.

Abraham and I were both being detained. We were in separate cells, which was a good thing because I was irate at what he had done. I had financed a heist that I didn't show up to participate in. I couldn't even begin to imagine how furious Double V would be with me. He had it in him to be a maniac and I know that I had jeopardized the entire operation. I had no idea when I would ever hear from him again.

To make matters worse, it was obvious that I had broken at least a couple of bones in my hand. There were lumps where there shouldn't have been and my hand was purple and swollen like a catcher's mitt. I was allowed ice while being questioned, but was told that I couldn't go get X-rays until my release.

The pulse from the pain in my hand made me lay as still as possible and as I tapped my feet on the floor of the cell floor, I began contemplating my life. It was my first time behind anyone's bars. I was thinking about how much time I deserved based on the crimes that I had committed in the last year. I wondered what the lives that I had taken were worth. I imagined a judge, like the one my grandfather faced, sitting up on a bench deciding my fate. I thought about Angel and her mother and a tear formed in my eye. I thought about my father and how I might have killed him if I had the chance to that day in Harlem. I know I would have, given half a chance without the police around. My mind began racing back to thoughts of my childhood and the preacher who told me that my gift would be revealed to me. I couldn't understand why God would create such a ruthless creature in me. What good was I to this Earth? I was a rapist, but a much worse rapist than Phil Boogie. I was raping God. I was destroying the lives and the gifts that he had created and given.

I sat staring at the bars, knowing that this was my future in this life if I kept my course. Then I started thinking about rapping and how Wild Steve was the first person to ever show me he believed in me. Ever. Everyone else who ever stood beside me, stood to gain from my actions. My mother, my grandfather, even Abraham. I led him his entire life. It wasn't until he met this girl Tasha that he was able to think on his own.

Then for some reason, I laughed aloud in my cell at how he must have gotten the information from Marcella. She wanted him to stop me bad enough to convince him to drive down to Atlantic City and kick my ass to save me from myself. I laughed some more.

I leaned back on the bench and began to make up a rhyme in my head about it. I wondered if I could rap about something that mattered to people one day. The strange thing was that it didn't matter if anyone ever heard me or not. I had never realized it before now, but the rapping made me feel good.

One of the officers was kind enough to give me a Tylenol 3 for my hand and I was able to doze off while I was waiting to be released. At about 4:00 in the morning, I was awakened when there was a huge uproar in the station. Officers began scrambling about. "Sign their paperwork and get them out of here!" I heard an officer yell to one of the clerks. "We have a major bust and we might need the space."

I stood and walked to the bars. In a few moments, I was being escorted out of booking. When I reached the lobby, I saw Abraham and Marcella waiting for me. Marcella ran up to me and gave me a hug. "I'm sorry, Malik. I don't care about you making any money. I just don't want you to be in danger." I looked over at Abraham.

He started, "Look it's over and done. Let's go."

We sat in the waiting room at the Atlantic City Medical Center. The wind was howling so hard I could hear it inside the emergency room and it was starting to rain. I sat in the waiting room waiting to be treated. I wasn't speaking to Abraham or Marcella who sat directly across from me. I even pretended to be watching the weather report on television when the news tease for the 6:00 a.m. news came on.

"Over night, one man killed, one wounded and three arrested as an undercover investigation nets big results. Also, a man is stabbed to death after attending an after-party at the Sheraton Hotel. Many were on hand, including Denzel, Jay-Z, Allen Iverson and Donovan McNabb to see the big fight tonight. We'll see how Bernard Hopkins fared in his first fight in nearly two years, there was also much hype surrounding the Corey Spinks fight earlier."

The second anchor cut in, *"There were even bigger fights in the stands, and we'll have all that for you and more in the next hour."*

I didn't think anything of the news until the commercial went off and they showed an armored car. The news flashed to a live shot and my heart sank as the pain in my hand paled compared the stress that grabbed hold of me at that moment.

"What can you tell us?" the anchor asked the reporter.

"At this point, it appears that the police have foiled an attempt to rob a Bricks Armored truck. Right behind me," The field reporter pointed, *"is the home of Robert Webster, who is a seventeen-year veteran of the New Jersey State Police. He has been under the watch of the FBI for several years and it led them to this intricate plot. He was apparently involved in the plan to hijack the truck, which contained the take from five or six casinos. The gunmen were actually able to take*

possession of the truck, without harming either driver, and drive it to this location. This was the meeting place."

The anchor chimed in. *"We have reports that one man was killed."*

"Yes, Lynn. One man was shot while attempting to flee the scene in an eighteen-wheeler. He actually attempted to drive the truck through the barricade and the officers were forced to open fire on him. The wounded man was shot in the chest after he opened fire on the officers. He is believed to be in serious condition."

"You said that it was an ongoing investigation."

"Yes, the investigation of Mr. Webster led authorities to monitor his involvement. He seems to have been linked to a recently released felon, who may have been one of the men involved. We'll get more details to you as we have them."

"Thanks, Drew."

There was no reaction from Abraham or myself. We were both stunned. I almost didn't hear my name called to go to the back room for treatment. When I walked back there, I saw my grandfather in the far corner with an oxygen mask over his face and two nurses monitoring his breathing. He was surrounded by three officers, so I said nothing as I walked into my examining room. I attempted to get several looks at Double V but when my curtain was pulled, I didn't want to arouse any suspicion.

Forty-five minutes later, my hand was in a cast and I was cleared for release. As I made my way out of the room, I called the one black nurse I saw over there. Her name was Shakeema. "Excuse me."

"Yes," she said.

I signaled for her to come closer and she did. "Is that man over there gonna make it?" I pointed to Vincent.

She looked at me with a strange expression then she answered. "I think so."

I nodded and left. It was the last I would ever see or hear of Vincent Vaughn. He died on that table, alone, two hours later.

365 days later

"**Preaching** don't mean a thing if you ain't reaching."
The congregation erupted with a chorus of 'Amens.' "Can I
get a witness?" People were standing. I was in a high school
auditorium in Harlem. It had served as a church for the past
few months and no one could tell me that I wasn't dwelling in
the most lavish House of the Master. I didn't need stained
glass windows, oak pews, a grand pulpit or a cathedral to
spread the word of my transformation. Where I had come
from showed that GOD had a place and purpose for everyone.

"Today, I want to take a look at your life," I said in a
quiet tone. The microphone carried my voice through the
auditorium. I continued, "Not an examination for the purpose
of crucification... that's just fancy for judging folks." There
was laughter. "No, I want to take a look at your life and
hopefully show you where you're headed if you keep coming,
keep healing, keep believing." It was the middle of December
and even though it was New York cold out, the heat was
pumping in the auditorium. I pulled my handkerchief out and
wiped my forehead. I had a light coat of sweat on my face.

"Preach on, young man," a lady yelled.

"No... reach on," I shouted back.

"Amen."

"I just want to tell you that I understand that some of you
are going through it. I know that you are wrestling with
demons of addiction, materialism..." I looked at my best

friend who was seated in the front row and said, "...demons of violence." I took the mic from the podium. "I know some of you have lost your way and you came here today looking for a spark of light. Well I'm here to tell you that you came to the right place. Let my existence show you, I'm that spark of light. I am not *The* Light, I would never claim to be. I'm just a spark."

"Amen."

"Thank you, brother. People I want to show you where to find *it*. I said I want to help you find *it!*" I shouted *it* the second time. "*It* is going to give you the happiness you've been longing for. The money you've been needing, the love you've been lacking. Oh yeah, if you search hard and long enough, you can certainly find it and more." I winked at Sondra who was rocking little Abraham Jr. in her arms trying to hush his cries. "I know because I found it. I found it amidst the darkness of the ghetto streets. I found it even through the snares of the devil. I found it even though I was misdirected, misguided, hated, abandoned, and attacked at every turn. The greatest feat was that I found it even through my own foolishness and stupidity. You see, I was a soldier in the Devil's army. Some of us are drafted, while some of us enlist when we sell our souls for money, fame and ghetto celebrity." I looked at Tasha Robb. She had abandoned her rap career just like Mase. Unlike him though, she had only performed one show. "But the good news is that for a discharge, all you have to do is ask the Master."

"What is it?" I wiped my brow again. "Does anybody know?" The congregation was silent. Nobody wanted to yell the wrong answer. "The answer is peace."

The churched erupted again. "Amen! Peace!"

"You see, I have it now. And it's worth more than anything that money can buy. You can't buy peace. They don't sell it anywhere. You can't find it in a bag of dope. You can't drive it. You can't drink yourself to it. You can't meet it in a nightclub, you can't see it in a video, you can't get it at the ATM, you definitely can't live through anyone else's, you can't even vote for it."

"Amen! Thank you!" The people were shouting.

"YOU CAN'T TAKE IT FROM SOMEONE ELSE. YOU CAN'T STEAL IT!"

"AMEN!"

"THERE'S ONLY ONE WAY TO GET. HOLLAH IF YOU HEAR ME!"

"AAAAAMEENN! THANK YOU, THANK YOU!"

"PREACH, BOY, PREACH!"

"NO, REACH, BOY, REACH!"

I shouted back, "That's it!" I waved my hands to calm the congregation down. The only way to get..." It was dead quiet. "I said the only way to get it... is to humble yourself and ask for it."

I looked at the crowd. I went on telling the congregation some of the things that I had seen in my life and how I had come to find peace and why I had to share it with them. I preached for another half an hour and when I finished, people had tears in their eyes. I then had them pull out their bibles and I shared a pertinent scripture that related to my journey.

Psalms 40:12, "For calamities encircled me until there was no numbering them. More errors of mine overtook me than I was able to see. They became more numerous than the hairs of my head, and my own heart left me." At that moment I used my handkerchief to wipe my own tears. I couldn't go on. I simply said, "Thank you so much for coming to share the Word with me today. The Master is good. Find peace with him. Amen." The walls shook as the hall filled with applause. I felt exhaustion and was ready to step away.

There was no Holy Ghost jumping around or loud singing, just people being filled with the strength and the power of my testimony. I had indeed been a spark of light because the entire place was lit and glowing.

Everyone stood and shouted, "Amen!" Shivers went through my body because I knew that I had reached someone if not everyone. I placed the microphone back on the podium and stepped away to take my seat. My wife greeted me with a hug as I found my way back to my seat on the stage. Abraham stood up and walked past me and headed toward the podium.

When he took hold of the microphone he said, "Please everyone, can I get another round of applause and thanks for Brother Malik and that powerful message he delivered this morning." Abraham led the congregation in clapping for me and a sea of thanks and blessings came my way.

"Thank you," I whispered back. Marcella reached out and took my hand.

"Let us join hands as we pray," Abraham led the congregation in one of his signature prayers. He was thorough and when he spoke to the Master, he was clear and inspiring. He ended the prayer and said, "We will see some of you Tuesday for Bible Study and the rest of you next Sunday."

It was a beautiful thing coming to know and love GOD. I had surprised many, including myself, when I accepted Abraham's offer to go to bible college with him. It was amazing the way my tortured soul had healed. It was still a battle everyday forgiving myself for all the evil that I had done, but I was beginning to learn.

I had donated large portions of the money to different youth centers around Brooklyn and Harlem. Almost all of the rest, I allowed Abraham to use in building our church. I had married Marcella and she was attending Columbia University, majoring in Journalism. After hearing all the details of Abraham's story, and mine too of course, she decided that she would some day write a book about it. I had made her a promise to change our names to protect the innocent and out of respect to the dead.

Speaking of the dead, I did hire a reputable law firm to set up a trust fund for Phil Boogie's daughter. I also sent money to the families of the slain officers. I, of course, had to do this anonymously. I would have tried to adopt her, but my guilt for my part in what happened to her family was too much. When it was all said and done, I had given away all of the money that I had stolen. All except for what was buried in my mother's backyard in Baltimore. The only person who knew about that was Abraham. That was our emergency money in case we needed it for legal fees.

Abraham was doing a great job as a father. I was truly impressed and a little envious. He was extremely active in his son's life and he and Sondra got along unusually well.

He was a great pastor as well and his first lady was his heart. He had married Tasha Robb. They say she could have been one of the best female rappers, but she chose Abraham and GOD instead. They had gotten married on New Year's Day last year and were coming up on their first anniversary.

Our congregation was growing and all of our needs were being met. I found that everything I did to take money was unnecessary. People willingly supplied enough for our congregation's needs plus enough to feed two families. We had over three hundred people come to see us on any given Sunday and had only been meeting for four months.

I was beginning to live for the preaching-reaching that I was doing. It filled me up. I would go out to the hood and invite anyone I saw on the corner. Today, I saw a face that I thought I recognized and couldn't wait to get a closer look.

As the people poured out of the auditorium, I headed for the fountain and there he was. He had grown almost an entire foot since I had seen him last. I walked up on him.

"Ferris," I said as I reached out to hug him. "Look at you, boy."

A smile slid across his face and he reached out to me. "Hey, Malik," he said. "He told me you and Abraham were up here preaching. You know I had to come and see this for myself."

"Who's *he*?"

"Wild Steve."

"Oh, you've seen him?" I asked.

"Yeah," Ferris nodded. "I saw him a month ago. He told me he was about to open a store down south. Some sort of..."

I cut him off. "Hunting Supplies?"

"Yeah," he said and we both laughed.

"So what have you been eating?" I asked looking at him. "You must be at least six feet tall now?"

"Six-one and a half," he said proudly.

"That's whoa," I shot back. "You balling?"

"Yeah, I'm getting into it. You know I'm supposed to have the last surgery to have the metal removed from my liver tissue. So I have to take it a little easy until that's done with."

"I see," I said, changing the subject to avoid another bout of guilt. He had suffered a serious wound saving my life. "I want you to meet my wife."

I took him over to Marcella and introduced him. When Abraham walked over holding his son, he didn't believe it was Ferris. He had grown so much since we'd seen him last. Abraham didn't contain his excitement and gave the baby to me so that he could embrace Ferris.

We talked for a good fifteen minutes before we were ready to head out. We always stayed to help the school custodian put the chairs away. It wasn't our job, but we felt it was appropriate. The wives were helping, so I told Marcella that I would be right back after I walked Ferris to his car. We talked and laughed about him growing up. He was about to turn sixteen.

"Malik, it is so crazy to see you up there preaching to people. I know you and..."

I had to stop him, "That was the old me. I'm not like that anymore. I have come to love GOD and I have repented for all of that."

When we got to his car, I added, "Ferris, I don't expect you to understand, but things can happen in your life, things that change you and make a difference in your life. The difference in the old personality and the new spirit can be as wide as the ocean and as grand as the sky. But it takes a different thinking and faith to understand that."

Ferris smiled at me. "I understand. I do. You know I've been through a lot myself."

"You know I do," I said. Just then, a young boy no older than twelve or thirteen, walked up to me and Ferris and handed me $26.30.

"What's this for?" I asked.

"Hey sir, that was a great message you gave in there and that is the all the money I have to my name," he said. "My brother really needed to hear it."

I looked at him and smiled. "Thanks for the money, but I don't want take your last." Then I added, "And why didn't you bring your brother?"

"Well you see, my brother is dead." Then he went on, "But I want you to keep the money because I swore on his grave that I would give my last dime to be able to find the man who killed him."

I looked into his eyes and I saw the face of every man that I had killed. He looked right into mine and there was no fear and I nodded my head. Things slowed down as I heard Ferris yelling my name, trying to save my life again, "Malik, noooooooooo!" He even lunged, but the youngster was too fast. He pulled the pistol from the pocket of his Northface and began to squeeze. I heard the clap and the thunder. I heard the thunder over and over. I felt nothing and everything at the same time as I felt myself falling toward destiny. Dying right there on the cold ground in Harlem after my first sermon was the most perfect thing that I had ever done. It truly was my finest day.

AMEN.

For Discussion:

- Questions by Tahisha Cunningham & Derek Lowe.

1. What impact did Abraham's spirituality have on his relationship with Malik?

2. What role did the desire for affluence play in the lives of both Malik and Abraham? Were Sondra and A.J. merely gold diggers or was there a genuine interest in Malik and Abraham on their part?

3. What factors do you think caused Malik to snap and become so violent? Was his grandfather's influence the real problem or was Malik inherently evil?

4. Do you think that Do or Die challenges the spirituality of the reader? What do you think the author's purpose of the intros in the beginning of each chapter was?

5. Ultimately was Cortez smart or lucky? Did he surprise you with his actions at all?

6. Do you feel the author wrote the novel with a particular audience in mind? Who else could identify with this novel? Would you recommend it as part of a college curriculum?

7. How do Abraham and Malik believe that respect is gained in the game of life? How closely do you think their ideas mirror the mindset of the hip-hop generation?

8. Why do you think that Malik continued to trust Angel after his near-assault from her? Was she trustworthy?

9. Who's life best fit the title "Do Or Die," Malik's or Abraham's?

10. Where would a guy like Wild Steve get his development from? Who was your favorite character? Least favorite?

11. What do you think Malik's interest in Angel was about? Was he merely chasing tail? Was it guilt from the deed?

12. How different are Malik and Abraham?

13. Is there any belief that the mayhem in the lives of Malik and Abraham was part of the 'Master Plan'?

14. Do you believe that the tendencies of these characters reflect a tug of war inside of each of us?

15. How significant was the appearance of Malik's father in the story? What about his death?

16. What was Malik's ultimate gift?

17. How did Ferris become so cold hearted at such a young age? Do you think there are children in the inner cities just like him? What did his appearance at the end of the book signify?

18. Do you think that Abraham's upbringing led to his behavior in the story? Did you think the author implied that he was in fact, saved by angels as a child?

19. Discuss the impact the book had on you.

20. What do you think the author's purpose for writing this story was? Do you feel as though he had a worthwhile message?

If you enjoyed Do Or Die, you <u>ABSOLUTLEY</u> have to read NO WAY OUT by Zach Tate.

Whatever you do... Don't sleep on this book. Visit a store near you or use the order form in the back of this book! Zach's follow up novel *'Lost & Turned Out'* hits stores this summer!